underneath it all

THE WALSH FAMILY

KATE CANTERBARY

VESPER PRESS

Copyright

Editing provided by Julia Ganis of JuliaEdits. www.juliaedits.com

about underneath it all

Matthew Walsh doesn't have feelings, and he likes it that way.

Between breathing life into his family's third generation Boston architecture shop, keeping the peace with his five siblings, and competing in triathlons, he doesn't have much time for feelings.

At least that's the case until Lauren Halsted tumbles into his life.

The feisty, beautiful blonde isn't what he wants and definitely not what he expects. She's so much more.

Lauren Halsted doesn't have time and that's turning into a real problem for her.

Losing focus isn't something Lauren does with any regularity. She has checklists and to-do lists and action plans a mile long. She doesn't have distractions and she doesn't let anyone tell her what to do.

When she trips down a flight of stairs and into her architect's arms, she gives into distraction for one night.

They weren't looking but they found each other anyway.

CW: *History of emotional and physical abuse by a parent; on-page moments of emotional and physical abuse by a parent; parent illness; parent loss; estranged family members*

For all the girls who know life never goes according to plan.

One

LAUREN

IF I HAD KNOWN I'd have a hot architect balls deep inside of me before the end of the weekend, I'd have made time for a pedicure. Also, a little chat about not losing my shit at all the wrong moments.

Hindsight was a bitch, and karma…well, I didn't know her story yet.

But instead of prioritizing that pedi, I was sobbing in a stairwell. It probably owed something to stress or sleepless nights or hormones or the freaking lunar cycle, but there I was, mascara smudged and nose running, crying it all the way out. Reacting this way to a missed deadline was ridiculous and childish, but the number of things going wrong today was obscene, and it wasn't even noon.

And this happened most days. Not the crying—that wasn't a regular occurrence for me—but the dead ends, the brick walls, the square pegs and round holes, the things that wouldn't go as planned.

It started innocently enough—all the best situations did. I used to teach third grade, and while I loved everything about it, I wanted to lead my own school. Conquer the world beyond my classroom. Do something incredible and bold and innovative.

For longer than I could remember, I'd toyed with applying for an absurdly competitive two-year paid fellowship program to launch a new school, and one day I finally did it. No one was more shocked than I was when the acceptance letter arrived. At the time, it didn't seem like I was embarking on the world's greatest obstacle course.

Part of me knew that receiving an offer to join this fellowship was a tremendous accomplishment and a validation of my hard work in the classroom, but most days I felt like a fraud. Someone would soon notice I wasn't nearly as smart or talented or driven as I led them to believe. They'd realize I was sitting at my kitchen table at one a.m., trying to make sense of state guidelines for school lunch programs or wrestling with five-year operating budgets, and rip those generous start-up grants right out from underneath me.

Not so long ago, I was good at everything. Not just good —awesome. Parents lobbied to get their kids on my roster. My students outperformed their peers across the city and state. I was engaging and creative in the classroom, and managed every committee, event, and initiative at my school. Five golden apples lined my desk, one for each year I received the district's Teacher of the Year award. The cognitive research I conducted for my Master's thesis was mentioned in prominent journals and blogs. A girl could get used to that level of wonderful, and it made the present state of affairs even more dismal.

I expected the fellowship to be demanding, and I knew all about demanding. I was the chick who taught the largest, neediest classes while simultaneously running the book and science fairs, and coaching the middle school's cheer squad, all while finishing my Master of Education degree and prepping for my principal licensure exams. But I never expected it to be quite like this. Working straight through weekends and holidays. Chained to my email. A slave to my action plan. Spending zero time in classrooms. Clinging to my sanity's last threads upon finding a state office unexpectedly closed on the day of a filing deadline.

But as my father liked to say, there were three choices in life: giving in, giving up, or giving it all you've got.

I wasn't giving in and I sure as hell wasn't giving up.

This school was part dream, part reality, and all mine. So what if I couldn't find time to collect my clothes from the dry cleaner or sleep more than a few hours each night? I could sleep when I was dead, and when that day rolled around, I didn't want to think about all the opportunities I passed up over some miserable moments in a stairwell.

The right amount of stubborn resistance had me swiping raspberry red gloss over my lips and wiggling my shoulders back. The hours, the hurdles, the hoops—they weren't stopping me, not when I had four inches of clear-ance rack Jimmy Choo goodness to get me through it.

A genuine smile fixed on my face, I sweet-talked my way through a few clerks to get what I needed. Within fifteen minutes, my documents were filed before the critical deadline and this particular fiasco was behind me, and I marched out of the state offices beaming. The satisfaction of crossing that off my list bordered on orgasmic, which was a commentary on either my work ethic or my shortage of orgasms. Couldn't be sure.

The sweet talk was a double-edged sword in my world. Some blamed it on the California in me, others said it was the elementary teacher, and an odd few thought I was trying to be a psychic medium, but I think I'd always seen just beyond the masks people wore, to where they were real and vulnerable. I stared too closely, watched too long, but it never took much to see what was right there. People revealed themselves in glimpses and flashes, and I believed they usually wanted to be seen.

I was good at it—knowing what to say in awkward moments, interpreting body language and subtle cues, figuring out what people needed—and it was my undoing. My tendencies to put people at ease and draw them out occasionally made me the world's greatest dumping ground. Add to that my inclination to adopt every project and solve every problem I encountered, and I neglected myself in the process. As my friends Steph and Amanda liked to remind me, those problems and projects occasionally took over, took all of me.

That was why I swore off men. I couldn't worry about fixing all the boys in Boston anymore. There were schools to open and shoe sales to find, and I didn't have the time to deal with man-children who owned a singular set of sheets and still called their hometown pediatrician for every sore throat.

I had an incredible group of friends, and a number of vibrators powerful enough to chip a tooth if not handled with care. There was no room in my life for men right now, and no need to make room.

With the meltdown behind me and two hours until my next appointment, I required a treat, and my first instinct pointed to cupcakes and tequila. While it seemed like the appropriate reward for navigating another mindlessly bureaucratic channel, I usually reserved the cake-and-liquor doubleheader for blue moons and holidays. Bypassing my preferred cupcakeries, I went in search of my other indulgence: lingerie.

My happiness was pegged to neither my measurements nor the number of pounds I wanted to drop, but I played the trade-off game, keeping my treats and cheats in some semblance of balance.

Croissant for breakfast, no drinks that evening. Cheesy enchiladas for lunch, no nibbling chocolate at midnight.

Of course, it didn't always work that way.

My father was a Navy man, and after years of deployment, he transitioned out of the field and into training new SEALs. Each batch of sailors endured months of conditioning, "the good kind of torture," my father would say, and his dinner table stories never skimped on the gory details.

That is, the details the government allowed him to share.

I wasn't joining the SEALs anytime soon—my girl parts saw to that—but my father didn't see gender as a reason to exclude me from the mock training operations he planned for my older brothers. He taught me how to use my height and low center of gravity to my advantage, but more importantly, he taught me to rely on myself.

Over and over, he told me there was nothing anyone could do for me that I couldn't do for myself. He and my mother raised me on that ethos, and I believed it every time I dropped his SEALs on their asses. They weren't comfortable perpetrating crimes against the commanding officer's daughter, but they armed me with the knowledge and skills necessary to fight off attackers, escape kidnappers, fashion weapons from random items, and treat any number of injuries with salt water and a belt. But more than the badass technique, they instilled confidence, the internal faith that I was capable of anything.

I knew from countless survival exercise that sailors often went into battle with little more than their wits, and if they did have a weapon, it needed to serve many purposes. My father saw to it that I had a small bunker of equipment at my disposal, but my armor was softer than anything Commodore Halsted would have recommended.

The streets of Boston were no battlefield and opening a school was not a covert op, but my weapons of choice were devastating heels and lacy undies. It wasn't about the designer brands or lusting after this season's hottest styles, and it wasn't about being anyone's eye candy. No, it was about the strength I felt when that sumptuous lace skimmed up my thighs and how only I'd know about those big girl panties swishing against my skirt. It was stepping into a platform heel and seeing the world from an entirely new vantage point, one where nobody ever mistook me for a college kid or intern.

Though the fellowship program paid me well, it wasn't Agent Provocateur or Christian Louboutin well, and my habit required a certain amount of sale stalking. Forty-five minutes of salivating over unimaginably expensive lingerie later, I laid my hands upon some of the most beautiful mesh and dot lace panties.

I was one of the odd few for whom nude-colored under-things nearly matched my bare skin, and when I picked up the panties, I knew I'd look naked wearing them, and I loved that idea. I couldn't contain the jolt of excitement rippling through me at the thought, a giggle slipping from my lips and attracting the side eye of the shopgirl. When I spied the matching bra in my size—finding 36DDs in La

Perla was like seeing the ghost of Paul Revere riding through downtown on a unicorn—I knew this treat was precisely proportional to today's victory.

Perhaps I wasn't on karma's shit list.

With my finery tissue-wrapped and stowed in my tote bag, I headed for my next appointment, and with any luck, an overdose of good news for my school.

Of all the issues I expected to encounter in my school-opening odyssey, finding a functional building or bare bit of land never cracked my short list. The fellowship established rigorous environmental and sustainability requirements, and the architects approved to handle that kind of work were few and far between—exactly seven in the state of Massachusetts with the mandated credentials. Two only touched multi-million dollar residential designs, two others weren't accepting new business, and the last three belonged to a single firm—Walsh Associates—specializing in historic preservation.

It sounded charming, really: a business focused exclusively on keeping Boston's old buildings looking new...ish. It was probably a New England thing; it seemed unlikely that a niche architect would find enough work in my home-town, San Diego, to stay in business.

They were located a few blocks from my apartment, and without knowing it, I had been walking past the Walsh Associates office every time I visited my favorite coffee shop.

It took several calls and a box of the best from Mike's Pastry to get on Matthew A. Walsh's calendar. His assistant had eyed the cream-filled sfogliatella, made me promise to "stop calling all damn day," and scribbled a date and time on the back of his business card.

Retrieving the card from my suit coat pocket, I studied the string of letters trailing after his name, denoting his credentials. He was an architect and engineer, he was an expert in sustainable design and preservation, and with any luck, he was the solution to all my problems.

If he wasn't, I'd research ways to operate a school from a quiet corner of my neighborhood Starbucks.

Two

MATTHEW

"WOULD you like to know what bullshit Angus is pulling now?" Shannon asked.

I rolled my eyes as her voice piped in through my phone's speaker. My older sister, Shannon, only referred to our father by first name. We all did. I couldn't tell you the last time I heard someone call him Dad, and all things considered, it was better than calling him Miserable Bastard.

Even if that was fitting.

After a shitty morning crammed with ornery inspectors and stop-work threats, Shannon's issues were par for the course.

"Go for it," I murmured. Peering over the steering wheel, I scanned Neponset Avenue for a shuttered church and my one o'clock appointment. "Can't be much worse than changing the designs on the Belmont project at the last minute. Again."

"Believe me, Matt, it *is* worse," she hissed. "He's picked

up four rehab and restore properties around Bunker Hill. Apparently, he wanted to. You know. Just because."

I turned down a side street and brought the Range Rover to a stop. My fingers curled around the steering wheel. Tension seized every muscle in my hand, up my arm, along my neck, and into my jaw. I didn't need this shit and I didn't need four bullshit projects clogging my days.

"Who's going to run that? Does he realize how much we're managing right now? Sam, Patrick, and me, we're fully booked. I've backed out of three marathons in the past few months! I have no time for anything, ever, and now I have four properties that will definitely fall to me because Sam's busy agreeing to random shit without discussing it with us first, and Patrick works twenty-nine hours a day, and no one stops to say this is insane."

"Exactly! And me, right now, I'm saying this is insane." Sharp clicks punctuated her angry sigh, her stilettos reverberating against the hardwood as she paced her office. "He just wants us to know he's still holding some of the cards and plenty of chips."

"A lot less than you think, Shan."

In the nine years since we—me, with my brothers Patrick and Sam, and my sister Shannon—put our stake in the ground and edged Angus onto the sidelines of our ailing third generation architecture shop, he never failed to concoct obstacles to our success. He hated that we were doing more with the family business than he ever did. Us kicking up some dust in the sustainable design world didn't meet with his favor either, and he made his displeasure clear every time he interfered with projects or bought crumbling buildings to add to our overflowing slate.

Externally, it appeared that visionary architect Angus

Walsh was simply staying engaged with the work in his retirement. What could be obnoxious about an old man who wanted nothing more than to preserve the city's forgotten architectural gems?

And he was brilliant when it came to keeping up appearances. Only a select few outside our family knew the truth of Angus's alcoholism, his vindictiveness, his violence. We went along with the ruse, even when that meant absorbing costly projects and covering up his public indiscretions.

I shook my head and drained the coffee from my afternoon stop at Dunkin's. I was always the intermediary, always stuck cleaning up Angus's messes. I didn't know when I earned that role but seeing as I never let him get to me it was mine to keep.

I felt a glimmer of wry relief Angus hadn't shown up at one of my properties to deliver the news of his acquisitions in person. Increasingly, his appearances were moving out of the office's controlled environment and into public venues. And after my face-off with the inspector, a visit from Angus would have gone down as smoothly as a shot of scotch and a handful of nails.

"Fuck," I sighed. "Just…fuck."

"You know there's nothing I enjoy more than Angus and his little visits. We need to hire a bouncer."

On most days, Shannon was a steamroller and that was putting it mildly, but when Angus was in the office, he usually raked her over the coals. He treated her with such derision and scorn I couldn't help but take those bullets for her. She shouldered more than her share of the work and family burdens.

"We probably should," I murmured. "Shan, I gotta go.

I'm late for a client and I'm lost in Dorchester. I'll figure out how to deal with him later. Be a duck. Don't let him get to you. He's not worth it."

"I don't want to hear about your fucking ducks, Matt."

After fifteen minutes circling the streets of Dorchester and some help from Siri, I scaled the steps of Saint Cosmas while pulling on the fleece vest embroidered with our new Walsh Associates logo—another in an endless line of changes to make the firm our own.

Weeds stood tall around the perimeter and vines roped up one side, over the roofline, and down the other. Small trees grew out of the parking lot, the roots leaving behind eruptions of concrete. The earth was repossessing the structure. A quick inventory of the church and the attached hall told me the work involved the two E's: extensive and expensive.

"Oh, hi, over here." I turned my focus away from the sagging roofline and stone pillars toward a female voice. "Hi, I'm Lauren Halsted."

She came in about nine, maybe ten inches under my six-three, though the energy she projected made up for the small package. Tucked into a navy skirt and jacket with her rich blonde hair loose at her shoulders, she turned a slow smile toward me. The professional suit did nothing to disguise her curves, and for a moment, I stared at her, wondering what a pin-up girl was doing at a Dorchester church.

My expectations had run closer to a graying librarian or grandmotherly type. Who else would want to convert an aging church hall into an elementary school?

"Miss Halsted, hi, Matt Walsh. I apologize, I didn't mean to keep you waiting." I squeezed her hand, but it was the shimmers of gold in her green eyes catching my attention. I'd never seen anything like it before, and I couldn't look away.

"Oh please don't give it a second thought. And call me Lauren. Let's get inside, and I'll tell you what I'm thinking."

I held open the heavy, warped door for Miss Halsted and found myself gazing at something even more captivating than her eyes: her ass. It was round and firm, and the craving to squeeze it—*hard*—left my fingers itching. And then her legs. Deeply tanned, natural and without a hint of that strange spray-on shit.

She was talking, but between her butterscotch-washed voice and the dark freckles on her calves, my brain didn't have the bandwidth to listen. Angry creaks echoed from the floorboards and plumes of dust swirled around her ankles, and then I noticed the leopard-print Come Fuck Me heels.

Those looked good on her.

Finding myself admiring the lilt in Lauren's voice and her sultry features was a surprise. She wasn't my type. Not even a little bit.

I liked beasts—ass-kicking, whey protein-and-oatmeal-guzzling beasts who preferred compression sleeves and hydration belts to jewelry and flowers. I liked women who planned their lives around Color Runs, Tough Mudders, and the Ironman circuit. I liked women who could bench press my weight, and those within a few inches of my height, and even the ones who liked to remind me they could knock my ass into next Friday. I was about hard-core athletic women, usually ones from my marathon and triathlon circles, and always ones who wanted only fast, stringless sex.

Maybe I was irreversibly fucked-up, but beast mode worked for me.

Lauren was short and soft, with generous, real curves. Everything about her screamed sexy as fuck, yet innocent and warm. Not even within striking distance of beastly.

And this was an architectural consult, for Christ's sake. I wasn't here to think about her or types or freckles or sexy-ass shoes. And women like her married young. Anyone with sense would have snapped her up the minute it was legal. She had naughty schoolteacher written all over that sunny blonde smile, and I was willing to bet she was bent over someone's knee every night.

Client, client, client.

Fuck, I needed to stop thinking about spanking this chick and get my head in the game.

Blowing out a frustrated breath, I turned away and inventoried the hall's structure. Rays of daylight shone through the ceiling. Crisp autumn air wafted in through broken stained glass windows. Beams listed at precarious angles. Water damage and wood rot long ago destroyed everything worth preserving. It was a train wreck—my favorite kind of project.

"...so this area could be divided into four classrooms and five small offices over there. I know the plumbing needs updating. What would it take to add another set of bathrooms down here?"

My phone's structural engineering apps came to life under my fingers while I eyed the space. Perhaps train wreck was a gracious characterization.

I looked up from my phone to watch Lauren traversing decayed stairs to a small alcove—in the CFMs, no less.

When she shot her left arm out to steady herself, there were exactly zero rings on those fingers.

Client, client, client.

Get through the consult, I thought. Plenty of time for thinking about fucking Little Miss Naughty Schoolteacher when she was out of sight.

I ran my hands along the pillars flanking the main room. The feel of an unstable load-bearing structure was unmistakable, and I stopped caring who Miss Halsted went home to at night. I jogged across the hall, slowing only when I reached her side. "Time to go."

Eyes narrowed, she studied my grip on her bicep. "Excuse me? What's going on?"

I yanked her outside and shook my head. "Miss Halsted. You need to stay away from this place. It's not stable. Go across the street. Now."

Lauren's lips fell into a tight line. Maybe she was the one doing the spanking. "I'm fine right here, thank you."

If this place wasn't a breath from caving in around us, my dick would have been standing at attention and waiting for marching orders, and I would've had only that sharp look and bossy tone to blame.

"The load on this structure"—I pointed to the roof—"is causing extensive stresses and deformations on the internal supports. The walls, the pillars. And I'd bet anything the foundation has deteriorated beyond repair. A strong gust and this place is coming down. I want you fifty feet away, Miss Halsted." I passed my fingers down the stone column for emphasis, a trail of sand and pebbles trickling to the ground.

"I'm only Miss Halsted inside the classroom. Call me

Lauren." Her smile was serene, yet wholly impatient. "Are you sure?"

"I make a point of knowing safe structures." I wanted to drag her across the street, lock her in the car, and then... well, those interests weren't part of a standard consult. "But let me take a closer look at the foundation. Stay right here."

The property borders told the same story. The site needed a full rebuild, if not a straight teardown and that was no surprise after surveying the interior. I debated how we'd get a team in place to preserve the only thing worth saving: a round, eastern-facing stained glass window. The time and money would be huge, and wouldn't help her project in the least.

Rounding the perimeter, my chest lurched when I noticed her staring at the structure, her plump, red lip trapped between her teeth. She looked frustrated and determined, and so fucking desirable, and even if it was a giant pain in my ass, I wanted to find a solution and make this right for her.

"I could run some more calculations at the office, see to a few variables. But," I hedged as the sparkle returned to her eyes, "I can't promise anything."

"Thank you. I knew we'd find a way to make this work," Lauren said.

She started down the church steps toward me but a worn patch of granite caught her heel and she shrieked, pitching forward. Her chin was headed for the sidewalk when my hand seized her elbow, and I jerked her against me. The adrenaline was pumping too fast, and my brain couldn't focus on the slide of her silky hair against my chin, or her sweet scent engraving itself on my memory.

"I was going to stick that landing," she said. Her expression was dead serious, but it wasn't until a shy smirk pulled at her lips that I understood the humor.

"I bet you were," I murmured. I kept my arm around her lower back, my hand cradling her waist. "Are you okay?"

Her palms laid flat against my chest and I didn't want her pulling away yet. My fingers had plans of their own, and they flexed, kneading the flesh beneath her suit coat. There was strength under all that softness.

And those eyes, they couldn't decide if they were green or gold.

She released a shaky laugh and looked up. "Quick reflexes. I knew you were the man for my project."

I was close enough to kiss her. She was short, and I'd have to bend down to meet her, but then I'd determine whether she tasted as sweet as she looked.

"Oh yeah?" I didn't know much about the correlation between reflexes and decent architects, but it seemed like something I wanted to hear. And if she noticed me rubbing her back or staring at her mouth, it didn't show.

"You're all over it and one step ahead, even when I knock myself down some stairs, which is not a new occurrence for me. Sadly." She paused, realizing her hands were on my chest, and pulled them away to rake through her hair. "I need people who won't give up on this project. I'm not stopping until I get a yes from you."

I reminded myself we were still talking about this shithole property, and not the seventy-two other activities to which I'd eagerly agree. But that bossy tone was addictive. Mesmerizing. Sexy as fuck. "I'll do my best."

"I know you will." Her arms wrapped around my shoulders and she folded me into a fierce hug. "Thank you," she said, her breath whispering over my ear. It was gentle and light, and if she didn't step back in the next three seconds, my hand was going to introduce itself to her ass.

Client, client, client.

"Okay, well, that's wonderful," I murmured.

Retreat. Disengage. Fall back.

Thirty was too old for midday erections on the sidewalk. A stiff pat to her shoulder, a giant step backward, and a notebook over my crotch kept my dignity intact.

For the moment.

Hugging clients wasn't a standard part of my consults. Neither was caring. I was good at numbers, structures, and ratios. It was a pleasant coincidence that I usually liked my clients, and because I was good at getting shit done, and delivering on time and under budget, they liked me. Somehow, I managed to both hug Miss Halsted and care about her happiness inside an hour.

And let's not forget the waking wet dream.

"I'll run some numbers. Probably get back to you in a day or two." I tried ignoring her smile—I could feel it piercing my skin, stabbing me like little pins of sweet, sinful joy—and gestured to the stone steps. "Watch out for stairs."

Lauren nodded and accepted my card. "Thank you so much. For everything." Her gaze swiveled between the steps and me, and she laughed. "I sent all of my information to your assistant last week, but if you need anything else…"

There was more, something she wanted to say, but it melted on her tongue and she presented her card instead. I felt only the brush of her fingertips against my palm, but it was enough to send electricity charging through my veins.

I didn't know what the naughty schoolteacher was doing to me.

"Call me. Day or night. This project is my life. Really. Anytime."

But I didn't think I wanted it to stop.

I WENT a couple more rounds with the inspector on the Back Bay brownstone restorations that were giving me hell, but after six hours of fixing mistakes and chewing some general contractor ass, all I had to show for it was a pounding headache. Making tracks on at least ten miles of pavement was the only answer, but at the rate my day was going, I'd be running at midnight. Exhausted, I climbed the stairs to the Beacon Hill headquarters of Walsh Associates and waved to Shannon and Patrick when I passed her office. Inviting myself into their weekly budget-and-sushi meeting was the last thing any sane person needed.

Settling into my desk, I stared out the eyebrow dormer windows at the night sky. Why did I do this? Insane hours, impossible expectations, bitch-ass inspectors. Why did I put up with this?

There was always Lauren Halsted.

If pulling a bubbly blonde from an unstable building and subsequently preventing her from eating concrete were the highlights of my day, I was calling it a memorable day. The full-body embrace put an interesting spin on things. A scarf camouflaged the finer aspects of her chest, but the second she was up against me, her full breasts were unmistakable.

Something else unmistakable? The semi I got from those tits and the vision of my hands all over them while she rode me. I couldn't remember the last time my hands explored a body like Lauren's, if ever. She wasn't sculpted or race-hardened. She was real, all feminine, and completely foreign to me. And a client and not my type and I needed something else to occupy my mind.

Fast.

I demolished a Reuben sandwich while listening to voicemails, and sighed—and couldn't repress a smile—when her voice filled the room.

"Hi, Mr. Walsh, this is Lauren Halsted. From the Saint Cosmas property. Touching base to see if you have any updates for me. Looking forward to hearing from you."

I pulled up the specs of her project on my laptop.

"Mr. Walsh, this is Lauren Halsted again. Please feel free to reach out with updates. I'm free anytime. Looking forward to hearing from you. About the Saint Cosmas project."

I checked the timestamp on her calls. Thirty-five minutes apart. "She wasn't joking when she said it was her life," I murmured.

"Mr. Walsh, this is Lauren Halsted calling. Sorry to trouble you. I've emailed some information gathered from a feasibility study completed on the site a few years ago. Again, please call me. Anytime. Looking forward to hearing from you."

I crumpled the sandwich wrappings and turned my attention to the Saint Cosmas project. The calculations were quick, and confirmed everything I suspected: the site was completely unstable. The costs of rehab far exceeded Lauren's budget, and that was before we started talking about restoration or turning it green.

Annoyed, I rolled my eyes at the screen. I probably would have been prepared with that information before this afternoon's meeting if I wasn't managing a ridiculous project load and incapable of seeing more than four minutes ahead at any given time. Regardless, I wanted another visit with Miss Halsted, and I wanted to touch her again.

And I figured she'd want to go through the data in person, piece by piece. She seemed thorough like that. Flicking a glimpse at my watch, I decided it wasn't too late to call.

"Hi, this is Lauren."

Fuck, I wanted to know what she was wearing. In detail. The conservative suit made me think of cotton panties in safe, subtle colors, but those heels said red thong. And I wanted to get to the bottom of that controversy.

Client, client, client.

"Miss Halsted, Matt Walsh. How are you this evening?"

"We're not in my classroom, Matt. Lauren is fine," she laughed, but her tone was no nonsense. It went in my ear and straight down to my dick. "So great to hear from you so soon. Any news on the site?"

We were pushing and pulling against a strange layer of formality. Was she still Miss Halsted because I was imagining her underwear, and fighting like hell not to? Or because she was my only full-body contact since the triathlon chick in July? Or was it the naughty schoolteacher thing?

If anyone asked, I was totally down for exploring the naughty schoolteacher thing.

"Still running scenarios. Can you meet me tomorrow?" I toggled to my calendar. "Around five?"

"Of course. At Saint Cosmas?"

"No!" I cried, imagining the floor dissolving into splinters under our feet. "Can you make it to our Beacon Hill offices? Off Cambridge Street?"

"Definitely. Thank you again for everything, Matt."

A smile spread across my face as I sat back in my chair. "Goodnight, Lauren."

She paused and I thought I heard her smile. Was that possible? To *hear* a smile? "Goodnight, Matt."

I definitely heard a smile.

She was contagious. It was viral, her juju, her mojo, her sparkle, her hip-swiveling swagger. Whatever it was, it was on me.

I needed a little swagger for the deluge ahead.

Seventeen messages from sub-contractors, all requiring immediate attention.

Five budget updates from Shannon, plus a rundown on Angus's new Bunker Hill properties and the associated screaming match, but I knew those issues would keep for another day. He liked to disrupt our work with time intensive, expensive properties, but he usually managed a few drunken rounds of golf in between the surprise attacks.

Eleven designs requiring structural analysis from my brother Sam, the sustainable design specialist. If that runt continued accepting new work without getting the entire team's approval first, I was drop-kicking his skinny ass into the harbor.

Six frighteningly basic questions on restoration projects from my brother Riley, the youngest architect on the Walsh Associates team and Patrick's slave.

Twelve one-line messages from my older brother Patrick, the senior architect and de facto chief executive, all bitching about progress on my Back Bay brownstone restorations. Bitching suited him. He liked freaking out over minute details.

I spent two hours deep in calculations for Sam, and updated my partners on the brownstone issues.

And that left one message from my little sister, Erin, with a photo album from her research trip to São Jorge Island, off the coast of Portugal, and its trio of volcanic complexes on the Azorean archipelago. I saved her for last.

Me and Erin, we got each other. We were the youngest, in a way, and being at the bottom of our respective heaps always brought us together. Patrick, Shannon, and I were born one after another, inside three years. Sam came along about two years later, then Riley, and finally Erin.

From: Matthew Walsh
To: Erin Walsh
Date: September 23 at 22:43 EDT
Subject: RE: Back from the Azores

E -
Good to hear you're back on the mainland. The pictures of that lava flow are sick. How do you even get close enough to take those shots?

Crazy, crazy day here today. I just about dislocated a client's arm when she tried to take a header down some stone steps. I think I've seen you do the same.

Miss you. We need to Skype soon.

Find a way to get your ass back here for Thanksgiving or Christmas this year. Pick one and show up.

M

I REREAD the message before clicking Send. I didn't know why I mentioned Lauren; I just knew I wanted to tell someone about her and Erin was my most trusted someone.

Three

LAUREN

I SAT cross-legged on my antique velvet sofa, staring at the cover of my latest book club selection. Another meeting with Matthew A. Walsh. *Matt.* I was more than happy to give him an hour of my day, especially if it involved good news. I needed good news, and sharing his company was no hardship.

He was one of those guys you met and immediately thought, "Wow. Let me take off your pants. And yeah, the shirt too."

Or, in my case, "Let me throw myself down some stairs and rub up against your chest."

Given his kindness in keeping me from becoming a sidewalk stain, I was tempted to thank Matt with coffee after our meeting, but I'd hesitated, and the moment had slipped away.

I was curious about him. He wasn't the type of architect I had expected—no tweed jacket, no suede elbow patches, no tortoiseshell glasses, no ill-fitting pleated khakis. Instead, he was an architectural superhero, all muscles and dark hair and throbbing annoyance at the building for failing to meet his expectations. His smile was scorching, but his intense gaze hit me hardest. When those blue eyes landed on me, serious and heavy, it was as if he was sifting through my every thought.

My phone vibrated across the table, and my heart leapt just as quickly. I rolled my eyes, laughing at myself and shaking free from my daydream. Time to shut down all thoughts of Matt Walsh's chiseled chest.

I studied the readout and smiled. "If it isn't the road warriors!"

"Hi, honey! It's your Mom and me, we're on the speaker-phone," my father announced. For a guy who trained Navy SEALs for over twenty years, he sounded quite impressed with the capabilities of his cell phone.

"Hi, Dad. Hi, Mom. Where are you today?"

"We're in the Anza-Borrego Desert, in the mountains outside Palm Springs. Amazing country up here. You'd love the hiking."

I snorted, imagining myself tumbling down the trail and landing in a bank of jumping cholla cactus. My brothers liked to say I tripped over dust. It wasn't that I was clumsy —ten years of gymnastics and competitive cheerleading proved I could control my body—it was that I managed to stumble at inopportune times, and those times were typi-cally when I was nervous.

Or distracted by the dress shirt pulled tight across Matt's chest, and the thought of peeling it away and tasting him just beneath his collar.

"And the views for miles!" Mom added. "The natural landscape is gorgeous. I can't stop taking pictures."

"How long are you staying there?"

"Well..." Dad released a good-natured chuckle. "We've scrapped the itinerary for the moment. Your mother has persuaded me to follow the good weather."

"That sounds reasonable," I said.

"But we'll be spending some time in Palm Springs to visit with the Rosses. And then down to Mexico. I'd like to stop in Rosarito, and then Ensenada. Along Highway One. Probably ending in Cabo San Lucas around Thanksgiving. Maybe later. I want some sunny holidays this year."

"You're welcome to join us anytime, honey," Dad said. "Just say the word, and we'll have a ticket waiting for you. I hope you're not worrying about money."

He trusted me with firearms, yet doubted my ability to balance a checkbook. Was it a protective dad thing? An only daughter thing? Or was it that he truly doubted I had my shit together?

Not that my shit was remotely together, but still.

"I know, Dad," I sighed. "I'm doing fine. You don't need to worry about me—"

"I know you can handle yourself, but I've seen more than enough evil out there. You're still carrying that pepper spray, correct?"

It was always a matter of time until he went there. Commodore Halsted and his "the world is brimming with danger and therefore my daughter needs a thigh-holstered k-bar to walk around the corner" speech. He liked to spice it up with stories cherry-picked from his missions, although I was fairly certain he tossed in plotlines from spy novels and war movies.

I also believed at least half of what he said, although it was more than likely the spy novel half.

"Yes, Dad. Please remember I'm twenty-eight and I've lived in the city for—"

"None of that matters. Predators strike the moment you drop your guard," he said. "Think about a Krav Maga refresher course. You need to keep those skills sharp. You never know what's lurking when you least expect it."

"Bill, stop with the dramatics. What's new with you, sweetheart?" Mom asked.

"We're having a party for Steph and Amanda this weekend, before they leave town. I've been busy finding a building, and meeting with an architect to get it ready for kids. I have meetings lined up for tomorrow with donors interested in funding some of the classroom research we'll be conducting."

"Be yourself, Lolo. They'd be fools not to donate," Dad said.

"I know, Dad, but sometimes it's a little more complicated than being friendly."

"You tell me if you want me to make some calls," he continued. "I have a lot of buddies from the service who want to see kids off the streets and getting a decent education. We've seen plenty of sailors who coulda used a teacher like you to set them straight."

"Thanks, Dad. I don't want any favors, though—"

"Not a favor, Lauren. That's how it's done. It's all about who you know and calling in the right contacts at the right time."

"Bill, let me talk to my Lolo. Go play with your new binoculars," Mom said. The speakerphone connection clicked off. "He's outside now. Probably being a weirdo and spying on the other campers. Is everything okay?"

"Yeah, Mom, everything's fine."

"Are you sure? You sound a little ruffled, Lolo, a little off. It must be rough on you, with Stephanie and Amanda moving away."

My oldest friends, Amanda and Steph, were my home away from home. The sisters I never had. The bitches in my back pocket. We roomed together in college then moved to Boston over six years ago, where we shared the darkest, dampest subterranean apartment in town. It earned every ounce of its nickname, The Dungeon. Over the years, we celebrated successes big and small, and endured heartaches in careers and friendships and relationships. We grew up together—the growing up you did when it was time to figure out life.

And now we were growing apart.

Amanda was engaged, pregnant, and moving with her fiancé, Phil. We always knew Phil's job as lobbyist for a consortium of cutting-edge pharmaceutical firms took priority in their relationship, and that his work would eventually take him and Amanda to Washington, DC. Expecting it to happen didn't mean it wasn't leaving a cannonball-sized hole in me.

We also knew Steph and her husband Dan intended to return home to Chicago when they started a family, and I was surprised they stayed so long after Madison's birth. Steph's pregnancy was difficult, her labor was complicated, and baby Madison struggled with reflux and colic and ear infections right from the start. We pitched in to provide Steph with meals, help around the house, and babysitting, but Steph and Dan needed their big families back in Chicago, and I wanted them to have that.

But like I said: cannonballs.

And if I was being honest with myself, we'd been

growing apart by feet and inches since moving out of The Dungeon. Marriage, careers, babies—these things changed us, and our relationships with each other were evolving, too. It wasn't bad; it was just different.

"No, it's not that," I said. "I mean, yes, it's going to be tough, but life is taking them on some new adventures. It's what they need to do and I shouldn't be sad about that."

"Sounds like a new project would be good for you. Something to mix up your routine. You need a man in your life. Men are great distractions."

I laughed at my mother's suggestive tone but couldn't ignore the image of Matt Walsh and his broad shoulders. Or that chest. Give me some dirty laundry and a shirtless Matt, and I'd happily spend my day testing out those washboard abs.

My mother would love his dark, wavy hair and blue eyes, and she'd make plenty of naughty comments about his lean body. He'd meet her criteria for beefcake status. I used to turn seven shades of red when she'd thumb through *People* magazine, telling my friends she thought Brad Pitt and George Clooney were hunky, and that she wouldn't mind a weekend alone with either. Or both.

I didn't understand the part about both until my twenties, and for everyone involved, that was probably best.

"I'll keep that in mind," I murmured. "I do have a bunch of travel for conferences over the next few weeks, so I'll be busy and finally spending some time in classrooms again."

"Enjoy it! When I was your age, I was pregnant with Wesley. All I knew was the base, and the other wives in the unit. Will was crawling, and your father was deployed on one of his missions. I had no idea when he'd be back. If he'd be back," she added, her voice turning somber. "You have so many options, so much freedom. Enjoy it."

"I do, Mom."

"Good. Now, if you do want to spend some time in Mexico, email us. Your father says we can't rely on cell service in Mexico, but what does he know?"

I laughed. "Have you heard from Will or Wes recently?"

"Yeah, your father spoke to them when we were leaving home. He has some theories about where they're stationed at the moment, but didn't mention specifics. Says they're both well, keeping their heads in the mission."

"Okay," I murmured. I couldn't understand how my mother accepted the dangers my brothers confronted on a daily basis. I didn't truly, deeply, fully understand the nature of my father's work until after his retirement, and was shocked when my parents wholeheartedly supported Will and Wes when they joined the SEALs after graduating from UC-San Diego. "Let me know if you hear anything new."

"Of course," Mom said. "I'll be updating our little website with photos from our journeys. I can't wait to hear what you think of my new posts!"

"I will, Mom," I laughed. My mother, the travel blogger. A few years ago, she kicked off their retirement road trip with a new camera, and hasn't stopped photographing since. What started as Wes's suggestion to post her shots to a blog rather than crashing our email accounts with a terabyte of attachments each week was now a thriving blog complete with voracious followers and advertisers.

"I'll let you go, it's late. Sleep tight, sweetheart. Love you. Daddy says he loves you, too."

"Love you both."

"Find a distraction, Lolo. Men are the best kind."

I leaned back and drummed my fingers against the book's cover, dismissing my mother's comments. No time for men. No time for distractions. Not even time to read this month's book.

The book club was a throwback to our days in The Dungeon, and grew over time to include Phil and Dan's friends' girlfriends and an assortment of colleagues and acquaintances. We came together each month but spent most of the time guzzling wine and catching up.

Was it crazy that I faithfully read the books—even if I hated them, even if I lurked in a few online forums to borrow insightful comments—or was it crazy that we didn't simply retitle the event?

Hanging out and drinking wine without the pretense of literature sounded superb, but I doubted I'd continue going without Steph and Amanda. It was our thing, and without them it didn't hold the same appeal.

And it wasn't as if I needed anyone else trying to fix me up.

The old 'always a bridesmaid' adage wasn't lost on me. I dated plenty but finding The One was the least of my worries. I was as single as single could be: not seeing anyone, no compatibility matches from dating portals, no singles mixer booze cruises on my calendar, and I liked it that way.

Regardless of sad-faced inquiries, the singleton life worked for me. It was my prerogative to shave—or not shave—my legs. I could go on last-minute trips to Martha's Vineyard or New York City or back home to San Diego without including anyone else in those decisions. Dinner often consisted of sliced cucumbers and carrots dipped in chipotle ranch dressing, and there was no one to complain about that.

I was free to watch *Pretty Little Liars* and *The Vampire Diaries* and every other slightly ridiculous show. I was under no obligation to share the bed, closets, or bathroom. I decided how to spend my money, á la three hundred dollars on one incredible pair of shoes. If I wanted to dedicate my entire Saturday to researching elementary math programs or trying on every pair of peep-toes in Boston, I wasn't cramping anyone's style. And most importantly, I had the freedom to whip off my bra and pull on yoga pants the second I walked through the door of my apartment.

There was the crux of it for me: I didn't like being told what to do or following anyone's rules, and it was that kind of rebelliousness that uniquely suited me for opening a radically new type of school. Without a healthy supply of oppositional defiance to challenge the status quo, I wouldn't be able to question long-held beliefs about teaching and learning, even if some of those questions were uncomfortable and disruptive.

Don't get me wrong, I was a good girl at heart—I had the Type A personality straight from my father to prove it. I waited at red lights, even if it was two in the morning and the roads were deserted. I paid all of my bills on time. I never had one-night stands. I always sent handwritten thank-you notes. I religiously kept annual appointments for teeth cleaning and Pap smears—though never on the same day.

I was a rule-follower…and a rebel.

I wandered into my bedroom and gazed into my closet, waiting for inspiration to strike. The right look always kicked my confidence into high gear, and with the way tomorrow was shaping up, I needed the extra boost. The dry cleaner was holding all my favorite dresses hostage, and the go-to uniform of depressing skirt suits and statement necklaces was tired. Not even Jimmy Choo was changing that.

A shock of red toward the back caught my eye and I drew the fit-and-flare dress off the rod. A substantial amount of peer pressure went into the purchase, and I struggled to find the right opportunity to wear it these days. The retro styling reminded me of June Cleaver, but modern touches edged it toward Michelle Obama.

Hanging the dress on my closet door, I added a navy scarf with silver stars, my favorite stiletto Mary Janes, a funky little artisan necklace from a July trip to Provincetown, and those fancy new undies.

No one would see my panties, but I'd know about their sheer silkiness. And that? That was exactly the armor I required to conquer the battles ahead.

Four

MATTHEW

"GOT A MINUTE FOR ME?"

I looked up from my double screens and rubbed my eyes. "Yeah, come on in," I called to my assistant, Theresa. "What's up?"

She dropped several thick folders onto my desk and settled into a chair. "Files on the new Bunker Hill properties. Angus asked me to pull the permit history."

"And where would we be without his thoughtfulness?" I dragged my hands through my hair and grunted. There were enough problems with my Back Bay projects without worrying about Bunker Hill, too. "What else?"

"I need your signature on all of these." She pointed to another file. "And these are draft bids. Patrick told Riley not to send anything without your approval."

I met Theresa's fake cheerfulness with a raised eyebrow. I didn't know what I'd do without her blocking and defending my door most days. Numbers and shapes were my domain, and Theresa took care of the organizing, ordering, and scheduling. "That kid needs to get some shit done without me," I said.

"I tried to tell him that, boss. But remember, he's still learning and he knows he has some big footsteps to follow." Theresa shuffled loose papers into neat piles and folders, and tidied the markers and mechanical pencils scattered over my drafting table. "Are you closing up shop for the weekend soon? Or should I order a sandwich for you?"

I ran a hand over the light scruff on my jaw and shook my head. I spent an extra nine minutes in bed this morning, forfeiting a decent shave to contemplate whether I'd ever had erotic dreams about clients prior to Little Miss Naughty Schoolteacher. None came to mind, and on further review, I was convinced the 'wake me up with your mouth on my dick' fantasy lived beyond the realm of the beasts, too. Not that I spent much time in beds with them, but that was aside the point. "Nah. I've got a client at five."

"All right," she murmured as she continued straightening my things. "I'll stay until your client arrives. Get out of the office this weekend, please. As the kids say, get a life."

Theresa's Boston accent was everything I loved about her and this town, right there in a few garbled sounds. She was scrappy and didn't give a fuck what anyone thought about her, or the threadbare Red Sox hoodies she wore as World Series good luck charms. She joined the firm years before any of us were born, and served her time under Angus. She didn't take any shit from anyone—my father included—and knew every single Walsh secret worth keeping.

"I don't think Patrick allows those," I muttered before my attention snapped back to my assistant. "Theresa, one more thing. My afternoon appointment yesterday? The church hall in Dorchester? How did that get on my calendar?"

Thirteen miles this morning did nothing to slow the Lauren Halsted fantasy montage in my head. Despite Patrick's rampant bitching, I had extended the route but there was no shaking that naughty schoolteacher sparkle.

"Halsted?" I nodded. "Last winter you were yappin' about being tired of dealing with rich assholes all the time, and wanting a few community projects. First that came along. That young lady is also quite persistent." After a shrug, she said, "And knows her pastries."

I murmured in acknowledgement and turned back to my designs. Staring at the screens, I debated a handful of scenarios. I knew some of the client's requests would have to go, or some of the restoration would; the structure couldn't handle both. Neither made me happy, and the client would be less than understanding considering the amount of money he was paying to have it all.

"This motherfucker is going to be the death of me," I moaned.

"I hope that's not my project."

Blinking at the sound of Lauren's voice, I shot out of my chair and heard it crash into the wall behind me. If yesterday's suit was an attempt to disguise her curves, today's dress was an ode to them. Every step toward her increased my desire to touch her. I didn't want her falling down stairs again, but if the opportunity presented itself, I was going to be there to catch her.

"Miss Halsted. I'm sorry, no, another project entirely."

"Didn't I tell you yesterday? You're only required to call me Miss Halsted in my classroom." Her tone teased, offering access to an inside joke and ignoring our narrow knowledge of each other. "Here, Lauren is fine."

She extended her hand toward me, but I didn't notice, instead standing there and staring at the golden hair tumbling softly around her shoulders. Before this moment, I hadn't given women's hair much thought. It was nice enough, but I never wanted it gliding through my fingers or tickling my chest. Not until I imagined burying my face in Lauren's hair while I buried myself inside her.

Shit. That spiraled out of control quickly.

"Mr. Walsh?"

Her eyebrows winged up, and I was betting she knew exactly what I was thinking. Narrating that fantasy out loud was the only way to make it more obvious.

"Matt," I croaked. "Call me Matt. Or Matthew. Around here, Mr. Walsh is my father."

And I'd rather you not confuse the two.

I gestured to the seats in front of the desk and tracked her hourglass shape as she sat, watching her movements, studying her hands, admiring today's Come Fuck Me heels. The red dress accented a narrow waist rising from flared hips that called out to my hands. I saw myself bending her over the desk, hiking up her dress, and taking her right now. And I saw her liking it.

I spent a full minute on that thought before groaning inwardly. I was a dick. An unprofessional, single-minded dick and I didn't like small, curvy girls who left their mojo all over me.

"Matthew, I really hope you have some good news for me."

On her lips, my name was a purred commandment, and

I wanted to hear it like that, the confluence of gentle and firm, again.

"I ran some scenarios," I began, spreading site plans on the desk between us.

I expected the linear order of shapes and structures to take over and cool my nerves, but Lauren tucked her hair over her ears and smiled, and there was no unwinding the lust in my belly. I wanted to touch her and taste her, and I wanted it very soon.

"That structure is barely standing. I looked for options, but I cannot see anything salvageable in the structure."

Lauren's fingers moved over the plans and she studied them carefully, and it was all I could do not to grab that hand and press it to my crotch. It was absurd and wrong to obsess over her this way, and I knew it, but there was no beating back the hunger surging through my veins, overtaking me. She did something to me, something I didn't understand, but I definitely wanted to figure it out.

"The architects who looked at it before and the people who told me to check out that property, they didn't mention any of this."

"Yeah," I nodded. "That's because most architects—I love them, but physics isn't their primary concern. I wear both hats: architect and structural engineer. You could have spent a fortune on rehab only for the foundation to crumble with the first heavy rainstorm. And that roof won't survive the winter."

Minutes passed in silence and Lauren continued looking at the plans. The optimism drained from her expression until her full lips pursed in a grim line.

Those lips. Rosy and plump, and I wanted to taste them,

feel them between my teeth, on my cock, against my thumb.

"Lauren? Do you have any questions? Anything I can talk through with you?"

She inhaled deeply and shrugged. For a second, all that confidence vanished, and she looked young, vulnerable.

"I was hoping for better news." A sigh propelled her back into the seat. "I've searched everywhere for a workable site and someone to help me. This was my last hope. I was convinced you were the guy to get it done, that you had the goods to make anything possible."

I hated disappointing her, and I hated that her words made me feel things. I was quite content without regularly experiencing strong feelings. Numbers usually made it easy. Counting, measuring, estimating, solving. It occupied my brain enough to tune out most everything else. When that didn't work, I went running. The math and the miles, they never let me down.

Sucking a fresh breath of air into my chest, I fought for the calm that usually came so naturally, the calm Miss Halsted destroyed every time I was within five feet of her.

"Well…thank you, Matthew. I wish things could have worked out differently, but it seems like I've hit another roadblock."

She personified pin-up, but as I crossed my arm over my chest and propped my chin on my fist, I sensed something different, distinctive, something I wanted to uncover. She wasn't just sexy, she was beautiful and smart and her own special version of beastly.

She collected her folders, and I knew I needed to get out of my head and seize control of the situation soon if I wanted to spend another minute with the naughty school-teacher.

I skirted my desk and sat beside Lauren. Breeching the architect-client desk etiquette veered into creeper territory, and if the warning grimace she fired at me was any indication, I needed to be damn sure I was done with that element of our relationship before I went any further. Her fingers were folded around the smartphone in her lap, and I layered my hand over hers.

Not an architect move.

Not even a Matt move.

"Let me take you out for a drink, Lauren. You can tell me more about your project. It's the least I can do."

"Is there a possibility that Saint Cosmas can be rehabbed?"

"I'm good, but not that good. However," I hedged, "I know every vacant lot and available building in Suffolk County. Most of Middlesex and Norfolk, too." I gently squeezed her fingers. "Let's figure something else out. I know there's a solution. There has to be."

Her slim, ringless fingers curled around mine, and that connection spread over my skin and around my mind. With that singular touch, I sensed myself losing my grip on the world I knew, the world I understood, and getting lost in Miss Halsted.

"Just a drink. I'd hate to think I didn't help you in some way."

LAUREN QUIRKED a brow as I held the door to The Red Hat open. "I've never heard of this place before," she said, her eyes narrowing.

"An old Scollay Square gem. Trust me."

Happy hour crowds from City Hall and the nearby courthouse clogged the bar, and I should have accounted for typical Friday evening bar noise and rerouted this activity sooner, but I'd spent the entire trip from my office convincing myself I could behave.

I paused, scanning for an empty table or quiet corner. I wasn't interested in competing with anyone else for her attention. Spotting a newly vacated private booth, I settled my hand on the small of her back and directed her through the room.

"What can I get you?" Being a gentleman—not a horny dickhead determined to touch her by any means necessary—I helped her out of her belted raincoat, but the thought of her showing up at my loft wearing that coat and nothing beneath turned my manners to shit.

Wait, no. The raincoat and those leopard-print heels.

"Tequila," she said. "Tequila. On the rocks. No salt. A lot of it, in a really big glass."

I couldn't hide my shocked smile. Pinot grigio or fruity mixed drinks would have made more sense, but there was something to be said for a woman who ordered hard liquor like that.

I returned to the table with the tequila and a bottle of Heineken, and Lauren knocked back half the tumbler before my ass hit the seat. A droplet of liquid lingered on the corner of her mouth and I gazed at her lips while she batted her straw around the glass. I didn't know what I wanted more: her tongue darting out and wiping it away, or seeing it roll down her chin.

I waited twenty-nine seconds. That seemed like an

appropriate amount of time to stare at her mouth before acting. Reaching across the table, my fingers cupped her chin and my thumb passed over her lips. My hold lingered a few moments, and I saw my seed dripping from her pouty lips instead of tequila.

That looked *really* good in my head.

"Mr. Walsh?"

My gaze broke away from her mouth and met the challenge in her eyes. I let my fingers graze her neck and brush her collarbone before retreating. Any further and I'd be diving into the deep end of her cleavage and we didn't need an audience for that. "We're not in your classroom and I'm not my father. I asked you to call me Matthew."

"Matthew. You're looking at me as though you're the big bad wolf and you intend to eat me whole."

I nodded at her red dress. Heat rushed to her cheeks and a tight, new tension ignited between us. "Would that be bad?"

Lauren raised her eyebrows but didn't respond. She didn't need to. I smiled around the mouth of my beer bottle and took a long drink when her attention shifted. I was neither gentlemanly nor well-behaved, and I was enjoying the hell out of it.

Since meeting her yesterday, there were only a few instances when her smartphone hadn't been glued to her palm. As I watched her fidgeting with the device, her fingers flying over the screen and her expression morphing in reaction to each message, I wanted to know what it would take for her to put it down. My thumb on her lips didn't do it, and neither did my comment on the topic of eating her. What more did she require to tune everything out and turn off the world?

She caught me staring, and placed the phone beside her newly refilled drink.

"I'd really like to hear about all those lots and buildings you have committed to memory now."

Much to my relief, she sipped at the second tumbler. I didn't know many small women who handled their liquor —let alone tequila—well. Liking her ass and mouth and her sparkle didn't mean I liked the idea of watching her vomit all over the sidewalk.

I leaned forward to study the gold in her eyes, those little flares that drew me in and took me prisoner. "Of course. Tell me about this school you want to open."

She lit up when she talked about creating an innovative school, and her authoritative tone was hypnotic, but there was no shortage of defeats and obstacles in her path. I never knew there was so much behind-the-scenes work associated with running schools, but Lauren's hands were full with recruiting students, hiring teachers, finding board members, writing grants, and designing the educational philosophy, and that didn't even include the physical space. Her quest to open this school was grueling, and I had no shortage of respect for her work.

I'd figured Saint Cosmas was the first site she visited— try fourteenth—and she claimed it was the best-looking one she'd seen, by far. If Saint Cosmas was decent, I was afraid to see the other flaming heaps of rubble. I also discovered I actually *was* the only person for this work, save for Sam and Patrick, and I knew I wasn't leaving Lauren without some feasible options. Regardless of whether she was my naughty schoolteacher and her ass was ruling my fantasies, she needed someone on her side, and I was going to be her someone.

"Have you been doing this long? And how old are you?"

Lauren cringed but tried to hide it behind her drink. Shannon would have beaten me for that question, reminded me never to ask women about age or weight, and then beaten me some more.

"Twenty-eight. I've spent the past year in the fellowship I mentioned. That's where I've been learning how to do all of this."

"And you need a site in Dorchester?" I pulled my phone from my pocket and zoomed in on an area map.

"Around there," she said, "and parts of Roxbury, and the surrounding neighborhoods. But at this point, Matthew, I'll take anything you want to give me."

"I'm thinking of three warehouses, and two vacant mills. The rehab on church complexes is through the roof. Extensive and expensive. Stick with mills." I jotted notes on a damp cocktail napkin and pretended her last comment didn't land right between my legs. "We could schedule time next week to walk the sites. Or…tomorrow. If you're up for it."

"I'm up for anything. If you are."

A smirk pulled at her lips and I coughed to disguise my growl. She knew what she was doing, and she was enjoying it, too. "I don't know what to expect from any of these." I waved the napkin before tucking it into my pocket. "I won't know much of anything until I walk the sites, but I can help with the architectural and structural sides of the project. If you want me, that is."

Because I definitely want you. Anywhere you'll have me.

And that shocked the shit out of me. She was cute and sensual, and short, and I didn't like any of that. But I had to wonder: did I even know my type anymore? Did it matter?

Weren't the beasts just fulfilling a post-race adrenaline surge, and wasn't I doing the same for them?

I didn't actually like any of them, and I knew they didn't give me a second thought. It was just sex, cold and mechanical, and I was intentional in choosing not to care about them. It was the most disconnected form of connection possible, and I liked it that way.

But right now, I couldn't understand why I ever liked anything cold or mechanical when women like Lauren Halsted existed.

"I might." Lauren nodded and reached for her drink. She met my eyes from behind the glass, and I swore I saw desire flicker in her gaze. Spending the better part of the past twenty-four hours swimming in my personal Lauren spank bank might have made me a pervy dickhead, but that one look told me I wasn't there alone. "How did you get into this work?"

The Walsh history was the opposite of happy hour. It belonged with campfire horror stories.

"Birth. Let's get some food. I can't remember eating today." I flagged down the waitress to order.

I was aware of all things Lauren in our shadowy booth. Her scent—like sugar and sweetness. Her skin—smooth and tanned, and sprinkled with just a few pea-sized dark brown freckles. Her smile—brighter than the sunrise, with just a bit of smirk. Her sparkle—a fucking force field I was powerless to resist, though I wasn't sure why I bothered resisting in the first place.

Lauren asked, "You were just born into architecture and structural engineering?"

"Basically."

"So, what?" she laughed. "I can drop my hot messery in

your lap, but you're empty-handed? Come on, Matthew."

I turned my attention to the pulled pork sliders and fresh round of drinks when they arrived at our table. "Try one. They're awesome."

Lauren waved a hand. "I'm fine, thanks."

She was on her third round of tequila, and looked as sober as a saint. "Have you eaten yet?"

Lauren squared her shoulders and sent me a firm stare. That expression probably brought most people to heel in an instant; I was halfway there myself. She didn't need to be eight inches taller or bench two-twenty to kick my ass. I drank in the set of her jaw and decided I liked seeing her in control. She was intelligent and quick-witted, and bossy as hell, and I wanted to touch her again.

I also wanted to fuck her until she lost her voice from screaming my name, but I'd start with touching.

"No, but—"

"Please. Considering I'm the guy who figures out how to ignore the laws of physics on a daily basis, I'm not in the business of saying no very often, especially not to beautiful women. Drinks and bar food are the least I can do, and my sister would belt me for not taking you somewhere decent like No. 9 Park or XV Beacon."

"You're a little demanding," she laughed while selecting a slider. "And you just rattled off the only two places in Boston with numbers in their name."

Grinning, I rubbed the back of my neck. "There's also 75 Chestnut, and Twenty-First Amendment, and 29 Newbury. And a few others."

Lauren folded her arms on the table and leaned forward. "So you're a freak. This puts things in a new light."

"Something like that, yeah." I raised my beer to her

glass. "Not sure I can compete with hot messery, but I'll sure as hell try."

We covered the basics—our siblings, our work, our general interests—but didn't delve further. No fucked-up family stories, no exes, no hopes or dreams.

The history of Walsh Associates was fairly straightforward, mostly because it didn't turn pear-shaped until recently. The firm dated back to the fifties when my grandfather and his brothers started out as architects preserving and restoring historic buildings in the Boston area. My father, uncle, and aunts carried on the work, but Angus wouldn't play nice in the sandbox, and over the past two decades, my uncle and aunts left for greener pastures. I didn't get into Angus's preference for pissing his money away at the dog track or his day-drunkenness, and there was no talk of his screaming matches with Shannon or his tendency to throw things at people.

I opted for stories of us growing up surrounded by architecture, and getting conscripted into grunt work as children. It felt good talking about my love for building and designing, and creating ways to modernize within the constraints of restoration.

Dozens of people and loud bar music surrounded us, but her gaze never wavered from mine. She listened, savoring every word, and made me feel like there was nothing she'd rather hear.

I stared at my beer bottle for a second. Five-point-four percent alcohol by volume. I didn't need to run that equation to know the prickly heat crawling over my skin wasn't from the beer.

It was from Lauren.

And the best part? I didn't want it to stop.

TIPSY. I was definitely tipsy.

Tequila was to blame for the current state of blissfully inebriated affairs, such as they were. His tie sat crisply folded beside his beer bottle, green with small pink shapes, and the collar of his white shirt gaped open. And I wanted to taste him right there.

It was late, the bar nearly empty, and far, far past the proper end for a normal business meeting, but this stopped being a business meeting when we walked through the door.

None of my other first dates—or fourths, for that matter—involved hole-in-the-wall bars or innuendo-laced discussions of architecture. They never involved Matthew Walsh either. This was all rather peculiar, much like that fun, buzzy feeling in my body.

He smiled at me, a smug, knowing expression that told me he was watching my inhibitions evaporate by the minute.

"If you hadn't come out with me? What would you be doing tonight?"

"I'm not winning at work-life balance these days," I said with a grimace. "I'd probably be working on a few overdue projects."

Matthew held up his palm and I stared at it for an embarrassingly long time before meeting his high five. His fingers laced with mine, and for a moment, I could only gape at the way they layered together. He was touching me and I liked it, and somewhere in my head I knew this was strange. I wasn't into boys right now. I mean, I wasn't into girls, either, but I wasn't doing the whole boys and dates and worry about whether I shaved my legs thing.

"Balance is overrated."

I laughed. "Yeah? And what would you be doing? If you didn't maneuver me into drinking with you all night, that is."

"Maneuver? That's strong."

He rubbed his thumb against my palm, and I bit down on my lip to prevent the tipsy giggles from leaking out.

It was just a thumb circling a palm, and it shouldn't have been especially delightful, but if confronted with a choice between this and calorie-free cupcakes, I saw no contest. I liked this, and I didn't want it to stop.

"Some new projects landed on my desk this afternoon. Probably digging into those." He finished his beer and shrugged. "It's what I love, but I don't balance work and life either. Actually, I hate the phrase 'work-life balance.'"

"Why?" I set my empty glass aside, a clear signal for a refill. Considering the painfully overt manner in which the waitress mentally undressed Matthew and then threw some boob action in his direction each time she dropped off another round, I was surprised we weren't getting more of her attention. A greedy part of me knew it owed something to the heavy, hungry gleam in his eyes, and the methodical way in which he watched my every move, as if he was stalking his prey.

I liked that, too. Rationally, I knew there was something unusual about liking some late night prey-stalking, but unusual was my operating speed. The Commodore's idea of an exciting family adventure was getting lost in the desert with nothing more than a compass and Swiss Army knife. Bizarre? Yes. Traumatic? Not even close, but it meant some of my thoughts followed slightly unorthodox paths.

Matthew gesticulated as if trying to reach for something, and sighed. "It's probably semantics, but work-life balance presumes that you're reaching a homeostatic level, where things are in perfect proportion. It never happens, not for anyone I know, but people are constantly beating themselves up and feeling guilty when it's unrealistic in the first place."

I didn't understand half of what he said, but he looked damn sexy saying it. He gestured when he talked. A lot. It was adorable and I wanted my mouth on him.

Like, right now.

"So...you're good with crazy hours?"

He shrugged. "Like I said, I don't see it as balance. It's about the fulcrum." I shook my head, not following his reference. "A fulcrum is the point where a lever rests, is supported, and pivots. Think about a seesaw. It's just a lever positioned over a fulcrum. Force on either side pivots the lever. On a seesaw, the fulcrum is always in the same place—the midpoint. But in life, and other mechanical applications, the fulcrum moves. Sometimes it's far to one side because force is exerted there. That's been my life for just about a decade now. There are days, sometimes a lot of days, when I hate it. But I mostly love it."

He motioned with his hands, miming his seesaw example.

"Some days, I hate it, too," I sighed. "But mostly love. You could probably teach me a few things about enduring the hate days."

Matthew's eyes seemed to darken, turning a deeper, more brilliant blue, and a slight smile pulled at his lips. "I'd teach you anything you wanted, Lauren."

Silence fell between us, though Matthew kept his eyes fixed on me. This would have been a great time for tequila to magically appear in my hand. It wasn't cheating; I skipped lunch and my skinny latte breakfast meant there was room for splurging tonight.

"I met you yesterday. Why does it feel like I've known you, I don't know, longer than that?" Matthew asked.

"Maybe you knew me in a past life."

"You believe in reincarnation? All that stuff?"

I shrugged, thinking a moment. "I have to believe there's something bigger than me, bigger than us. Maybe we're just recycled versions of ourselves, floating around the universe, trying to make sense of it all."

"You believe in soul mates, too? Isn't that why we're all floating around?"

Matthew sounded both skeptical and hopeful, and I didn't know what he wanted me to say. "It's a possibility."

"Mathematically speaking, a rather unlikely possibility."

I studied our joined hands, the bar, the people laughing and talking, and I felt as though I was watching myself from a distance. I wanted to remember the way my foot bumped Matthew's knee and my hair fell across my face and his eyes sparkled every time I laughed.

This moment, this night—they were proof I was still me, that I hadn't lost myself to the deadlines and deliverables and action plans. Not yet.

I knew this school required me to give it my all, and I knew I was losing some of myself in the process. I'd wake up some morning, not able to remember anything I once loved about schools and kids and learning, and I'd be trapped in a hollow wasteland of spreadsheets and strategic priorities. I was sliding down that slope, the slippery one no one ever managed to climb. I didn't know what would be left of me if I fell all the way to the bottom, but I didn't have to worry about any of that tonight.

"You're doing it again."

"What's that?" he asked.

My eyebrows arched upward. He had to know what he was doing. No one could stare that hard, look that heated without putting some effort into it. That kind of eye action burned calories. "The way you're looking at me."

"Lauren, please tell me you want to get out of here."

———

THE BRISK AUTUMN air whipped along Cambridge Street in sharp contrast to the overheated bar. Or maybe I was a little hot and bothered, and the bar was the best excuse. Wind blew through my hair and I struggled to smooth it into place while my new architect friend was trying to melt my undies off with a few smoldering looks.

I glanced up at Matthew, his tall frame sheltering me from the wind. My gaze lingered on the exposed hollow of his throat where his top button gaped open, then the way his belt rode low on his hips, and then the bulge just below the brushed steel buckle.

Scrumptious.

"What would happen if..." I bit my lip, hoping I was interpreting his signals the right way, hoping my tequila-infused courage would see me through. I stretched up on my toes, and Matthew's hands went to my waist. "If I did this?"

Digging his fingers into my hips, he pulled me against him, and there was no misinterpreting that signal. Our lips brushed together, and I hesitated, wanting more—*so* much more—but not knowing the right way to play this game.

"If you do that, I'm doing this," Matthew whispered against my lips. Tugging my hair, he tipped my head back and slipped his tongue past my teeth, and it was exactly as I suspected: he wanted to swallow me whole. A strong gust forced me against him, and I shivered, at once relieved he was taking the lead and wondering if it was the lead I wanted.

"Let's get you out of this wind tunnel," he said, his hand rubbing in a circular pattern against my back.

"Mmm, not yet," I murmured. My lips found Matthew's again, and we were rooted to the sidewalk, our arms locked around each other, and I felt fully and completely awake, aware, *alive*. And I was doing this—kissing a stranger on a street corner, surrendering to my desires, letting my instincts make the decisions—and I wasn't second-guessing myself.

"Didn't say you had to stop," he laughed. "Definitely didn't say that. Just relocating."

Matthew signaled for a cab, and shepherded me inside

when it jerked to a stop at the curb. "Burroughs Wharf," he called to the driver.

I didn't know our destination, but being pressed against a hot guy on a Friday night meant I didn't need an itinerary. Right? This was fine. Normal. Totally normal. There was no way this could end in Matthew killing me in the woods and wearing my skin as a scarf.

Enough with the greatest hits of Commodore Halsted's Tales of Evil.

Even if Matthew was a serial killer, it would never get that far. I could break his fingers in eleven seconds if needed.

I pulled him to me again, my hand snaking around his neck, just under his starched collar, and our lips met. With his mouth locked on mine, Matthew was different. He wasn't the Serious Architect with his technical vocabulary and curious, thoughtful expression, and he wasn't the Serious Guy with his intense gaze and endless undercurrents. No, when he kissed me, he was thorough and insistent and affectionate, and this version of him intrigued me the most.

Matthew dragged his teeth over my bottom lip, and I groaned when the cab stopped. "Of course we found the one cabbie in Boston who knows every shortcut between Beacon Hill and the Waterfront," he said.

"Burroughs Wharf," the driver yelled.

Matthew plucked me from the cab and lifted me over the curb as if I were a small sack of potatoes. I looked up after cinching my raincoat's belt, and stared at the building. This was a super swanky condo building, not a cozy tavern or thumping club. This was where he *lived*. "Where are we going?"

"My place," he said. "We can have a drink and talk and stare at the ocean and…whatever. Whatever you want."

I stopped walking, my fingers slipping out of his grip. This wasn't what I anticipated when I turned the decision-making over to my instincts.

Shameless bar flirting? No big deal. Street corner kissing followed by cab kissing? Slightly bigger deal. Going to a guy's home little more than twenty-four hours after meeting him? Huge deal.

At least for me.

When did I give him the impression I was ready to go home with him? Was there a switch I flipped between talk of seesaws and soul mates? And he was evidently a manwhore. Only a manwhore would toss me in a cab and assume I wanted to go to his apartment for sex.

Sex. I did not want that at all. Lots of sex. Good sex. Dirty sex. Hot sex.

Matthew looked like *very* good sex.

Gulp. Okay, so that didn't sound terrible.

"What's wrong, Lauren?"

"I should go." I nodded to myself and hitched my tote bag higher on my shoulder. Too much, too fast. I was already feeling tomorrow's pangs of regret. Oh, but when Matthew aimed that stare at me, that drop-your-panties-right-now look, I sensed myself drowning in his desire.

"This thing you're doing," the manwhore smirked, gesturing up and down my body. "It's insanely sexy."

I looked over his shoulder, avoiding his eyes. I didn't do this sort of thing for a reason. "Mr. Walsh. Thank you for everything. I'm going to go."

Never make eye contact with the manwhore. He'll turn you

into an irrational swoon-puddle concerned only with getting your hands on his rear end.

As I turned away, my narrow heel wedged between the cobblestones and this sack of potatoes hit the ground.

I couldn't even walk away from the hottest, manwhoriest body I'd ever touched and stand behind my principles without going splat. Apparently the universe wasn't granting me any graceful exits this evening.

I heard the manwhore swearing under his breath before his arm circled my waist and he lifted me from the ground. "Easy there," he said.

He ignored thin rivulets of blood trickling down my bare legs and staining his dark gray trousers while I brushed the pebbles from my palms. "This seems to happen a lot, sweetness. Let's get you upstairs and take care of those scrapes."

"I'm fine. Just a skinned knee, no big deal. I'm going to get a cab," I insisted, staring at his shirt's buttons.

He dipped to meet my eyes, his brows furrowed. The pads of his thumbs brushed across my cheeks, my lips, and down my neck. "What is your deal? Are you with someone?"

"No!" I laughed at the definitive tone in my voice. I didn't mean to sound so emphatic, and any minute Matthew was going to realize I wasn't the kind of girl he wanted to take home. I didn't do this—I didn't know *how*—and this entire exchange was stepping far beyond my sphere of expertise. He'd feel it or sense it or taste it, and he'd send me on my way with a pat on my naïve little head. "I mean…no, I'm not seeing anyone right now."

"Good. Good." Matthew framed my face with his hands and brought his lips a breath from mine. "I'm going to kiss you again," he murmured, sliding his fingers along the base of my neck. "And I'd rather you not run away this time."

I dodged his mouth. "Is this some kind of thorough, manwhorish customer service?"

"Hell no." He bent his head to my level and found my lips, and it wasn't a kiss—it was an experience. Kissing involved lips and tongues, but this was teeth and growls, fingers carving notches into my ass and impatient hips bumping against mine for more friction. This was my heart crawling all the way up my throat and pounding there, suffocating me in these breathless seconds.

He groaned when my nails scraped under his collar and over his scalp, and that sound unfurled something tight, something desperate inside me.

"Do you do this a lot?"

Matthew's hands moved to my shoulders and he edged us apart. "I *never* do this. My sisters are the only women who have seen the inside of my place. Okay? This is about you. You're hot as fuck, all sexy and bossy. That strict teacher voice? I've been hard as a fucking stone since yesterday because of it, plus the fact you're so insanely fucking hot. I don't like the implication that this is happening for any reason other than you."

Lifting my chin, I glimpsed the rise in Matthew's trousers. It was amazing, really, how everything changed in a blink of an eye. Perhaps it wasn't that quickly, but it didn't take long and I was watching from a distance again, willing myself to be brave, be bold.

My boundaries, my hot mess, my control freak, my crazy thoughts, my good girl, even the blood drying on my leg…all gone. Now it was me, bare without all that noise, and I couldn't stop the brazen smile from pulling at my mouth.

I heard the words and I sensed them vibrating across my lips, but I didn't believe them as mine. "So that's what you like, Mr. Walsh?"

He growled and seized my hips, grinding me against his hardening length. His mouth hovered over my ear, and he whispered, "You wouldn't believe the long list of obscene things I want to do to you."

My response was ready on my tongue, but I bit my lip, hesitating for a moment. I didn't know much about sex beyond some college hook-ups and *Sex and the City* reruns. Sure, there were plenty of secret cravings and dirty thoughts, but not much experience to back them up. I didn't know what I was doing here, and the fear of doing the wrong thing left me doubting my instincts all over again.

"I saw that." Matthew rolled his hips, pressing himself against me. My lips parted on a gasp, my eyes wide. "Say what you want to say, sweetness. You can't scare me away."

I didn't have to be a sex expert to know that erection was *from* me and *for* me, and it was all the reassurance I needed. "How much longer do I have to wait to hear about this list? I might want to make some additions."

"Oh, holy fuck, Lauren."

Six

MATTHEW

THE FIRST TIME I rode the elevator to my loft was when my sister, Shannon, was walking me through the unit. I preferred stairs, but Shannon liked to say her sky-high heels were "for show, not go" and I bowed to her request to take the elevator.

She scouted the property about five years ago. The previous owner was a little old lady who kept a couple litters of cats and every edition of the *Boston Herald* published in the past thirty years. She died in her sleep, but her nieces and nephews didn't notice for weeks. The place needed a complete overhaul and extensive fumigation but the price was far below market value. The two hundred and seventy degree views of Boston Harbor sold me on the unit at first glance. I bought it, gutted it to the studs, and replaced everything.

My second ride in that elevator was with Lauren. By my estimate, it lasted just under ninety seconds, but I wouldn't be looking at elevators the same way again.

We were backed into the corner, her leg hooked over my

hip and her hands flat against the walls. Heat radiated from between her legs and I leaned into it, groaning as I crouched down and buried my face in her neck. Her height was an obstacle. Even in ass-kicking heels, she barely reached my chin but touching her was worth the challenge.

Lauren's hands attacked the top buttons of my shirt and she kissed from my collarbone to the shell of my ear, her lips urgent and demanding, and I fucking loved it. My hand ran under her dress and up her thigh, and I savored the reward of her rocking against my palm. She was hot and wet there, and I entertained some panty-ripping scenarios on the ride to the fifth floor.

We stumbled from the elevator, laughing into each other's mouths, our hands busy stroking, tugging, exploring. I walked backward in the general vicinity of my place, my shoulder eventually connecting with the doorframe. "This is me," I said against her cheek.

Lauren craned her neck over my shoulder. "This isn't happening in the hallway, Matthew."

She was honey in my hands, and so fucking bossy, and it all destroyed any semblance of ordered thought. "Keys. In my pocket."

Lauren didn't skip a beat. She went for the wrong pocket, but didn't retreat when she found it empty. Instead, she scraped her nails up and down my inner thigh while fishing the keys from the other side. Her knuckles grazed my cock, and it didn't matter that a layer of clothing separated us, her touch was a heated, impatient caress, and I wanted her. I bit down on her lip with a growl, and then she did it again.

Pivoting, I pressed Lauren against the door and fumbled with the keys. Her hand moved down my chest and over my belt, her palm covering me. She squeezed, dragging the pressure from root to tip, and sent me a shameless smile that said she knew exactly what she intended to do with me.

"When you open that door, decide what you want from your long, filthy list." She pumped twice, and I started begging myself to stay in control. "I want it to include plenty of this." She gripped me again, hard. "Inside me."

"I have a pretty good idea what you want, sweetness," I said, and pushed open the door. "Don't worry about that."

Apparently, I did like short girls. Bossy ones, too.

A TRAIL of coats and bags began inside the door and followed us to the sofa parallel to the harborside floor-to-ceiling windows. The loft was dark, the only light coming from boats on the water and the gas fireplace I switched on when we moved through the hall and into the living room.

I had forgotten the simple pleasure of a thick beer buzz and a gorgeous woman in my lap. I untied the scarf around her neck and tossed it to the coffee table. Four small buttons separated me from her breasts, and I was determined to get on a first name basis with those peaches. My eyes stayed on Lauren as the buttons popped free, each one drawing the air closer, heat crawling around us when her dress gaped open. It was the first I saw of her delicate silver necklace, and I traced it to where it disappeared into her bra.

"This is what I was talking about…" My tongue dipped into the hollow between her breasts where she was slightly salty and entirely perfect. "…when I said you are hot as fuck."

I closed my mouth over her nipple, sucking and pulling through the bra's mesh fabric, and Lauren's hips rocked forward.

"Oh my God," she panted, her head falling back.

My teeth connected with her skin, and I knew it was a little wrong but absolutely fucking right. Her body vibrated, a subtle pulse moving through her muscles and stuttering out in a gasp, and I smiled at the faint mark on her skin.

"Did you just bite me?" she squealed. Her eyes sparkled, a combination of shock and amusement, and it was obvious her head was in this game now. I wasn't competing with a smartphone or her better judgment against going home with me anymore. She was all mine, and now I knew what it took to shut off her world.

"Yes." I searched for the mechanisms that would free her from the dress. "Don't even pretend you didn't like it."

Giggling, Lauren slapped my hands away. "What kind of vampire are you? Do you usually go around biting people?"

I unknotted the sash at her waist and returned to the remaining buttons while I considered her question. I definitely didn't bite the triathlon chick I hung out with this summer. The others were local marathon beasts with benefits. No biting there, although one of them did like slapping me when she came. Most of the time, I didn't bother taking off their sports bras, and they were fine with that.

The last button slipped from its casing, and the dress was hanging open from her shoulders. I needed an outlet for everything I was feeling, a place to deposit this heaving energy. My mouth moved to her other breast for a matching bite. "No, sweetness. Just you."

I couldn't explain any of it; I just knew I wanted to leave my mark on her. Bites, scratches, swollen lips, messy hair. I wanted to see it all.

Her hips swayed against my erection. "You're a strange creature."

"And you're insanely sexy."

Blushing and diverting her eyes as if no one had ever spoken those words to her before, Lauren jerked the shirt-tails from my pants and struggled with the buttons while I raked my chin scruff against her skin.

"Not so fast," I groaned, tugging her fingers out of my trousers.

I lifted Lauren off my lap and eyed the nude mesh boy shorts hugging her hips. The color blended with her skin and if not for the random splattering of embroidered dots, they would have created the illusion she was naked under that dress. It was beautiful and startling and yet again, I wanted nothing more than those fucking panties shredded in my fingers.

Kneeling before her, I unfastened the tiny buckles around her ankles and set the ass-kickers on the floor. Her knees were more bruised than scraped, and the blood long since dried. "I'm amazed you didn't blow out your ankle on that fall. I'm not letting you get on your knees tonight, sweetness."

"I've survived worse," she said. She nodded toward the shoes. "Didn't want to leave them on?"

I trailed kisses up her thighs before hooking my fingers in her panties. "We'll save that for another night. It's a very long list, after all."

"I bet it's huge," she purred. Fuck me running, this girl

knew her way around a double entendre. "But I don't remember signing up for repeat performances."

"Then it's a good thing you like me because this might take a while."

I couldn't tear my eyes away from Lauren's while I tugged her panties down. I needed to see the way my words affected her, and I needed her to know we were a breath away from something we wouldn't be able to control, and I needed her there with me.

"And I thought you'd be all wholesome pink cotton. Never expected this."

I lifted the fabric to my face and inhaled her musky scent. No ordinary panties for Miss Halsted. They were fragile and lovely, and required the proper amount of admiration before this turned indecent. We stared at each other, her underwear pressed to my face and her body exposed before me.

I tucked them into my pocket and nudged her legs apart, and nothing could have prepared me for that treat when I finally broke away from her eyes. "And I certainly didn't expect this."

Recently and quite thoroughly waxed. So many contradictions in one woman but I couldn't be sure which side of her dominated as she seemed to fight off both in equal measure. I teased my tongue down her slit, and her essence washed over me.

"Oh my God," she gasped, her hands seizing my hair.

I leaned back and aimed a hard gaze at her. "God has nothing to do with this. You want to thank someone, I'll be right here, worshipping you and your outrageous body for the foreseeable future. God isn't involved."

I latched my mouth on her clit, sucking and stroking

until her legs tightened around my head, and she shrieked, "Matthew!"

I smiled against her, enjoying the sound of my name in her trembling voice. It was the best oral sex anthem I'd ever heard. Goosebumps spread over her skin, her eyes screwed shut, and I knew she was close when her nails bit into my scalp.

"Lauren," I commanded. "Look at me."

Her eyes fluttered open, hazed over with need and bright, bright green. The tousle of her hair, the flush riding along her cheeks, the erratic rise and fall of her chest— seeing it all from between her thighs was a new level of insanely sexy. She held my gaze as she rode the spasms, her eyes full and lips parted, then she slumped back against the sofa with a shuddering moan. She held nothing back, and I loved it.

The past day didn't give me time to know everything about Lauren, and I wasn't about to discover them all tonight, but I sensed we knew each other, recognized each other, and a few things were clear. First, she was under my skin and in my blood, and as much as I hated talking about spiritual shit, there was a possibility she knew me in another life. Second, she played the part of the wholesome schoolteacher, but pull back the boy shorts and she was very, very naughty. Third—and most importantly—no one was giving this woman what she needed. The way she came apart in my hands and the astonished reaction to her orgasm made that abundantly clear.

She raked her hands through my hair, and I interpreted her grip as an invitation to continue licking. Her tissues pulsed under my tongue, and that response felt better than finishing any triathlon.

"Oh my…Matthew," she sighed.

Possessiveness spread out from my chest and through my limbs, and the air around me tasted different, new. I didn't care whether it was only tonight; she could be mine right now. My teeth connected with Lauren's inner thigh, and I nipped the tender skin there, raining kisses over the blossoming welt. "That's right," I growled.

My hands ran up her legs, palming the globes of her ass. I fought the urge to plunge into her right there but I wanted more than messy sofa sex. I wanted messy bed sex where there was enough room to spread her out and move in her, and then fall asleep with her wrapped around me, and then do it all over again. And after that we'd try it again with the ass-kicking heels.

I secured Lauren's legs around my waist and lifted her into my arms. My cock throbbed miserably, and nestling against the soft rise of her belly only made it worse. As much as I wanted to see a puddle on her stomach, I wanted it after my cock spent an extensive amount of time inside her. Striding toward the bedroom, I pulled her dress down her arms and tossed it in my wake.

"This is like Carly Rae Jepsen crazy, right?" she laughed, her mouth pressed against the pounding pulse on my throat while I relieved her of her bra.

"What's that?"

"I just met you, and we're… It's not 'Call Me Maybe' but it's crazy. Do you do this a lot?"

"You need to stop asking that," I said, my mouth against Lauren's. "Do you not recall me telling you you're hot as fuck?"

My fingers continued their descent and trailed along the seam of her ass to brush back and forth there. Her legs tightened and she rocked against my fingers. Another thing I didn't expect from Lauren.

I deposited her on the bed, her skin gleaming in the darkness.

"Men always have such big beds," she murmured. Her hand cruised over the dark blankets.

I stopped, my fingers frozen on my half-buttoned shirt. "For our purposes right now, let's not discuss you in anyone else's bed." Circling my hand in that direction, I shook my head. "In fact, I'd be good letting myself believe there haven't been any others."

She was all pin-up, all the time, but her innocence lingered around the edges, and I preferred it that way.

Lauren murmured something under her breath, looked up from beneath her lashes, and reached for me. "You sound like a caveman. I should *not* like that so much."

Her hair tumbled over her shoulders and she was bare save for the necklace nestled between her breasts. My fingers coasted down her chest and traced the rose quartz pendant crowned with a tiny pearl. "What is this?"

Lauren smirked and watched my finger moving over the shape. It was familiar, but I couldn't place it. "I think you know."

Lifting the pendant, I studied it in the moonlight. It resembled a flower, maybe a lily or even a conch shell, and my thumb circled the pearl again.

"You're good at that," she laughed. She unbuttoned my shirt and pushed it down my arms.

And then I figured it out. It wasn't a flower. It was a pussy, an artfully carved pussy complete with a pearl clit, and she kept it hidden between her tits.

"You're a filthy, filthy girl. Pull back the sheets," I barked when she reached for my belt. I didn't know where I found the steely command, but I'd show her something about cavemen.

Grinning, Lauren crawled away from me. While I struggled to shuck my pants, she folded the bed coverings and sat back. I felt saliva pooling in my mouth and I pursed my lips to keep from drooling. The sight of Lauren kneeling on my bed, her voluptuous body exposed and patiently awaiting instructions, left my brain screaming *now* and *mine*.

"What would you like me to do, Matthew?"

Absently throwing my pants toward the corner, I choked down the frantic desire throbbing in my veins, the drumbeat vibrating in my muscles and nerves, the energy pulsing from my fingertips. She was sweet and pure and obscene, and nothing like what I knew. "Lie back," I ground out. "I want to watch you touching yourself."

Lauren's eyebrows quirked at my request and she paused, blinking. There she was again with that innocence, and for a second, I doubted my request. Her suggestive comments were equally matched by timid ones, her bold touches balanced out by the tentative, but something about that pale pink necklace revealed the true Lauren.

Or maybe it was the Lauren she wanted to be.

"I'm waiting," I said.

Her gaze fixed on me, she licked her lips and allowed her hands to skim along her belly and hips. She brushed her fingers on her outer folds, and I growled when she shuddered and moaned. Her breathing quickened, and a flush covered her body. It wasn't a game to her. This was as much for her pleasure as it was for mine. She wasn't angling for porn star choreography or even shy seductiveness. She was only concerned with getting off on her own fingers, and that honesty made for a rare flavor of foreplay.

Two fingers slipped inside and her thumb circled her clit, moving with measured strokes. Time slowed to the pace of my ragged breaths yet I felt it blurring and screeching past me. I concentrated on memorizing every inch, every movement, every sound.

Underneath her sassy sweetness Lauren was bold and wicked and precious. I loved it, I loved that there was no time for taboos, and I loved the way she watched me watching her. It was sexy as hell but best of all, it was instructive.

"Don't be so shy," Lauren whispered.

I gazed at her, unblinking and speechless. My cock was begging for her, straining and weeping from behind my boxer briefs. They hit the floor, and I groaned when my fist jerked down my throbbing length.

The sounds of skin sliding over skin were spellbinding, and we fell into a staccato rhythm, watching each other. I didn't pay much attention to what I was doing, but Lauren studied my hand as it glided up and down. Her fingers moved quickly, instinctively, and I saw her fighting the balance between learning how I liked it and surrendering to her body and her needs.

And I didn't want her making that choice.

"Tell me what you want."

Confusion flashed through her eyes before her head lolled back on a throaty wail. "Matthew," she moaned. "Get your cock and fuck me with it *now*."

If there were better words to hear, I didn't know them.

I snagged a condom from the bedside drawer and knelt between Lauren's shaking legs as I rolled it down. Her deep hum of agreement and self-satisfied smile when she saw my cock pointed directly at her sent tingles through my body. I pushed into her on a rough grunt, and her incredible tightness was unlike anything. Urgent, eager sensations bit at the base of my spine and I traced the pulse hammering in her wrists, inhaling and exhaling to slow it all down.

"Is this what you wanted, filthy girl?"

She wrapped her legs around me in response, and my arm cradled her hips. I lifted her to me, angling her body to receive me, take me deeper, take all of me. She clenched, and the constricting pressure was divine. Prickles of release shot along my spine again, and my next thrust pushed us to the other side of the bed.

I held her hands down, my mouth sucking hard at her taut nipple as thin spasms rolled through her core. She arched against my mouth, clawing at my hands, whispering stuttered pleas into my ear. "Tell me how you want me, Matthew."

The droplet of tequila clinging to her lip forced its way into my mind, followed by the greatest hits of every scrap of porn I'd ever seen.

"Fuck, sweetness. I don't think you're ready for that."

And I didn't think she was. The things I wanted were wild and hedonistic. It didn't matter how many taboos we crushed; I was essentially having a threesome with Lauren and her naïveté right now, and I wasn't about to ask if I could come on her tits. I wasn't going to be the asshole who took it too far when this was already fucking phenomenal.

"Maybe I am," she said. "Maybe I want you to fuck me like I'm your dirty little slut."

Looking up from between her breasts, I stared at Lauren, uncertainty and discomfort ticking away and multiplying between us as her words spread over me, sinking into my skin and claiming space in my vocabulary. They were wrong—so much of this was wrong—and the opposite of my expectations, yet exactly what I needed, and the slight smirk pulling at her lips told me it was what she needed, too.

"You're all mine." I growled against her neck and rocked into her hard, quietly begging her to utter that raw request over and over.

"Is that what you want?" she whispered.

I groaned into her mouth, kissing and biting and murmuring that it was exactly what I wanted, that she was what I wanted. Pumping frantically as I neared the end, I laced Lauren's fingers with mine, our eyes locked, and she whispered those words again, soft and low, and nothing like the bomb she dropped earlier.

One hard thrust and we were falling from the bed, tumbling to the floor with a thud, a heap of sheets and pillows and blankets cushioning our fall. That didn't stop the lightning zipping through me, or the explosion leaving my brain blank and muscles numb, or the rolling, pulsing spasm in her center.

Breathless, I collapsed on top of her, my face buried in the crook of her neck. Everything about Lauren was orders of magnitude better than I imagined when she walked into my office earlier today, and now I knew the taste of her skin, the scent of her hair, and the beautiful obscenity of her mind. "Are you all right?"

Lauren nodded, and I estimated how long she'd let me stay this way. It was a funny thought, actually; staying rarely crossed my mind. I was usually concerned with getting off, getting up, getting out.

I pressed my lips to her pulse and rolled, slipping free from the vise grip of her heat. "Stay here. Don't move a muscle," I said.

The short trip to the bathroom was grueling. My legs barely propelled me forward, a gelatinous feeling taking up residence in my muscles. Discarding the condom and running a damp washcloth over my dick bordered on torture. The orgasm wrung me out, and I needed some down time in the form of my head on Lauren's soft belly and my fingers tracing the lines of her body, and with any luck, her hands in my hair. Boobs were also excellent pillows—hers in particular.

I found her standing at the floor-to-ceiling windows, gazing into the harbor. It was the type of image photographers and painters waited entire careers to capture, and it was here, for me. She looked over her shoulder, licked her lips, and beckoned me closer. Heat spread through me like a fever, and I was stirring to life at the sight of her lush curves bracketed by the night sky.

Maybe I didn't need that snugglenap as much as I originally thought.

"When did you start on your long," her eyes dropped to my crotch as I approached, "list of dirty things?"

"When you opened the door to the church hall. Your ass. In that skirt."

"That skirt makes me look short and boxy."

"I respectfully disagree, Miss Halsted." I swatted her ass and pressed myself against her back, bringing my arms around her waist.

Even shorter without the ass-kicking heels, Lauren's head rested low on my chest and my cock made itself comfortable against her back. Reaching between us, she gripped me, caressing lazily. "So tell me: what went on the list first?"

"An ass as fine as yours should be worshipped by taking you from behind."

"What did you have in mind?"

"Kneeling, your back against my chest, so I can hold your tits," I hissed, her fingers shifting lower, cupping my balls. "Because I've been thinking about them since yesterday. And facedown, hands tied."

"I think I like that list." Her strokes increased, and though I didn't think it was possible to come again so soon, I was teetering on the brink. Wrapping my fingers around her wrist, I stopped her movement and pressed her hand to the glass.

"Don't move," I whispered against her ear. A condom snatched from the bedside table, I was sheathed and leaning into her, her body against the window.

"Your rebound time is impressive."

I pressed my mouth to her shoulder. I didn't know whether I wanted to bite her or kiss her or just fucking howl against her skin, but I needed to be inside her. *Now*. Gripping Lauren's hips, I shifted her, trying to find the right angle. It was something of an engineering problem.

"I promise you, sweetness, it owes everything to you."

"I bet you say that to all the girls," she laughed.

"No other girls. You're my only girl," I said. Braced on her toes, she followed my lead, letting me cant her hips and angle her legs, but it wasn't working. There was no resolving a twelve-inch height differential when the heels were off, and the position that served me so well before was unavailable with Lauren. "Now get on your knees."

I don't know where I found the restraint to watch her

dropping to the ground, but I stood there, my arms crossed over my chest and my cock twitching and pleading for her attention. It was only when she winced that I realized my mistake.

"Oh shit, no, wait, your poor knees."

"You threw me off the bed not too long ago, Matthew. And then you landed on me. I'll be fine," she said, her nails scraping my inner thighs. "Now don't leave me all alone down here."

And naturally, I complied. There was no denying the very naughty schoolteacher.

My cock molded itself into the cleft of her ass, and I savored that warm pressure before easing toward her wetness. I watched her reflection in the window, the way her eyes closed and her lips parted, and I brushed my mouth over her neck. "Tell me what you want."

Lauren's arm curled around my neck, and I waited, wanting to be inside her but wanting to her hear demanding it even more. She glanced over her shoulder, brows lifted, and I heard the questions in her eyes.

You want to play like this?

You want it fun and rough and dirty, and maybe a little dangerous?

I nodded, and a gentle kiss told her I understood, that I'd remember the rules for next time.

"Fuck me until I can't walk, I can't breathe, I can't do anything but ask for more. Fuck me until I'm yours."

Her soft delivery of coarse words made them more profound, more electric than any mid-fuck requests or screaming demands.

She shifted to her hands and knees, her backside angling toward me, and there was no waiting. My fingers gripped her hips relentlessly as she ground into me with a measured rhythm, taking me inside, and again, her tightness lit stars behind my eyelids.

Lauren set the pace, and my thoughts hovered in a hot, hazy place. My body had never performed so thoroughly, so flawlessly before this night, but I managed only grunts and gasps, echoed murmurs for *more* and *oh, fuck, yes*. And though I probably couldn't spell my own name, I knew with absolute certainty this wasn't straight-up p-in-the-v sex. This was a spiritual event, and I, for one, wouldn't have been surprised if some druids started chanting behind us.

I was ready to blow, and each of her cries and moans kicked me closer to the edge. Desperate to prolong this moment, I yanked Lauren against my chest. My arm snaked across her chest to control her rhythm with a hand locked on her shoulder. My other arm traversed her belly, my fingers spreading her folds.

"Better," I sighed, kissing the slope of Lauren's neck.

"What?" she pouted. "You didn't like that?"

Lauren dragged her teeth across my bicep, leaving stinging bites in her wake. Another reminder that she was a complete contradiction—one minute it looked like she didn't know what to expect from my tongue on her clit, and the next she was biting and talking dirrrty.

Sugar and spice, all of it nice.

"I loved it," I groaned, our pace quickening. "But I was going to come all over you within thirty seconds."

She moved against me, and I pistoned up to meet her, my fingers moving fast over her clit. "Maybe I wanted you to come all over me."

I gripped her shoulders and angled her to face me.

"Maybe we should combine lists and eliminate these missed opportunities."

My hand shifted from her shoulder, tracing the line of her collarbone down, down, registering the contours of her skin, and stopping between her breasts. Lacing that necklace around my fingers, I held tight, bracing her. My body was moving, thrusting, fucking *pounding* without my brain's involvement.

"And I wanted to enjoy your amazing body and filthy mind a little longer this time."

"The only filthy mind here is yours," she laughed, her head falling against my arm.

I wanted to laugh but my body's need to mate, to mark, closed in on me, and I lost myself there. My hold on the necklace tightened, the chain taut and tense, then snapping and pooling in my fist.

Roaring my release, my fingers scribbled over her twice before submitting to a full-body shiver that bordered on seizure.

It wasn't *if* there would be a next time.

It was *when*.

FINGER-COMBING my hair in the elevator's mirrored walls was my new reality. All things considered, it was only worse than crying in a stairwell or shopping away my feelings in that I smelled and looked like stale sex.

Oh, and I wasn't wearing any panties.

Minor details.

I clutched my shoes under my arm and balanced the handles of my tote in the crook of my elbow while thumbing mascara smudges from under my eyes. My wrinkly raincoat slipped over the sides of the tote, raspberry welts stained my neck, collarbone, and chest, and there was no mistaking it: I was embarking upon my first walk of shame.

The elevator arrived at the lobby of Matthew's building and my bare feet marched straight to the security desk. "I need a cab. Could you request one for me?"

Ignoring the guard's knowing grin as he lifted the phone, I wiggled into my shoes and winced at patches of blue and purple on my shins.

"Two or three minutes, miss," the guard announced.

I murmured my thanks and set to righting my raincoat, and dismissed the idea of asking whether Matthew welcomed many guests of the ridden-hard-and-put-up-wet variety.

This little activity was over, and Matthew's social life was none of my business.

I stepped out into the morning fog as it rolled off the harbor, the air of confidence in my steps entirely hollow. I avoided the cobblestones but memories of his hands on my waist, his arms holding me close, and his lips against mine swirled around me.

Glancing back at Matthew's building before settling into the cab, I saw the first rays of sunlight cresting the horizon. "Beacon Hill. Chestnut at River Street," I called to the cabbie.

Six feet separated Matthew's bed from the bank of windows but it had taken us hours to get there. The memories were fuzzy yet oddly vivid, not unlike riding a high-speed roller coaster and seeing specific faces in the crowd below, but I wasn't able to distinguish the second time from the third or fourth, or the quiet, close moments in between when laughed and touched and kissed.

Once we made our way to the bed, Matthew fit my body against his, my back connecting with his strong chest and his arms crisscrossed over my torso.

"Stay," he whispered into my hair. "We're not done. Not even close. Stay right here. Promise me."

My fingers reached over my shoulder and kneaded the muscles at the nape of his neck. He hid all of his tension there. "Okay."

He fell asleep quickly and I tried to follow, but my brain

shot into overdrive. When the adrenaline and pheromones crashed, the reality of our wild night hit me dead center. I stared at Matthew's arms and the way they locked around me, caging me. My chest started heaving, and it wouldn't have surprised me to see my heart pounding up through layers of muscle and tissue, bursting out of my chest, sprouting legs, and scrambling out the door.

I didn't do this. I didn't have one-night stands. I didn't go home with men I barely knew. I didn't have sex, period.

Especially not *that* kind of sex.

Everything I *said*, everything I *did*—none of it was me, and I needed to forget the entire night. Chalk it up to a moment of weakness. A first time for everything. A lapse in otherwise spotless judgment. A wild oat, or whatever.

And handling the morning after? Oh God, help me. I didn't want to navigate any awkward discussions about our very important and very imaginary Saturday morning responsibilities, and I really didn't want to crawl around looking for my panties while he admired the handprints he left on my ass. Hollow promises to call or connect later would have only made a weird situation worse.

Breaking out from under his bear trap arms, grabbing whichever pieces of clothing I could find, and getting the hell out of there had been the only option. Writing a note crossed my mind, but with the pen poised over the page of my notebook, I couldn't find the words. Was there an apropos morning-after message?

Thanks for a fun time, but I will die of mortification if you ever make eye contact with me again.

Or something along the lines of: *Sorry for leaving but I need to go burst into flame now.*

Or maybe this: *I'm actually off men right now, even though*

I spent the night all over you.

Instead, I had cast a quick glance at his place, realizing I allocated no part of last night to observing my surroundings. The Commodore wouldn't have been pleased—it was important to identify multiple escape routes upon arrival—but he wouldn't be getting wind of this.

The loft was cool and open, and surprisingly modern for a guy who spent his days restoring historic homes. His furniture was dark and angular, and everything was positioned for maximum ocean viewing. My eyes had swept over the living room and white marble kitchen, and back again, but I couldn't find any hints of Matthew. No photos or books, no magnets on the refrigerator, not even a messy dish of keys and coins. Aside from the suit coat in the hallway and black messenger bag by the door, no trace of him existed there.

And I removed every trace of me, too.

I tiptoed into my apartment and headed straight for my bedroom. I lived alone but the Beacon Hill brownstone was at least one hundred years old and I didn't need to wake the downstairs neighbors at this hour.

I was still a good girl, even with the dirty, dirty sex and…oh God, the things I did.

Who *was* that person? And what the hell had she *said*?

I stripped off my coat, dress, and what was left of my underwear, and tossed them in the dry cleaning bag. While the bath filled, I scrolled through emails and text messages about Steph and Amanda's going away party this evening to divert my mind. Analyzing last night further would only lead to stress-eating a brick of chocolate before six in the morning.

I dropped into the apartment's original claw-foot tub

and, as if I didn't have enough reminders of Matthew, every inch of my body felt supremely used. My hips were dotted with fingertip bruises from his unrelenting hold. Stinging bite marks throbbed against the bath salts. Overextended abdominal muscles shrieked in protest, a reminder that I'd effectively avoided sit-ups of all manner since high school gym class. I groaned at the aching in my center from Matthew's insistent pummeling and the introduction of his fingers to my rear end.

I wasn't ready to think about that particular moment.

Okay, fine, I loved it, and much like rest of that night, I didn't know what to do with that information. I didn't want to think about the ways in which everything with Matthew was natural, if not enormously shameful. I wanted to disregard the moments when our bodies met, our eyes locked, and the electricity between us was the only thing that mattered.

But I had real priorities—finding a facility, educating children—and I couldn't let some electricity or hormones get in the way. I didn't have time for one-night stands or boys with ridiculous policies on biting and growling.

And I didn't do this sort of thing. It was untidy and sticky and awkward, and not at all for me.

Neither were relationships. I made my choice when I joined this fellowship, and I knew I couldn't have it all right now.

I didn't know how or when, but I knew a future version of me would be able to manage my school masterfully, and I'd find the time to meet the ideal guy and build a healthy, normal relationship. It would happen when the time was right for those pieces to fall into place.

And the time just wasn't right.

From: Erin Walsh
To: Matthew Walsh
Date: September 24 at 11:03 WEST
Subject: RE: Back from the Azores

Kid, if you think I'm having Christmas or Thanksgiving with the tribe, you have lost your ever-loving mind. Surely, you're asking for comedic purposes only. Yep. That's what I'm going with.

And I've told you before: I can walk on lava. It's one of my superpowers. All gingers have them.

I picked up a Portuguese translation of *Flowers in the Attic*. I discovered two things. One, my Portuguesa is no bueno. Two, I prefer my campy novels in American. <<momentarily homesick>>

Keep scraping damsels-in-distress off the sidewalk, or whatever the hell you're doing.
- e

From: Matthew Walsh
To: Erin Walsh
Date: September 25 at 08:18 EDT
Subject: RE: Back from the Azores

E –
I really hope you're up because I need you to help me sort out my life. Can I call you?
M

From: Erin Walsh
To: Matthew Walsh
Date: September 25 at 13:21 WEST
Subject: RE: Back from the Azores

Unlikely. I drank my weight in the Portuguese equivalent of moonshine last night and I might have fried the speech portion of my brain.

Also: I'm getting on a bullet train to Italy. My capacity for support is limited.

And by sort out your life, you mean...what, exactly?

If you think for a second that I want to hear about how the Black Widow is ruining your life, you've really lost your fucking mind.

From: Matthew Walsh
To: Erin Walsh
Date: September 25 at 08:25 EDT
Subject: RE: Back from the Azores

No, Shannon is fine. She's not ruining my life. You'd know that if you called her.

I met someone.

She showed up at my office yesterday in this dress, and we went to The Red Hat and she can pound tequila like a frat boy. Then she tripped and I brought her upstairs and my keys were in my pocket and she's so fucking hot, and we hooked up and now she's gone.

I should be over it, I get that, but I'm not. Not at all. I just don't know what to do right now.

From: Erin Walsh
To: Matthew Walsh
Date: September 25 at 13:32 WEST
Subject: Matt's mental breakdown

Stream of consciousness much?

Clearly, you're distraught. Maybe hungover. Maybe both.

Ok. I need a minute to process this. Are you saying that you like chica? I didn't think you were a hook-up and hang-out kind of kid.

And P.S.: The Red Hat? Classy, Matt. Classy. No wonder chica ditched your ass.

From: Matthew Walsh
To: Erin Walsh
Date: September 25 at 08:36 EDT
Subject: RE: Matt's mental breakdown

I'm not hungover and I'm not having a mental breakdown. I can't explain this, and that is why I'm asking YOU to sort ME out. By my count, you owe me a few.

From: Erin Walsh
To: Matthew Walsh
Date: September 25 at 13:41 WEST
Subject: RE: Matt's mental breakdown

Wow. Way to get all loan shark on me, kid.

Don't you have chica's number? CALL HER.

Say, Hey, chica. It seems we had an eventful day together and then you ghosted. WTF?

Or text her. Or go to her house.

If she wants to see you, she will. If she doesn't…find a new one.

———

From: Erin Walsh
To: Matthew Walsh
Date: September 25 at 13:59 WEST
Subject: RE: Matt's mental breakdown

You better tell me what happens. Don't think I won't send Sam to find you, and I know he'd feast all over this gossip.

I SET one copy of *Oh, The Places You'll Go!* aside for Steph and picked up the other to write a message inside the cover for Amanda when my phone signaled an incoming text. Pen between my teeth, I froze, seeing Matthew's name flash across the screen.

In the hours since fleeing his bed, my thoughts volleyed between estimating when he would call, debating if he would, and trying to decide which I wanted more.

The messages from Matthew kept coming until I set my phone face down and headed for the kitchen. I nibbled a square of dark chocolate—reminding myself it would be a morsel and not the entire bar—while the chirps seemed to amplify until they were reverberating off the walls. Flying into distraction mode, I washed a week's worth of dishes and edited my sloppy mail pile. I kept cleaning when the chirps stopped, suddenly concerned with polishing the bathroom faucets until they sparkled, but the quiet was strangling me and I dashed for the phone.

Matthew: Lauren, it's Matt. what happened? where are you?

Matthew: you have to know how truly mind-blowing and incredible last night was.

Matthew: I think it was good for you too.

"Don't worry, Matthew," I announced to my chocolate. "Mind-blowing and incredible all around.

Matthew: It scared the shit out of me when I woke up and you were gone.

Matthew: If there is anything I did or said that made you upset, I want to know.

Matthew: I was rough with you and I'm sorry for that. Please tell me you're ok.

Matthew: Lauren, please, I need to know you're all right. I'm going a little crazy here.

Matthew: Fuck, Lauren, do you have any idea what could have happened to you on the streets last night?

"Don't even start with that," I muttered. The role of Overbearing Male was already filled, and the Commodore had two promising understudies in Will and Wes. And it wasn't as if I couldn't handle myself.

Matthew: Lauren, please. Talk to me.

What was there to say? I didn't go home with guys I'd known for all of one hot second? Or I didn't know *how* to have a one-night stand? Or it hadn't been weeks or months since last having sex, it had been years.

Or maybe this was the time to tell him I was a hot messy

mess and between crying in stairwells and stumbling around like a wobbly drunk girl, I was failing at damn near everything.

Or perhaps he wanted to hear that last night scared me. It was all well and good to flirt your pants off, but there was nothing flirty about the shit that went down between us. That kind of sex required agendas and protocols and some kind of how-to guide.

Matthew: I need to hear from you.
Matthew: I will meet you anywhere at any time. I'll come to you.
Matthew: Please just let me know you made it home.
Matthew: Lauren…please. I just want to make sure you're alive.
Matthew: and I know your phone is never more than 3 ft away from you so if you don't respond soon I'm going to assume you're dead and not ignoring me.

I could hear the tension coiling between his shoulders with each message, and though I wanted to unknot every muscle, I wanted to smack some sense into him. Roaming the streets while female didn't require a chaperone.

I stared at his phone number alongside the string of texts, debating whether I should add him to my Address Book. The gesture was inconsequential but after last night, it was loaded with significance—I was deciding whether I intended to communicate with him ever again, and while I considered this, I barely registered the knocking at my door. I didn't consider the holey yoga pants and tank top I was wearing when I answered.

I probably should have.

"You left a few things behind, Miss Halsted."

Matthew leaned against the doorframe, and hanging from his fingers were my panties. My very expensive, very pretty panties. They glared back at me, all judgey and sanctimonious. It was my karmic punishment for sneaking out, for leaving a perfectly scrumptious naked man, and I could hear those panties condemning me.

"Unless, of course, you wanted me to keep them," he said, a playful edge creeping into his voice. "I'll take good care of them."

"I don't even want to know what that means!" I said, snatching the skivvies from him and tossing them into my apartment. I couldn't burst into those flames quickly enough, and that was before I determined what he'd do with my undies. "What are you doing here, Matthew? How do you even know where I live?"

Straightening, the mischievous glimmer in his eyes vanished. "I wanted to make sure you made it home, Lauren, and your address is on your business card."

"Fine, so that proves you didn't inject me with a tracking device. Magnificent." I shook my head and pointed to my door. "I'm home."

He glanced inside my apartment, and nodded in that direction. "Can we talk, or…something? We were going to hang out today."

Why couldn't he let me crawl under a rug and die, like I wanted? Why did he need to show up holding my panties and looking adorable? This had to violate numerous one-night stand rules.

"Before you say no," he said, holding up a hand. "Just say yes instead."

Part of me wanted to close the door on him, close the

book on this whole encounter, but another part of me wanted to kick it wide open, and I knew we'd be naked within five minutes if that happened.

And if I stepped back from it all—the chaos in my head, the ache between my legs, the swaying in my stomach from the tequila, chocolate, and not enough sleep—I wanted the naked option.

I also wanted a croissant, and if there was one thing I knew well, it was playing the trade-off game. Matthew was my treat yesterday; today it would be a croissant.

Easy enough.

"All right. But not here. No, you can go and, um, I'll meet you at the Frog Pond in a little while. Practice not being a creeper."

"Half an hour," he said. It was delivered as a statement, a warning: *I won't wait for you all day*. "Oh, and sweetness? You might have those panties back, but this?" Matthew's hand dipped into his pocket, and in an achingly slow movement, like a lurching movie in my mind, too slow to be real, he held my rose quartz necklace up by the chain. "I'm keeping this."

A HAPPY PERK of subletting from a colleague of my brothers' was living a block away from the Boston Common and the Public Gardens. It was my spot. I loved the Swan Boats, the *Make Way for Ducklings* statues, and the skating rink constructed over the Frog Pond every winter.

Not that I was cut out for ice skating, but I did enjoy the hot chocolate sold nearby.

I entered the park at the Charles Street Gate and

adjusted the plaid scarf around my neck, my clothes strate-gically selected as an extra layer of confidence. Power heels and fancy panties didn't jive with weekend wear, so I need every scrap of fashion armor I could find.

Who did he think he was, showing up with my freaking underwear in his hand? And announcing he intended to keep my necklace? I was going to have some words with him.

Matthew was easy to spot, pacing in front of the pond, his hands perched on his hips and his long legs eating up the path. I watched him for several quiet minutes, trying to piece together why I agreed to this. I didn't get involved with this kind of drama, and I didn't let beautiful boys take over my life.

Just when I convinced myself to stop this ridiculous flir-tation and leave, Matthew looked up, his eyes giving it all away. He was confused and annoyed and relieved, and behind that was a twinge of hurt. And I was responsible for all of it.

The distance between us evaporated, and he reached for me, running his hands from my shoulders to my fingertips and back up again. It was a decent response, considering I kicked him out of my apartment. Regardless of what he said in his texts, I expected to hear I was an awful hook-up and he was dumping me as a client and telling all his archi-tect-engineer friends to steer clear.

"Miss Halsted," he sighed. He studied me, shaking his head while his hands skimmed up and down my arms.

"Mr. Walsh."

"Do you have any idea what you put me through? You leave in the middle of the night, then you don't respond to my texts? What the fuck happened?"

His sharp tone didn't align with his gentle hands as they pulled me closer, working over my shoulders and down the planes of my back, settling on my waist. He was a demanding little shit, but at least he was sweet about it.

"Nothing. I'm fine." I rolled my eyes. "You don't think this is all a bit much? Showing up at my place? The texts? My panties, my necklace? Aren't you coming on a little strong?"

Matthew tilted his head and shot me a measured glance. "I think last night was a little…strong."

It didn't matter whether I agreed with him—I did—but what I really wanted to know was whether last night was normal. What he liked, what he wanted, what he fantasized about. And perhaps the question wasn't about last night so much as it was about me: was *I* what he liked, what he wanted, what he fantasized about? Or was I convenient? Was it possible he did this, this whole crazy production, on a regular basis?

Or was it something else? Something different?

"Don't do this, Matthew. Don't go all caveman on me. You do not get to call the shots. I didn't mean to scare you, however you cannot send me, like, three dozen texts. I don't care *what* happened last night. It's ludicrous and over-bearing and suffocating, and I don't put up with that shit."

"Are you kidding me? You actually believe I shouldn't freak out when you disappear from my bed in the middle of the night after promising to stay and you don't respond to my texts?"

"Well, yes."

He crossed his arms over his chest and stared at me. "Miss Halsted, that's bullshit and you know it."

I gazed at his long-sleeved Cornell t-shirt, and my argument dried on my tongue. I didn't know why he generated such strong reactions in me, but there was no in-between.

I told myself to stop analyzing, stop dissecting. The day was crisp and sunny, and these jeans did amazing things for my legs, and this scrumptious man wanted my attention. It didn't have to fit into an agenda, and it didn't have to mean anything.

"Do you like croissants?"

"Hmm?" He squinted at me.

"Croissants. One of my favorite bakeries is over on Charles Street, and they have the best croissants, and I'd rather have a croissant than yell at you in the middle of the Common."

"Fine, but you need to promise me you'll never do that again."

I couldn't help but roll my eyes. "Fine, but you need to promise you're not telling me what to do, or blowing up my phone with obsessive and stalkery texts again."

"Fine, and just so you know? All that eye rolling is adorable. Keep doing it."

"Fine, I will," I snapped, my voice cracking into a laugh at the end. "You're a caveman."

"You're bossy. I have to keep up."

Matthew smiled, and brushed his lips against mine. A hot blush stole across my cheeks and I studied the wash-weathered lettering on Matthew's shirt.

"I'm sorry I freaked out, Miss Halsted. I kept thinking you'd trip into the harbor and be swept out to sea. And then pretend you did it on purpose."

Another eye roll. "Can we talk about that croissant now?"

Matthew's fingers laced with mine as we walked to the

bakery, and they stayed that way while we ordered and chose a sun-drenched table outside. He tore into his sandwich as I slathered apricot jam on my croissant, and from the right angle, we were a regular couple out for brunch. The unlikely history of us fell away, and we weren't trying to formulate the right words without the shelters of night and alcohol.

"You're not from around here," he said.

I unwound my scarf and dropped it to my lap. "Why do you say that?"

Matthew watched as I adjusted my chair in the direction of the sun's rays. "I know Boston people. You're not Boston people." He rubbed his knuckles over his jaw. "And you'd never heard of The Red Hat. So where are you from?"

"I grew up in California. Outside of San Diego."

He nodded and sipped his coffee. "And you're here because…why? You have a problem with great weather and beaches?"

"No. I love all beaches. They're my favorite places. And sunshine, too, but I'm into seasons. San Diego is summery and slightly less summery. I came out here to go to Williams College, and I wanted to work in urban schools, which is how I made my way to Boston. Chelsea, actually."

"Do you visit California much?" Matthew leaned back, his ankles crossed over each other and his arms folded against his chest.

Licking my lips, I tried to remember the question. Too scrumptious. "No, not much. My parents are mostly retired, and they do this whole motor-home-and-road-trip thing. My dad does some consulting, and my mother's blog is basically five minutes from being featured on the Travel Channel, so they're busy."

Matthew's eyes narrowed. "Not even for the holidays?"

Frowning, I sipped my latte and mentally scrolled through my calendar. Surviving September was my top priority. "Uh, no, I hadn't planned on it. My parents are touring Baja California for the next few months. A group of friends usually get together for Thanksgiving and some form of mash-up of winter holidays, and..."

I trailed off, realizing that we wouldn't be hosting a Christma-Hanu-Festivus party this year. Not with Steph in Chicago and Amanda in DC. Sure, other friends would extend invitations to their celebrations, or try to recreate our festivities. Not so unlike book club, it wasn't the same, and I wanted—maybe I was being a petulant child—to remember the way we did it, not the spin-off.

"I like this area," he said, looking around. "My sister lives on Mt. Vernon, near Louisburg Square. She's obsessed with Beacon Hill."

I hated the idea of dismissing his comments, but I didn't want all of these personal details. I couldn't pretend this never happened if I picked up another uniquely Matthew story. "You said you wanted to hang out today?"

Matthew nodded and reached into his pocket, retrieving a neatly folded cocktail napkin from The Red Hat. "We could walk a few properties."

"Oh, so you're here in a professional capacity? When you showed up with my panties I figured you were in manwhore mode."

He grabbed the arm of my chair and dragged me closer, a metal-on-stone screech whipping through the courtyard and drawing every eye toward us. He brushed my hair over my ear, leaning in until I could feel his breath on my skin.

"You're a mouthy little thing, you know that? I don't

know why, but I like it a lot." My teeth sank into my lower lip to repress a broad smile. "You'll be getting a bill. I think it will come out to…" He brushed a few croissant crumbs from my shirt and twisted my nipple in the process. "Drinks with me."

"I don't have time for drinks with you. I barely have time for drinks with myself. I have too much—"

"Yeah," he interrupted. "We work too much and neither of us has a life. We covered that last night. Doesn't have to be drinks. Maybe just my cock in your mouth, and just because you want to."

I turned and stared at Matthew's defined jaw, and the way the sun illuminated his dark, wavy hair, and those blue eyes that told so many stories. I couldn't have it all, that I knew. But I could have a little treat. "Drinks? Just for fun? Just for now?"

"Yeah," he said. "It's only as complicated as you make it."

As much as I wanted to lock Matthew in the First Time for Everything vault and throw away the key, I didn't want that at all.

"GOOD BONES," I declared, my hand slapping the brick wall with reverence. I appreciated many things about old Boston architecture and construction, and diehard brick walls was one of them. "A wrecking ball's the only thing taking down this place."

Over my shoulder I saw Lauren, her head shaking. She stared at the abandoned button mill's broken windows and released a strangled sigh.

"Okay, explain to me what's wrong with this site," I said. "Because this will work *and* it won't cost half of what the last three sites would have. And it's solid. I walked the roofline twice, and it's the most stable roof I've seen in months. And that's saying something because I climb a lot of roofs."

She waved at the cavernous space. "I don't see it the way you do, Matthew, I don't get it. How am I supposed to make this into classrooms? Where's the playground going to go? And do you see how the floors slant? That's gotta be expensive to fix."

I paused, expecting a dozen more complaints. Despite wanting to peel her jeans off and fuck her against one of those brick walls, I was also in architect mode and trying to keep my client happy. My brain blew up a few times attempting to manage that line, and counting bricks was the only thing keeping me from doing wind sprints up and down the mill floor.

As if I needed to make matters more complex, there was a pussy necklace in my pocket. It was all too easy for my hand to slide in there and, without thinking, let my thumb glide over the stone.

"Those are reasonable concerns, and they're solvable. I sketched a rough plan. You'll see all the classrooms you requested here, along this half of the building. Look." I handed over my graphing notebook. "And the offices and gymnasium and cafeteria here, along this side. By my math —which tends to be correct—you have space for more classrooms or offices, if you want them. And flooring is a fast fix. It doesn't require a quarter million in steel, unlike everything else we've seen."

Lauren's arms crossed over her chest while she turned a critical eye to the design. I knew this wasn't exactly what she wanted, and the degree of abandonment was pretty high—the rusted-out water heaters piled along one side of the building weren't helping my case, and neither were the raccoons defending their territory in the basement.

"Oh," she said at length. "Okay. I like that."

"All you need here is upgraded flooring, drywall, and ventilation, and a couple green improvements. Altogether, that will cost less than the steel on the last property we checked out. You can afford this."

"How much?"

"All in? I could ballpark it," I shrugged. Staring at the walls, I visualized a few cost structures and scribbled a number beside the blueprint before handing it to Lauren. "Fully loaded."

"You did that in your head." She pointed at the number. "I didn't see you write anything down, or use a calculator."

Watching Lauren's eyebrow arch, I chuckled and slipped my hands into my pockets. "Well, yeah. It's mostly addition. Some multiplication."

"Don't let anyone tell you you're anything less than freakish."

"I'll keep that in mind," I laughed. "I can give you something more precise when I draw this up, and do some more research on the lot. The estimate might be a bit high."

Lauren nodded and paced the perimeter. The mill's interior was huge, and when she wandered out of sight, a thin sheen of doubt trickled into my stomach. I had seen her debating with herself at the park, and I had seen her turn to walk away. Even when she excused herself to the ladies' room at the bakery, I contemplated whether she'd sneak out through the kitchen.

I couldn't understand what kept pulling her away from me when all I wanted was to pull her closer.

After waking up alone, I had surveyed the wreckage of my loft—note to self: never, ever leave used condoms on the floor where it was all too easy to step on them—and took a long shower. I expected the hot spray to wash away the night, to clear my head, but if anything, each drop of water left me more tightly wound. Pacing, push-ups, emailing Erin, more push-ups, manically texting Lauren, none of it helped. Not until Erin suggested seeing Lauren.

I knew it was far from rational, but showing up with her

underwear in my hand was my admittedly inarticulate way of asking "When can we do that again?"

The mechanics were secondary.

We were each too damn busy for our own good, but I'd forgo food and sleep to get her naked again, to be with her again. I didn't care what we called it. I wanted more of those jarringly intense nights with her, but if the cautious glint in her eyes was any indication, I should have turned the project over to Patrick and let it go down as the best one-night stand in recorded history.

Lauren's shoulder bumped mine and she handed the notebook back to me. Warmth radiated from the subtle touch, and I bumped her in return. "So, what now? You'll call me with the final number tomorrow or Monday, and we'll figure out how to get started here?"

I grinned. "Or you can just come back to my place and I'll do it today."

"I can't."

I waited for more explanation, but Lauren offered nothing.

"Okay." I nodded and stepped away from her, deciding to focus on photographing the plumbing and duct work instead of deciphering another layer of Lauren. I pointed my phone at a serpentine cluster of pipes in the corner and snapped a few pictures before turning back to her. "Actually, no. Is that you can't—you don't want to? Or is that you can't—you have something else going on?"

"I have a thing."

Tell me you don't have a date. Say you're not seeing some guy tonight.

I crossed one arm over my chest and rasped my other hand against my jaw, waiting, while Lauren fidgeted with her scarf. Those fucking scarves. It was as if she was intentionally putting a barrier between her breasts and me, intentionally killing my joy. "I can find some tequila if that sways the odds in my favor."

"Hilarious as always, Matthew."

She walked toward the windows, the afternoon sun catching her hair and illuminating every shade of blonde. Her phone in her hands, she typed and toggled through screens, the topic dismissed.

I continued measuring, photographing, sketching, and Lauren didn't look up from her phone. Reciting numbers aloud and noisily retracting my tape measure didn't draw her attention, and when I had more data than necessary, I said, "I'm good. We can probably—"

She whirled around, her hands on her hips and forehead wrinkled. "What's your middle initial stand for?"

"What?" I heard the question; I really didn't want to answer it. Lauren stared at me, and somehow this one inquiry was the test. I groaned and crossed my arms over my chest. "Listen. I don't let this out much but you're nice. I'll tell you mine if you tell me yours."

"What are you? Eleven?"

"Thirty," I said. "Now, you first."

"Olivia. Your turn." She gestured, urging me to answer.

"Antrim."

She stepped closer, shaking her head. "What was that?"

"Antrim. My mother, she came here alone from Ireland when she was fifteen, and gave all six of us ridiculous Irish middle names, all starting with A. I got stuck with Antrim. I frequently draw the short straw."

Lauren nodded, her eyes cast downward at the dingy concrete flooring. She was carrying on a full conversation with herself, complete with raised eyebrows and head shaking.

"So like I said, I've got everything I need, and—"

"Don't you want a night off? Maybe some time away from me?"

My gaze swept over the mill's interior, as if I'd find something in the empty space to diffuse my exasperation. Why the fuck would she think that?

"No. Definitely not." I scratched my chin, not wanting to ask the question but knowing it was necessary. "Do you?"

She studied her scarf, the fabric twisting around her fingers and then unfurling. "It's a thing, a big thing, actually. Tonight. My friends, Amanda and Stephanie, they're both moving in the next few weeks, and we're having a party for them. And..." She sighed and tore her eyes away from her scarf. "And you could come. With me, that is. For a drink."

I didn't know what to make of meeting her friends when she barely agreed to see me today, and I didn't know whether drinks meant *drinks*, but I knew Lauren was predictably unpredictable. No rational order to be found.

But at least I knew she wasn't seeing some random guy tonight.

"I think I will come with you."

FIFTEEN MILES of pavement always did me good, and tonight was no exception. As usual, it tied off my lingering annoyance with Angus over the Bunker Hill properties and other stresses from the week. It helped that Patrick's ass was parked in a British pub in Cambridge that broadcast his favorite soccer leagues, and not bitching about my route choice.

Back inside my loft, I grabbed a beer before stepping into the shower and spent a few minutes drinking under the water. It would have driven my mother crazy, and if she had lived to see me drinking in the shower, I'm certain she would have taken one of her wooden spoons to my ass because of it.

The places where my mother should have been were everywhere, but it wasn't the big moments—graduations, birthdays, holidays—that haunted me. It was the everyday moments, when I craved her spaghetti or needed to know the right gift to send for the birth of an old friend's baby, when I felt it the most.

The thought lodged in my throat, and I choked down the remnants of the beer. I dried off and headed for the den, knowing I owed Erin a response.

Her emails flashed across my phone all day, along with a torrent of calls and texts from Shannon about getting my shit together on the Bunker Hill properties before Angus went postal. Patrick wanted status reports on the brownstones, Sam needed me looking at a foundational decay issue, and Riley was very concerned about getting my take on his Fantasy Football league. All said, I had nineteen missed calls, thirty-two texts, and fifty-one emails from my siblings.

From: Erin Walsh
To: Matthew Walsh
Date: September 25 at 17:03 CEST
Subject: RE: Matt's mental breakdown

Since you haven't updated me on chica, I presume you've decided to climb Mount Washington together, or swim to Quincy Bay, or whatever you athletic types do, and you're living happily ever after.

(have I mentioned that I find that bizarre—isn't life difficult enough without choosing to climb things?)

Or chica kicked you in the balls and you're lying in a gutter somewhere and she wasn't as incredible you thought she was. BTW—In Italia now.

From: Matthew Walsh
To: Erin Walsh
Date: September 25 at 18:31 EDT
Subject: Not climbing Mt Washington

E –
Everything's awesome.
M

I PULLED another beer from the refrigerator when I heard my phone ringing, and answered without looking at the screen. Odds were high Lauren was calling to cancel or a sibling was in need of something completely unessential. "Hello?"

"Everything's awesome? That's all I get? It's been ten hours, and I get a one-line response with zero descriptive details? Really, Matt?"

"But at least I know what it takes to get you on the phone." Smiling at Erin's ever-present piss and vinegar, I edged my hip on the counter and sipped my beer. "What would you like to know?"

"What does she look like? Give me a point of reference."

I ran my hand through my damp hair, thinking. "She's blonde, green eyes, twenty-eight, a little shorter than you, wears a lot of scarves—"

"Okay, scarves, that tells me everything. So you're *with* her now? You're dating?"

"Do people still use that term?"

"Jesus, Mary, and Joseph," Erin muttered. "Matt, you're making it hard for me to tolerate you right now."

"Why are you being such a bitch about this?"

"I'm not! I just think you're getting a little carried away with chica—"

"Her name is Lauren," I snapped.

"Okay, great, you're getting a little carried away with *Lauren*. I mean, come on, you hooked up with her and then went into meltdown mode this morning. Do you even know her birthday? Her favorite citrus fruit? These are the important things, Matt, and it would suck to realize after a few months that she loves pomelos and you're all about tangerines. Take your pussy goggles off."

I wanted—no, needed—Erin on my side. "I don't ask you for much, E, and right now, I'm asking you not to analyze it. We're just hanging out. That's it."

"All right," Erin sighed. "But you better not—"

"I gotta go, E," I interrupted as the doorbell rang. "I'll keep you posted."

"I want proof of this in the form of pictures! You and chica, ASAP!"

A towel knotted on my hips and a half-empty beer bottle in my hand, I swung open the door to find Lauren in a blue sequined dress that barely covered her ass. "Holy fuck," I groaned.

Her eyes landed on my chest and then traveled lower, staring at the towel as she shut the door behind her. "Uh-huh."

I leaned against the wall and polished off my beer, somewhat surprised she chose to show up at all. "Where are your pants, sweetness?"

"Where are yours?"

That bossy little mouth. I wanted to hate it, I wanted to shove my cock in it, but more than anything, I loved it.

Locking a hand on her elbow, I pulled her to me, and lifted the loaded tote and silver gift bags from her. We watched each other for a heavy minute, the air between us shifting, heating. And then we attacked each other. Our lips crashed together, urgent and hungry, as if we spent three years apart instead of three hours.

Lauren's back against the wall, I dropped to my knees and hiked that blood-quickening excuse for a dress over her waist, and I found pale pink panties waiting for me. "Are these for my benefit, Miss Halsted?"

Her shoulders squared, she gazed down at me with a solemn expression. "I can't imagine why you'd think that, Mr. Walsh."

"Filthy, filthy girl," I said. The silky fabric slipped to her ankles and I hooked her leg over my shoulder, her laughter ringing around us. Her fingers dug into my hair when my tongue swiped her bare folds, and it was everything I craved about her—her taste, her sounds, her shivers.

"We should go-*ooo*," Lauren moaned. I glanced up at her from my knees but kept my tongue fused to her clit. "You really need to get dressed."

Lauren halfheartedly pushed away from the wall, and I tightened my grip on her ass. I growled against her before looking up again. "Is this not working for you? Your pussy seems to be enjoying it."

The conflict was clear in her eyes, and I wondered whether I should feel the same, but I didn't understand what she found so problematical. I didn't see what could be wrong with this when we both wanted it, and we knew the rules of the game.

Her fingers curled around my hair, pulling me closer, directing me where she needed me, all while she shook her head. "No," she whispered.

"That's bullshit. Now stay right here," I said. "I know what you need."

"And what's that?" Her fingers attacked a knot in my shoulder while I returned to her folds, nipping and licking until we were both breathing hard.

I wanted her obscene words, but I knew if I asked for them they'd take over, and there were a few things I wanted to know before that happened.

"You need to be fucked properly, and I sincerely doubt anyone's ever done that for you." Two fingers pushed inside her, and her body immediately found its rhythm. "At least not before last night."

"Oh really?"

I nodded, my tongue teasing her. Last night with Lauren was indescribable. It redefined everything I knew about sex, adding layers of complexity and connection I never thought possible. And then there was her quietly obvious inexperience, and the unrestricted trust she placed in my hands. She was far from pure, but fuck, she was innocent.

"I knew last night. Either no one's ever gone down on you before, or you've never come from it. Which one is it?"

Lauren's head fell against the wall and her eyes closed, and for several minutes, the only sounds were her frantic murmurs and pleas for more. Then she ran her hands through my hair, canted my head to meet her eyes, and said, "You were my first."

"I like that." My tongue pressed against Lauren's clit, and I felt her orgasm pulsating around my fingers. In the distance I could hear her speaking, feel her clawing at my shoulders, but all I could hear was *mine, mine, mine.* It was the only thing I heard when Miss Halsted was around.

"Get up here," she demanded, her hand twisted tight around my hair.

That bossy girl.

As I stood, she tore the towel from my waist, closed her hand around me, and scraped her teeth over my earlobe. She whispered, "Why do you like it?"

Her grip tightened and I groaned against her neck, my hips pumping into her hand. The sequined dress bunched under her breasts, and I wanted it gone, out of sight. Once the zipper was down, I yanked it over her head and it joined my towel and her panties on the floor. "I don't want anyone else tasting your sweet pussy. It's just for me."

"You're such a caveman," she hissed. "Why do I like that so fucking much?"

"It doesn't have to make sense, sweetness. Just enjoy it."

Lauren's knees tightened around my hips, and she

dragged me through her slit. I shuddered, and bucked into her hand with a sharp grunt.

"How many other girls do you have drinks with?"

My teeth pressed against her collarbone, and I growled. "How many times have I told you there are no others?"

She smiled, offering a small shrug. "I'm on the pill. Are you going to give me herpes or anything gross like that?"

"What? No, no, definitely not—"

Her fist tightened around me, drawing me into her heat. "Are you sure?"

"Of course I'm fucking sure, Laur—" Before I could say anything else, she aimed my cock at her entrance, pressed her heels into my ass, and I was inside her.

Bare.

"Fuck, Lauren," I bellowed.

I didn't move. I wanted to remember every hot, clenching ounce of her. Thinking about baseball would buy me a few more minutes. It always worked under the condom regime. The wearing a raincoat in the shower regime. "Goddamn it, sweetness, you feel so tight and hot and wet, and perfect, and unbelievable, and if you behave, I might let you come soon."

She drove her fingers through my hair, scraping her nails along my scalp until I shivered under her hands. I wasn't ready for this. I didn't know how to handle the dizzy sensation wrapping around my brain. I wasn't even sure I could stay standing.

"I don't think I can behave, Mr. Walsh."

I heard everything she wasn't saying—her desire for something raw and real, something that didn't require definition—and I swallowed it all. I pulled all the way out before spearing into her, her breath catching as I filled her.

Our eyes met, and I repeated the motion, wanting her gasps and moans, wanting to own them.

"You're right," I said, my teeth clenched and jaw rigid. "And you'd rather have it this way, wouldn't you?"

Lauren nodded, a shy, devious smile dancing on the corners of her lips. She held my gaze while her orgasm vibrated around me and I exploded inside her, her hums and shrieking whimpers filling the space between us in concert with my guttural rumbles.

Her hands traced my spine up to my neck and into my scalp and back down, and we stayed calmly entwined as our bodies quaked with aftershocks. From the crook of her neck, I inhaled the sweet scent of Lauren laced with sex and sweat, and wondered if she could feel my heart hammering against my chest.

I attacked her mouth and dug my fingers into the supple skin of her ass. The kiss started with teeth and lips and tongues warring, but it mellowed and ended with Lauren's forehead pressed to mine and our lips barely touching. "You were saying something about me getting dressed?"

A sated, drowsy smile filled Lauren's face. "In a couple of minutes," she murmured.

Eleven

LAUREN

SHIT.

Shit, shit, shit, shit, shit.

Shit.

How did I go wrong with the 'croissant for breakfast, no dirty sex with Matthew' plan? It wasn't even a small cheat, like grabbing a few chocolate-covered almonds in the name of late afternoon protein. No, this was ordering lo mein, kung pao chicken, and beef with broccoli, and letting the delivery guy believe I had four friends hiding in my apartment.

I was really racking up points in the Didn't Think This One Through category, but it wasn't just the sex. No, I had other issues on my hands while we walked to the party.

First, it was too cold to be wearing this dress without tights, and the chilly evening air left my nipples painfully, awkwardly hard. Instead of honoring any after-sex customs like speaking or hand-holding, my arms were crossed over my chest while I stared at the pavement. I felt Matthew's gaze on me, his raised eyebrows and expectant glances begging for some indication of why I'd shut down but I couldn't tell him about my chilly nips, or that I shouldn't have dragged him along to this party. Inviting him meant seeing my friends, and that meant they'd want *all* the details, and I could barely explain this situation to myself. Beyond that, going away parties were the territory of couples, not fucked-up 'drinks but I actually mean sex' arrangements.

And I needed a nap.

Specifically, a naked nap with Matthew as my blanket, and maybe some more wall sex.

"You ready?" he asked, his hand holding the door to the venue, Tia's, open.

I eyed his dark jeans, white Oxford open at the collar, and charcoal suit coat with a pouty shrug.

"What the fuck does that mean, sweetness?"

It means my friends are going to want to know who you are and where you came from and why they've never heard of you.

It means they'll ask questions about you next week, next month — when this little game is over — and they'll want to know what happened.

It means my work is overwhelming, my friends are moving on, I don't want my one-night stand to end, and my world is sliding into barely controlled chaos.

"Nothing," I said, and ducked under Matthew's arm into the restaurant.

Looking around at the floral arrangements and photo slideshow projected on the wall, I was relieved Steph, Amanda, and I made time last week for dinner together at Sonsie. This party was for everyone else, and it never would have given us the quiet moments we needed.

In reality, the past four months were our long farewell.

Their announcements both landed in June, and from that point onward we arranged dinners, long beach weekends, and plenty of packing parties.

I was also thrilled I handed off the planning of this event to Elsie Moor. She organized parties by trade, and she approached every backyard barbeque with the same level of preparation she would for a massive charity ball. In fact, *Coastal Living* magazine photographed her Fourth of July party on Cape Cod. She'd worked that morsel into every conversation in recent memory.

Elsie knew Steph through one of those arbitrary connections that made you realize exactly how small the world was, and when she and her husband moved to Boston last year, she folded into our circle. Her personality was shiny, animated, and over the top, and I knew she was just waiting to star in her own reality series.

The second Matthew's hand curled around my waist, I spotted Steph and Amanda gaping at us from the opposite side of the restaurant. They excused themselves from their conversations, elbowing through the crowd.

"We were just wondering where you were, and now you're here! And looking freakin' sexypants as usual!" Amanda's chestnut hair fell in glossy waves over her shoulders as she motioned at my dress, then turned to Matthew. "Well hello there."

I gestured between him and my friends. "Matthew Walsh, these are my friends—"

"From your freshman dorm at Williams," he added. He'd pumped me for information about Steph and Amanda on the way back from the button mill but his sketches caught my attention, and I didn't notice how much I shared while envisioning my school. "And The Dungeon?"

"That's right," I said. Steph and Amanda exchanged loaded glances and didn't bother containing their amusement. "My friends, Amanda Rier, Steph Grasiani."

His eyes twinkled as he pulled me closer, his palm spreading across my hip and his fingers an inch away from starting something naughty. It was still surprising to feel those butterflies beating against my chest. It was even more surprising to discover I liked the butterflies.

I didn't want a relationship, I didn't have time for a relationship, but the fact we were here together, his fingers tapping out a beat on my hipbone while he met my friends, only established that my head and my ladybits needed to calibrate their decision-making.

My friends kept glancing at me while Matthew asked about Amanda's work as a financial consultant, and Steph discovered he managed the remodel—he called it a rehab and restore—two houses down from hers.

When another guest caught Steph and Amanda's attention for a moment, Matthew turned his head and brushed his lips over my ear. "How about that drink, sweetness? The usual?" I nodded, refusing to acknowledge the layers of meaning in his question even when I felt him staring, waiting for a reaction. Finally, he pivoted toward Steph and Amanda. "Ladies, can I get you anything from the bar?"

"Pregnant," Amanda said, pointing to her small belly.

"Breastfeeding." Steph pointed to her chest.

"Uh, all right then," Matthew murmured. "Congratulations."

I watched as he moved through the restaurant before turning to face Steph and Amanda. I forgot all about texting them with a heads-up around the time my leg went over

Matthew's shoulder, and I was bracing for their barrage of questions.

"You have sex hair," Steph announced.

"You totally have sex hair," Amanda said.

"I do not have sex hair," I said, but still ran a hand through my flat-ironed-straight strands.

"Where did you get that chunk of man candy?" Amanda asked. "And why the hell didn't I get a memo about this? This is the kind of shit I'm going to miss out on in DC. You're going to get freaking engaged and I won't even know until I get the freaking Save the Date."

I plucked Steph's sparkling water from her hand and sipped, inwardly snorting at the idea. Not a month went by without a bridal or baby shower in our extended circles, and though I was happy to be finished with wedding season for a while, it was a matter of time until the pastel cardstock started rolling in again. Everyone was moving into quiet, wooded communities, shuttling between holidays with the in-laws instead of our Friendsgivings inevitably composed of eight different types of pie, three potato variations, vegan green bean casserole, and a partially burnt, partially rare turkey.

I was going to miss those pies. There was nothing better than cold pie for breakfast. Apple, pumpkin, blueberry, coconut cream. Why bother with bagels when you could have pie?

"I don't care where she found him, I just want to know what's under the hood and whether he knows how to use it," Steph said.

"Oh, he knows how to use it," Amanda purred. She wrapped her arm around Steph's shoulders and they murmured in lusty agreement. "I bet he can use it. All.

Night. Long." She frowned at Steph. "Did I just say that out loud?"

I studied Matthew leaning against the bar, chatting with someone while he waited for our drinks. He glanced in my direction and met my gaze, but he didn't offer an easy smile. The look he gave me was intense and searing, and it spoke words I was unprepared to hear.

"No but seriously, Lauren, where did that beautiful boy come from?" Steph asked. "We had dinner on Tuesday. Why didn't you mention him?"

"We're just having fun," I said, my eyes still fixed on Matthew. "He helped me find a building for my school. It's not a big deal."

As the words left my mouth, I knew they were lies.

"You seem to have this under control," Amanda said. "Is it?"

"What do you mean?" I asked.

"This is a major shift in strategy," Steph said. "That chastity belt hasn't come off in years. You've been a season ticket holder to the Waiting Games since...well, I don't know. Since the summer we moved into The Dungeon, I think."

"Yeah..." Steph followed my gaze and smirked. "And Man Candy Matt is giving every guy in this place the 'she's mine' stare, he's eating out of your hand and knows your drink order, and you brought him here to meet us with your sex hair, so I have to assume you either have it all figured out, or he fucked the taskmaster right out of you."

Not terribly far from accurate.

The fucking part, not the figuring it out.

"Um, well—" I stammered.

"You know what? The waiting strategy needs a night off.

You have been going a hundred miles an hour for the last year with this fellowship, and you deserve to have fun. What have we told you about losing yourself in work? You earned that drool-bait boy."

"Yep," Steph murmured. "Presuming he's a decent guy and knows how to swing the hammer, don't talk yourself out of it."

Absurdly decent, and not even a little manwhorish.

"Of course he knows how to swing the hammer. Just look at her sex hair, Stephanie!"

Steph slapped a hand to Amanda's lips when Matthew returned, and I shook my head as they swallowed their laughter.

"Hi," he murmured. He kissed my temple and pressed a glass into my hands.

"Hi." I glanced at the tumbler and back up at Matthew. I quirked an eyebrow, and he grinned at the pair of cherries floating on top of the ice. And he called me devious and filthy.

"In honor of your first time," he whispered. "And your second. And *drinks*. And knowing what you need, even when you'd like to tell me otherwise."

"Tell me Matthew: what do I need right now?"

"You need to spend the night with me. The whole night," he said. His fingers brushed over the nape of my neck, and I leaned into him. "I wouldn't be against finding a dark corner in the next five minutes, but you're a bit of a screamer."

I laughed and clinked my glass against his beer bottle. "You say that to all the girls?"

"I believe I've told you already, sweetness, no other girls. Before I forget..." Matthew retrieved his phone from his pocket and swiped it to life. He handed it to Steph. "Would you?"

She nodded and snapped a few pictures before returning the phone to Matthew. I watched as he scrolled through the images and attached one to an email. He met my inquisitive stare with a smile. "My sister," he said, gesturing to the phone. "She asked for proof."

Before I could stop myself, another rendition of Commodore Halsted's Tales of Evil flew out of my mouth. "That makes me think you're going to drug me and sell me into the slave trade, and that picture's for your online auction."

Matthew glanced at Amanda and Steph, and back at me. "That's…no. No. My sister, she's working on her doctorate in Europe. She spends a lot of time around volcanoes and doesn't have much else in her life."

"You'll get used to it," Steph said to Matthew. "Just wait until you meet her brothers."

Yeah, that was going to happen right after I told my father I was having sex against walls. And windows. I still didn't know who that person was or how she came to inhabit my body, although I had to admit, many of her ideas were admirable.

"We have to go mingle," Amanda said. "In case we don't see you before you two sneak out…it was very, very nice meeting you, Matthew. It would be awesome to see you again."

"Enough with those comments," I murmured, pulling Amanda into a tight hug and rubbing her baby belly. "Take care of this little one."

Steph brushed her dark hair from her eyes and reached out for a hug. "I know we'll talk soon, but definitely send me the dates you're going to be in Chicago next month. I won't have furniture or food in the house, but we'll figure it out."

I watched as they embraced other guests, and knew we would never be this close, this involved in each others' lives again. And it hurt, a deep ache radiating from my bones. I leaned into Matthew, letting his warmth take the edge off.

"You're going to Chicago?"

"Yeah," I said, stalling with a sip of my drink. "It's conference season, and I'm making a small marathon of it."

"How does that work, exactly?"

I knew I should have brought it up sooner. Even if this was a one-night stand on steroids, a strange drinks-and-sex arrangement that couldn't last much longer, I probably should have mentioned the three weeks of travel ahead somewhere along the way. After the window sex, before the wall sex.

"Instead of going to one event and then flying back home for a day or two, I'm filling the time between events with by visiting schools with similar educational philosophies. Conference in San Francisco, then observing at schools in Denver. After that, I'm going to Chicago for a few more schools. New Orleans for another conference the following week."

"You won't be back until October." I nodded and met Matthew's eyes. "When do you leave?"

"Early Tuesday morning. That's part of my urgency around getting this building squared away."

"Remember how I said I know what you need?"

"Theory of the Caveman? Yes, you've mentioned this before," I laughed. My hand moved under his jacket and settled on his back, my fingers urging him closer.

"It's a pressure-tested proof, Miss Halsted," he said against my neck.

I slipped my hand lower, between his shirt and jeans, savoring the feel him, his heat. Being with him felt exquisite, or maybe it was that despite all of my single-minded, mission-focused days, I wasn't totally lost in my work. At least not tonight.

"And here's my addendum to that proof: if you're leaving in a few days, we need to get your designs finalized and approved. Stay with me this weekend, and I'll get it done. Then come to the office on Monday so my sister—"

"The one with the volcanoes?"

"No," he laughed. "Different sister—the CFO—and she handles all the real estate. She'll work on getting a clean title so we can order permits and start the work. This is the one thing I can take on for you. You have enough shit going on already so I want you to let me, even if that makes me a caveman."

My fingers continued traveling along his waist while I processed his words. I could spend the next couple of days indulging in Matthew, and then time zones and miles would separate us for weeks. This crazy, sexy pull would fizzle, and our demanding lives would take over again, and this would become a beautiful memory of a wild weekend.

It was no tiny cheat—more like a binge—but a three-week cleanse would balance it all out.

"You've thought of it all," I said, and tugged at Matthew's lapels to draw him closer. He smiled against my lips. "Come on. There are some friends I want you to meet, and I need another beverage, and if *you* can promise not to scream, we might go find that dark corner."

FOG WAFTED over Atlantic Avenue as Matthew and I embarked on the short walk to his building. Dipping my toes in the coupled pond—even if it was just for tonight—was wonderfully satisfying. I expected some relief from the constant fix-up attempts, but I never expected to feel so whole, so completely and thoroughly myself standing next to Matthew. But for every ounce of satisfaction, there was an equal amount of hesitation.

"I like your friends." Matthew shrugged, and he couldn't hold back a smug smile.

While most of my friends expressed some appreciation for the beauty that was Matthew Walsh, only Elsie set my teeth on edge. She went in for the hug instead of the hand-shake, and wrapped her hands around his bicep while she talked about some remodeling she and her husband, Kent, were considering.

I had no business being possessive or territorial or even jealous, but I was. At this moment, Matthew was with me, and she was a little too grabby for my liking.

I rolled my eyes. "My friends liked you, all right. They wanted to drag you out back and take turns on you. Do you always have that effect on married women?"

Matthew stopped in front of the marina outside his building and wrapped his arms around my shoulders, his face taking on a happy, serene quality that seemed unusual for him. "Marry me and find out."

"For the love of tiny purple ponies, Matthew."

I laughed and pushed out of his arms. If I didn't get out of these shoes soon, I was taking them off and walking down the street barefoot. According to the Commodore, that was the best way to pick up gangrene and lose a foot, and a girl needed both feet and all ten toes. He was also fundamentally opposed to my heels (too difficult to flee when the situation demanded it), necklaces (an invitation for strangulation), and long hair (something else attackers could grab).

"Is that a yes?"

"You really are a caveman," I said. "I'm tired, I'm cold, my feet hurt, I have to pee, and I want to be out of this dress and eating this cake"—I held up the leftovers from the party—"in the next ten minutes, and we agreed to drinks."

"And my cock in your mouth." He stretched his arm and peered at his watch. He nodded, and said, "By the way: when will that be starting?"

"Sometime after I change and go to the bathroom. And I really do want this cake."

He sighed. "Then we need to talk about citrus fruit."

Grabbing his hand, I towed him inside. "I'm not even going to ask what that means, Matthew."

He leaned against the elevator walls and crossed his arms, his brows pinched in thought. He didn't speak again until we reached his floor. "But I'm a little wounded you turned down my proposal. That shit was heartfelt."

Twelve

MATTHEW

MONDAY MORNING ARRIVED TOO SOON. The last thing I wanted to do was leave the protective bubble of my loft, but Lauren was awake and dressed before me, and if her clipped tone told me anything, it was that the bubble had long since burst. Even though we were heading in the same direction—she lived around the corner from my office —she invented some reason to leave before I hopped in the shower.

At least I saw her go this time.

Thumbing the email app on my phone open for the first time in thirty-six hours, I climbed the stairs to the small conference room on the top floor of the Walsh Associates offices and groaned at the landslide of new messages. I sank into my seat at the round reclaimed wood table, and if that table wasn't Sam's baby, I would have banged my head against it a few times.

Six or seven years ago, Sam stumbled upon the fallen red oak on a camping trip to Acadia National Forest in Maine and dragged it all the way home. He fashioned the table in his workshop, crafting the wood for months until it was just right. Getting the table to the top floor meant hiring a crane to move it out of Sam's shop and into Beacon Hill, blowing out a row of windows, and lifting the table from the narrow street below through the bank of windows. Much like every-thing Sam did, the event was a massive pain in the ass, but I readily admitted the table was gorgeous, and uniquely suited for our sustainable preservation work.

It also forced us to replace those windows, and back then, not a day went by without finding something new to replace. Those were long days, and they weren't easy.

The Beacon Hill home went into foreclosure during the last housing market crash, and Shannon pulled some strings to bid on the property right when it hit the market. The firm owned office space in downtown Wellesley, and had been headquartered there for almost six decades, but Shannon and Patrick always insisted it was critical that we establish ourselves without Angus's interference.

Getting out of Wellesley didn't remove Angus from the business as much as we expected, though.

We didn't realize the amount of work this place required until we peeled away the mustard yellow paisley wallpa-per, discovering decades of water damage and decayed structures. The wiring was one blown fuse away from an electrical fire, and at least eight layers of oil-based paint covered every old brick, every inch of hand-carved wood, and every pipe in the five thousand square foot home.

If we didn't know each other after growing up together, going away to college together, and then working together, living through that renovation taught us everything else we needed to know. There were more than a couple heated arguments, and even more drunk nights spent wondering whether we were crazy for doing this, and the one time when Patrick almost severed an artery with a jigsaw. Taking our degrees and finding normal architectural firms that weren't embedded in our blood and bones would have been the easier path, and some days, I thought I wanted that path.

But one look at the brick walls, the ones I spent weeks treating to remove the rainbow of paint, and I remembered how much I loved this work and this place. Even when I hated it.

After more than two years spent working out of Shannon's little apartment near Suffolk Law, where we couldn't move without tripping over each other or milk crates overflowing with blueprint canisters, we were desperate for more space. Sam was finishing school around that time, and after some high-profile restorations grabbed the media's attention, we were doing well enough to consider expanding.

That, and Patrick and I showed up at Shannon's place one morning to find ourselves face-to-face with a naked dude sipping juice in her kitchen like he owned the joint. He was as surprised to see us as we were him, yet he made no attempt to cover up. The three of us stared at each other in awful, naked silence until Shannon called out from the shower, inviting him to join her. He did, and Patrick and I spent the day working from a coffee shop, ignoring her calls, and murmuring that we were too old for this shit and we needed legitimate office space. At one point, we looked at each other, and I said, "We can agree that was the biggest dick in the universe, right?"

"Yes," Patrick said. "And I never want to talk about this again."

Open laptops, Starbucks and Dunkin Donuts coffee cups, and cell phones ringed the table, and I leaned back in my seat, surveying my partners. Directly across from me, Patrick scowled at his laptop screen and rubbed a hand over his auburn hair. He leaned against Shannon's shoulder and pointed to her screen while her fingers flew over her phone, her coppery red hair glinting in the morning sun.

Though her hair was styled in a trendy cut with waves and side-swept bangs framing her face, Shannon's resemblance to our mother was undeniable and at times, eerie. She shared many of Abigael Walsh's mannerisms and all of her passion, wrapped in a fireball personality that often scorched everyone in spitting distance.

Riley and Sam bracketed me at the table, their heads bent toward their screens. A printed call sheet flanked Sam's phone and I rolled my eyes at the extensive list of inquiries into his services. After gracing the cover of *Boston Magazine* three winters ago and showcasing a North End restoration outfitted with cutting-edge sustainability features, Sam's celebrity was born.

It didn't matter that I had the same skills and certifications with the added benefit of more experience. All the calls were for Sam. The team could stop working on individual projects and pick up Sam's excess, and we still wouldn't be able to handle the surplus.

It was probably a good thing. Annoying, but good.

It wasn't long ago that Patrick and I were restoring every random barn and boathouse that came our way while Shannon finished law school. We operated on the blind faith that we'd survive and find our niche. Eventually, the niche found us.

Staring at Riley while he yawned widely, I ignored the urge to slap my youngest brother upside the head. Unless he liked Patrick's method of asshole ripping, Riley's hungover frat boy routine needed to end. Patrick insisted we dress like we knew what we were doing, and he never tolerated anything short of professional.

Riley's shaggy, messy hair looked suspiciously like bedhead and it fell past the collar of his plaid shirt. A pronounced coffee stain traversed the leg of his wrinkled khakis and his fly gaped open, exposing a flash of Batman boxers. With his ankle crossed over his knee and sockless feet shoved into untied boat shoes, I shook my head.

We had a lot of work to do with this kid.

At the sound of a new text message arriving, I pulled my gaze away from the frayed hem of Riley's pants and swiveled toward my phone.

Lauren: hi.
Matthew: hi
Lauren: sorry I ran out. I just have a lot going on today.
Lauren: but I can meet you around 3

"You seem damn pleased with life for a Monday morning," Sam said. "Are you cutting your coffee with whiskey now? If that's your new normal, I'm good with it. Whatever it takes to make you smile, Matt. Most days I think you're plotting your escape."

I closed my fingers around my phone before turning to meet his amused expression. "No," I said evenly. "I don't need whiskey to be pleased with life today."

Sam's eyes glowed, and he leaned toward me. "Satiating weekend?" I tried hiding my grin behind my coffee and ignored Sam's chuckle. "That's splendid news."

"Something you need to share, Sam?"

Patrick's hazel eyes narrowed at Sam, and attention shifted to us. "It seems Jugger enjoyed the company of a woman this weekend, and I was congratulating him on ending the dry streak."

Of all the nicknames my siblings tried attaching to me, Jugger—as in Juggernaut, from *The X-Men*—was my least favorite.

"That's great," Patrick muttered. "At some point this morning I'd like this meeting to start because we have shit to discuss. So whenever this little tea party is over, let me know. I'll wait for you to finish."

Sam leaned back in his chair and fidgeted with his cuff-links. "You're one moody son of a bitch, Patrick. Honestly. Now that Matt's in the game, it's about time you start thinking about the opposite sex."

"Are you charging for that advice?" Patrick snapped.

"Perhaps I should be," Sam muttered. "I simply believe it is worth noting Matt's making time with a girl—" Sam swung back to look at me. "I shouldn't make assumptions about your sex life. We're talking about a female, yes?"

Throwing my phone at Sam would be bad, and I kept telling myself as much. There was no separating family from the business, and these were the moments when I craved the anonymity of a typical workplace. One where no one would stop to verify I was sleeping with women.

Make that *one* woman.

"Yes," I said at length.

My stomach sank, remembering that Lauren was

coming *here*. She wouldn't need to invent reasons to flee once she got a look at this crew.

For the most part, my brothers and sisters and I counted each other as friends, and we rarely looked beyond this circle. We were masters at covering up the broken, angry parts of our business and upbringing, and no one was the wiser. It was exhausting, and we diverted most of our energies into old buildings rather than friends or relationships. It was better that way, safer. It protected us from obligatory questions about family and childhood—too complicated, too cluttered, too depressing.

I spared Lauren the goriest details when we talked about the business and my family's inextricable ties to it on Friday night: the sisters who hadn't spoken in five years, the father who systematically expelled Shannon, Sam, and Erin from the family house and spent the majority of his miserable existence berating my siblings and desecrating the memory of my mother.

Regardless of the fast-approaching end—maybe in spite of it—I wanted to see her again, and I wanted to make good on that promise to take care of her building. Outside of the best sex I'd ever had, it seemed like the one tangible thing bringing us back together.

"Shut the hell up, Samuel Aidan. We have actual work to do here," Shannon said. "You don't have to be shameless all day, every day."

Chastened, Sam pressed his fist to his mouth and studied his laptop screen. Patrick talked through updates on a handful of projects, and I stole a glance at my phone. Texting was forbidden during our Monday morning status meetings.

Lauren: as long as that's still ok with you
Lauren: I might be able to do later but not earlier
Matthew: 3 will be fine
Matthew: i want dinner with you tonight.

"What's the story on the Bunker Hill properties?" Patrick asked, his eyes rounding the table before stopping on me.

"I pulled everything the city has. Each in the ballpark of three thousand square feet. Three to four levels. All multi-family. City had only a few work permits from the past fifty years. Mostly new water heaters, some main drain work. Nothing structural. Without walking the properties, I'm fairly certain we're talking original design and infrastructure, and full retrofitting."

Annoyance passed over Patrick's face. "Are you waiting for an invitation to get over there? Do you need someone holding your hand while you draft restoration plans or throw together a budget?"

And that's why we called him Optimus Prime. Serious about everything, perfectionist to no end, impatient as hell, and the most reluctant warrior I'd ever seen.

"Patrick, we acquired these properties on Thursday. They were relatively cheap, in decent shape, and won't take much to restore. They won't sit on the books for long. Unless I hear a compelling argument otherwise, I don't see why these are priorities. The Back Bay projects are far more urgent."

Patrick arched his eyebrows and stared at me for a long, hard second. "Fine. I'll let Angus know to check in with you directly when he wants updates. What else do you have?"

A sparkly blonde who will run screaming the second she meets this tribe.

"Shan, I have a client who needs representation on the acquisition of Trench Mills. Also looking for rehab. Conversion to a school. Can you meet after three today for that?"

Shannon scanned her calendar, nodding. "Three. Yeah, tight but I'll be here."

"We flip mills into schools now?" Riley asked.

"Apparently Matt does," Patrick said.

"My client came to us for rehab and restore on Saint Cosmas in Dorchester. School conversion. We discussed that *last* Monday," I said. "After the walking the property, it was clear Saint Cosmas would be a complete teardown and not within the client's project parameters. Walked a few more properties and Trench Mills is the best option. Floor plans drafted and approved by the client."

They didn't need to know the client and I discussed those floor plans in bed Sunday morning, or that she sat in my home office wearing only an old UCSD t-shirt, her legs folded beneath her and her hair tucked over her ears while I drafted them. They didn't need to know I checked every measurement three times because those swaths of bare skin were too distracting to be safe. She asked lots of questions, her finger tracing every line on the screen before tugging my shorts down, taking me in her mouth, and demanding —fucking *demanding*—I fill her throat with my orgasm.

And after she sucked me dry, I realized there was far more to Lauren than I first thought. More than the sweetness, the softness, the naughty schoolteacher. Maybe I knew it earlier, but a certain clarity came with an orgasm that blew through me like a goddamn tsunami. She was the size of a freaking fifth grader, but she was a force of nature.

"But we do residential, right?" Riley's brow furrowed in confusion.

"Yes," Patrick responded. He leaned back in his chair and thoughtfully unbuttoned his cuffs and folded his sleeves to his elbows. "But contributing to the community from time to time won't kill anyone. We should attempt to make more friends than enemies."

Patrick turned his attention to Sam's projects and I unlocked my phone under the table.

Lauren: that was a statement. maybe you meant to ask me a question, caveman.

I rubbed my brow and grinned. There was something about this girl I liked. Maybe numerous somethings.

Matthew: my apologies, Miss Halsted. Would you have dinner and drinks with me tonight?
Matthew: I actually mean dinner. You're absolutely welcome to suck my cock, but let's eat first.
Lauren: I'm not sure about that. My day is jammed. I fly out at 7 tomorrow morning and I haven't packed a thing, and most of my life is being held hostage at the dry cleaner
Matthew: here are the givens: you need to eat. I need to eat. We both work too fucking much.
Matthew: You'll be with my sister a few hours this afternoon and you probably need a ride to the airport tomorrow.
Matthew: and you really like my cock in your mouth.
Matthew: as I see it, we should hang out tonight
Matthew: get dinner with me and I'll bring you to the airport. Problems solved, cocks sucked.

"Patrick and I have been talking, and there some major

things to iron out," Shannon announced. She shuffled some papers and closed her laptop, her hands folded on the lid. "First, we need to hire some help. There's too much for us to do with just the five of us, and two assistants. We can afford it now, and we can't keep doing ninety-hour weeks."

"Preach," Riley responded.

Shannon glared at Riley for a beat before continuing. "And second, some of the architecture schools—Cornell in particular—have been hitting us hard to take apprentices or interns. Problem being that an apprenticeship requires a lot of time and attention. Those baby birds usually need lots of support before we can let them fly alone, and we can barely get out of our own ways on most days."

"And what is your recommendation?" Sam asked.

"Patrick and I are going to work on an intern or apprentice development model before we accept anyone, but expect to start seeing candidates in the office. Obviously," Shannon gestured to Sam while my leg bounced under the table in an attempt to distract myself from the vibrations pulsing off my phone. "We still have more demand than we can meet, even with some additional intern-level support. Thoughts on all this?"

"Why not just hire a couple architects?" Riley swirled his cup as uneasy glances darted across the table. Silence lingered, and I wondered how Riley could know so little about the firm. And it wasn't just that—how could he know so little about *us*? Hadn't he seen us busting our asses for years? Watching every last penny during those first years when it seemed like we weren't going to stay above water?

"This has been a family operation for nearly seventy years," Sam countered. "You weren't even in high school when we decided we were telling Angus to go pound sand

and taking over this place. But we made a plan to do this, and put everything into it *together* because we wouldn't let him run it into the ground. It should stay that way. Having a lot of inquiries," he waved his call sheet, "doesn't mean we should take every project. The money's great but I wouldn't trade that for the control we have over what we do and how we do it. We're the only firm in the region doing this, and I don't want to see us change. This is our place, and it needs to stay our place."

Patrick nodded. "I'd rather take on less work than take on new partners, but after everything we've been through, I can't believe I'm saying we should turn away business."

"So we agree?" Shannon paused for dissent, her eyebrows raised expectantly. "We'll look into interns and associates, but we're not hiring partners. Family operation. Sustainable prez for the win, like we planned."

"I agree with Sam, but what about you? If anyone needs more support, I think it's you, Shan," I countered. "And not interns. People who know what they're doing. You manage all the accounting, taxes, payroll, and real estate, and probably more that I don't even realize you do. You're great but it's too much."

Patrick closed his computer and leaned forward. "We're working on that."

"Get me some interns. I'll show 'em how it's done," Riley said.

"Speaking of which," Patrick barked, his coffee cup pointed at Riley. "RISD is riding with you, Matt. Maybe you can teach him to add or hold a ruler." Patrick jammed his phone into his slacks and collected his laptop and coffee before heading down the narrow stairs. Shannon and Sam followed, deep in conversation about the number of interns they could manage.

We all went through the Cornell architecture program—me and Patrick and Sam, and all the architects in my family back to my grandfather and great-uncles—everyone except Riley. I respected the hell out of the Rhode Island School of Design and their program, but I suspected his choice to head south to RISD was driven mostly by Angus's assholery.

I checked my watch to confirm the date. Just about four months. I was impressed Riley lasted that long with Patrick. He spent his first months on the job filing bluelines, waiting on permits, and picking up the scraps Patrick threw his way, and it had been a ticking time bomb.

I turned my gaze to Riley. "What did you do now?"

Riley blew out a breath as he collected his things. "I missed a few beams on a couple of designs. Screwed up a few cost estimates. Lost some progress tables. Forgot to run ratios on a couple others. Strayed from some parameters."

"As in, the parameters that would determine whether the building would withstand its own weight?"

"Yeah," Riley nodded, hipshot and hands fisted. "Those."

"What the fuck, Riley?"

"Maybe you could save me some time and tell me what you want me doing instead of telling me how much of a fucking moron I am?"

"Yeah. My office. I'll be there in ten. And Riley? Zip your pants. And get rid of that bracelet."

I pocketed the rubber 'Save the TaTas' wristband Riley tossed to the table. Once his footsteps on the stairs faded away, I swiped my phone's screen and read the new messages from Lauren.

Lauren: why am I not surprised you responded with some elaborate theory?

Lauren: and am I reading this correctly – you'd like me sucking multiple cocks?

Lauren: I signed up for drinks, not an orgy.

Lauren: but no, I really need to pack.

I wanted to respect the rules: raw, dirty sex, and sometimes partying with her friends or hanging out, and all of it on her highly random terms.

Easy, stingless sex—just the way I liked it.

But more than that, I wanted to demolish those rules.

Thirteen

LAUREN

I BURROWED into my red wool coat, the wind howling between the narrow streets and sending a chill through my bones as I rounded the corner to Matthew's office. An early winter was setting in but the threats of frost did nothing to dampen my spirits. My fellowship program signed off on acquiring the abandoned button mill, pending environmental and other standard safety inspections. My start-up facilities financing was approved and I only needed Matthew's sister—the CFO, not the volcano doctor—to write up an offer on the property.

As far as today was concerned, I had it all under control.

Everything except Matthew.

Waking up beside him for the third day in a row was a startling reminder that I couldn't do this. It was irrelevant whether I liked Matthew, and it only made it worse that I did. His sense of humor, intense vibe, nerdy quirks, bottomless blue eyes—I liked it all. But my ladybits were not in charge. I didn't have fuck buddies, and I couldn't carve any time or space for Matthew, not when everything else was barely held together with bubblegum and duct tape.

And he was a nice guy. He deserved a fuck buddy who could commit to regular, freak-out-free sex.

The kindest option for everyone was letting it fizzle out.

I pressed the buzzer at the Walsh Associates building and announced my appointment, and promptly heard the lock click open. Unwrapping my scarf and smoothing my hair in the office vestibule, a blur descended the stairs and pushed me against the door. My faux-combat training instincts kicked in, and my elbow pressed into his windpipe and my heel connected with his foot.

And then a hand wrapped around my wrist, and I noticed the TAG Heuer watch and its cobalt face. I knew that watch. I'd looked at that watch at the party, when the needy ache between my legs was too overwhelming and I wanted to be done with mindless chatting.

"Oh shit, it's you, I'm sorry!" I stepped back, my hands flying to my mouth.

I suppose attacking Matthew was one way of ending our little arrangement.

Matthew bent at the waist and coughed, his eyes flashing in my direction. "It's nice to see you too," he rasped. "What just happened?"

I rubbed his back as he coughed again. "I'm sorry, I didn't realize it was you. You caught me off guard."

"Where the fuck did you learn that?"

"My father, mostly." I shrugged and offered an apologetic smile. "And my brothers, and the Navy SEALs my dad used to train."

"There's a lot I don't know about you, Miss Halsted," he coughed. "Like your badass motherfucker training."

Straightening, he approached me, his hands outstretched in surrender. His lips hovered over mine for a moment before capturing my mouth in a kiss far too passionate for a Monday afternoon, for an office vestibule, for any part of my life.

His fingers moved beneath my suit coat and he yanked the satin blouse from my waistband, diving under to knead my lower back. His gaze was curious, confused, and though I knew I should tell him to stop, I wanted this one last treat.

"I don't know what that look means, sweetness."

"Nothing," I said. I enjoyed his chin stubble on my neck too much. This was getting too comfortable, too fast. "Just a lot to do before I leave. A lot on my mind. Let's…let's go upstairs."

Walsh Associates looked different after spending the weekend with Matthew. He offered limited details about his siblings—their birth order, areas of specialization, and the bizarre, semi-awful nicknames they had for each other.

It all made a little more sense when I noticed an artfully framed magazine spread on the wall reading 'Samuel Walsh: Beantown's Next Great Architectural Visionary.' Around the corner, I spotted another glossy print, this one featuring a petite redhead with her arms crossed over her chest and the headline 'The Hand That Holds It Down.' On the landing, I noticed an *Architectural Digest* spread filled with sweeping photos of a restored home and the heading 'Patrick Walsh's Midas Touch.'

Climbing another set of stairs to Matthew's office, his hands shifted from my waist to cup my rear end. Stopping, I turned to slide a glance over my shoulder, and his mischievous grin whipped that herd of butterflies in my chest into action. "What are you doing?" I asked, a laugh infused in my words.

"I'd rather you make it upstairs injury-free, although now I'm a little afraid of you. Please don't blind me with your heel."

"I'd wager you've stopped worrying about whether I can handle myself on the streets."

"Let's not talk about that," he murmured. He steered me toward his office and stopped at the desk outside his door. "Theresa, this is Lauren Halsted. Lauren, this is Theresa Sherill. She's the brains behind this operation."

"We've met," Theresa said. "Nice to see you again, Lauren. What, no Mike's? You spoiled me with those sfogliatella."

"Next time." I smiled at the plump, white-haired woman, but I wasn't convinced there'd be a next time. Once the construction on my building started, I wouldn't need to visit his office, and once things ended with Matthew...well, I could always drop off some pastries without seeing him.

"I'm holdin' you to that," she said.

"Let Shan know we'll be ready for her in about fifteen minutes," Matthew said. Theresa nodded in response while she eyed his hand on my back, and if I still cared whether he regularly fucked clients, her astonished expression shut it all down.

Inside his office, Matthew kicked the door shut and wrapped his arms around my waist, his chest warm against my back. "All I could think about last Friday was bending you over my desk and fucking you until you screamed. You in that little red dress? I was hard the minute you walked in. It was torture, and this isn't much better."

Okay, new plan: all fizzling out to begin tomorrow.

I reminded myself it wasn't wrong to enjoy the feel of his hands on my body or the heat of his words, and that I'd get my life in order after this. Until then, there was something hard and thick pressing against my lower back, and I wanted him bending me over that desk.

"Mr. Walsh, that sounds very inappropriate," I murmured.

"Let me show you how inappropriate," he growled. "I know you can feel me. How much I want you."

A throat cleared on the other side of Matthew's office and my eyes snapped open.

"I'm gonna go. I don't think you need me for this meeting," the young man said from the conference table.

I stifled an uncomfortable laugh and smiled, my face reddening. Matthew's arms locked around my body, and with a low snarl rumbling through his chest, I sensed he was devising ways to murder the man who bore more than a passing resemblance to him.

Whispering into my ear, he said, "I'm sorry. I didn't intend to grope you in front of my little brother."

"Well at least I didn't let you fuck me in front of him," I said. Matthew laughed, his body vibrating against mine, and his grasp tightened around my waist.

"Hey. I'm Riley. What's up?" he called, his fingers winging from his forehead in a casual salute.

"Riley, this is Miss Halsted. We're working on her project at Trench Mills."

"Nice," Riley trilled, his grin growing until a twinkle lit his eyes. That smirk was unambiguous—he heard every word—and if it was possible to feel blood pressure rising, I was feeling Matthew's. I busied myself in my tote bag, ducking out of the way of Matthew's death stare.

"Read this." He collected a file from his desk and slid it across the table to Riley. "Figure out where the collar ties are located, and which you think should be replaced. Determine how you'd do it without destroying the eaves. And in case you haven't heard, there are three vacant conference rooms in this place. Camp out in one of them."

Matthew motioned to the chairs and leaned against the edge of his desk while I sat. My foot grazed his trousers as I crossed my legs, and his gaze locked on my red patent leather platform stilettos. "Whose ass did you kick today? Other than mine, of course."

"Perseverance and a few extra inches. And the help of a good architect. It's all I need to rule the world," I laughed. "It was hard to believe, actually. I couldn't have imagined a smoother, more perfect sequence of events. Everything was approved, contingent upon all the usual—"

"Fucking hell," he sighed.

The door opened and I immediately recognized Sam and Patrick from the magazines in the hallway. And when they pulled up chairs to join us, I noticed fine threads of family resemblance tying them together. Where Riley and Matthew were nearly identical, they shared only a sharp, defined jaw with Sam and Patrick.

Patrick's short reddish-brown hair shone in the afternoon sunlight and his hard hazel eyes flashed with interest as he sat. His shirtsleeves were rolled up to his elbows, exposing a long stretch of freckled skin over rippling forearms. He came in around Matthew's height but his presence seemed larger, definitely unapproachable and certainly intimidating, and I figured he preferred it that way.

Where Patrick was aloof, Sam oozed trend and charm. His auburn hair was strategically sculpted into the perfect tousled look, and I was positive I saw his entire outfit—light gray glen plaid trousers and matching vest, crisp white shirt with funky cufflinks, and hot pink tie—in a boutique window on Newbury Street. He adjusted his cuffs, exposing two silver medical alert bracelets. Sam's frame was shorter and slimmer, a contrast to his brothers' broad, sculpted bodies, and though he most resembled Patrick, his look was all his own.

Matthew's expression turned impassive but I felt waves of tension radiating off him. "Sam. Patrick." Eyes rolling, he absently waved at his brothers. "This is Miss Halsted."

"Hello," I said, offering my hand with a smile. "Call me Lauren."

"She's from the Trench Mills project," said Riley.

"This meeting involves neither of you," Matthew said. I was waiting for him to sit down, but he continued leaning against the desk, his arms crossed over his chest. "And we have a critical timeline today."

"I'd like to hear more about that," Patrick said. "It's not every day we work on schools."

"As would I," Sam said.

His eyes traveled over my body in obvious appraisal and though it should have felt degrading when he studied my cleavage, it was clear he spent a few years smoothing it down to lightly obnoxious. But I was used to it. I stopped worrying about the boob ogling not long after my pair of hefty grapefruits came in, and my brothers taught me to execute a clean groin kick and broken nose combo around the same time. Sam—and anyone else who was interested—

could look, he could appreciate, but he wasn't getting on the short list of those approved to touch.

"I know incredible things are possible, and I know not every school is right for every kid, and that's where it all starts." I gave them my standard pitch—all kids deserve an excellent education, innovation in structured settings often leads to significant, breakthrough results, and growing this school in a green facility was essential to truly embracing a transformative approach to learning.

Patrick glanced to Sam and Matthew, and then back at me. "And you're doing this by yourself?"

"Yeah," I said. "I have some strategic support from my fellowship program, and they provide access to funding and researchers and people doing similar work in other parts of the country, but yeah...just me."

"That's extraordinary," Patrick murmured. "Really extraordinary. Do you need any help?"

"I really need a building," I said, laughing. "Preferably one that isn't home to a colony of possums—"

"Raccoons," Matthew said.

"Raccoons," I repeated, sharing a smile with him over my shoulder. "Though I wouldn't turn away prospective board members or donors."

"We can handle that," Sam said. He leaned forward, smiling. "I'd love to consult on this. Now that Matt's worked out the structural elements, let's talk about sustainability."

Matthew shifted beside me, sliding his hand to rest on the edge of my chair. I heard the brush of his fingers as they moved against the leather, and then felt them just beneath my shoulder blade. Sam, Patrick, and Riley tracked the movement, and though it was far less intimate than the moment Riley witnessed earlier, that quiet, loaded statement screeched across the room.

"I've got it under control, Sam," he said.

There was a decadence behind his softly possessive touch, a wonderful weight that brought a smile to my face and an unstoppable pack of gazelles—forget about the butterflies—charging across my chest.

But then my phone vibrated in my hand, signaling a new email, and I remembered this thing with Matthew wasn't for me, not really. My mission was opening a school and hiring teachers and fielding board members, and indulging in any degree of coupledom wasn't part of the operation. Not right now.

I caught Matthew's eye and nodded. "But thank you, Sam. You should come and talk about sustainability when we have our first college and career days."

"Sorry I'm late." The elfin redhead—Shannon—strode into the office and slammed the door behind her. "This day has been a special kind of clusterfuck."

"You know, Shannon, most professional adults don't enter a room that way," Patrick said. His teasing tone told me we were no longer in business territory, but firmly planted in family. I recognized it as a small victory, an acceptance into Matthew's private world that I never anticipated wanting but found I was thrilled to achieve.

"And lucky for you, I'm not most professional adults," she said.

Riley cleared his throat and jutted his chin toward me.

"Yeah, RISD, I got the text. You're free to stop being such a gossipy seventh grader." She scanned the room and braced her fists on her hips. Gesturing to Sam and Patrick, she sighed. "While this looks all nice and civilized, the two of you better get back upstairs. I know why you're here, and you're assholes. Get the fuck out."

Commodore Halsted would have liked her immediately, and I wasn't far behind. I could see him hiring her to yell at his sailors during Hell Week, and I could see her enjoying that.

"Splendid to meet you, Miss Halsted," Sam said as he shook my hand again.

"You," Shannon pointed at Riley. "You can stay as long as you keep your mouth shut. That includes tattle-tale texts, too. Don't do shit like that." Turning to Matthew and me, Shannon's irritated grimace transformed into a pleasant smile. "Hi, Shannon Walsh."

"Shan," Matthew started, "this is Lauren Halsted. We're handling her project at Trench Mills."

I extended my hand to Shannon. "Hello, I've heard a lot about you."

"All lies," Shannon laughed. "You know what?" She tapped her shellacked fingertips against her plum pencil skirt. "We're writing an offer? Let's take this to my office. Matt, you stay and deal with Bunker Hill. RISD, try to be useful."

"I don't mind. I have time," Matthew said.

Shannon held up a hand and shook her head once. "Bunker Hill. Don't argue with me today." Her diminutive frame forced her to tilt her head to look up at Matthew, but that didn't minimize anything about her orders. "Angus and I just screamed at each other for fifteen minutes so I am not having it right now. I promise I won't break your…friend."

I **WAITED**, watching while Shannon hunched over her laptop and furiously tapped at keys until her eyes narrowed and she studied the screen closely. After several more keystrokes, she pushed out of the chair. In a thin Southern accent called, "Tom, I have a few pages on the printer. Git 'em in here."

She returned to the table after pulling thick files from her desk and paging through them at lightning speed. A young man delivered freshly printed pages and she murmured in appreciation.

"Here's my recommendation. Come in at this," she pointed to a number and circled it with purple ink. Girl-friend liked her purple. Purple pens, purple nails, purple skirt, purple chairs, purple walls, purple phone case, purple calla lilies beneath a cloche, purple crystal paperweight. "And be prepared to negotiate within a swing of twenty-five thousand." She scribbled a number below the circled figure and pointed. "I would be happy shaking hands at this number. How does that sound?"

I beamed with relief. Shannon's figures were far below the listing price, far below the price Matthew estimated over the weekend, and far below my facilities grant from my fellowship program. "That sounds fantastic."

Shannon went to work drawing up the offer while I scanned a new stack of resumes for the teaching positions I needed to fill. While making notes on the documents, my phone buzzed in my pocket, and I knew without looking it was Matthew.

Matthew: hey.

Matthew: I am so sorry about Riley. And Sam. please tell me you're not inventing reasons to disappear

There was my trap door, my exit strategy. I could say goodbye to Matthew, cloak it in awkwardness and embarrassment, and walk away...but that felt unnecessarily cruel. I couldn't let him suffer, let him think his loud, unruly family was to blame when I was secretly loving their brash brand of hate-love.

And I still had until tomorrow before any fizzling was required.

Lauren: no worries. besides, your original ideas were very interesting.
Lauren: you think your desk can hold us? If it's anything like the desk at your place...

"A few signatures," Shannon announced, gesturing to the offer pages. I flipped through the pile of papers, smiling each time my phone alerted with a new message. "Tom will fax these and I'm going to call the seller's agent to get some balls rolling."

Matthew: I built it. It holds over 1000 pounds.
Matthew: So, yeah.
Matthew: if given the option, I'd take you back to my place and bend you over the dining room table.
Matthew: or any other surface. Several come to mind.
Matthew: this is torture.
Matthew: I want you.
Matthew: right. fucking. now.

I BIT my lip to hold back a laugh but couldn't control the heat spreading through my body. Part of me expected him to submit to his inner caveman and barrel into Shannon's office, throw me over his shoulder, and drag me off.

Part of me liked that idea.

Lauren: :)

"Offer is on its way and the agent thinks the seller is very motivated." Shannon dropped into her chair, crossed her legs, and set her hands on her knee, her gaze focused on me. "Now that's out of the way...I know he'd kill me for this, but would it be weird to ask about you and my brother? It seems like you've known each other a while."

I felt her comment like ice water in my veins before I comprehended it, and I knew my reaction was painted all over my face when Shannon leaned forward, her expression flustered.

"I'm sorry, it was weird. I shouldn't have said anything." She shook her head. "I'm rude and intrusive, and asking whether it would be weird meant I knew it would be, so I shouldn't have said anything. I'm sorry. It just...I don't know." Shannon kicked off her nude heels and tucked her legs underneath her. "I was only in there a minute, and I could be wrong, but I got the sense it was serious...yeah, I'm going to stop now."

How was that even possible?

My non-sexual knowledge of Matthew could fit into a dainty hand basket: his age (thirty), profession (architect-engineer), home (huge, covet-worthy waterfront loft), interests (showing up at doors with panties in hand, caveman-ning), alma maters (Cornell undergrad, MIT grad school), beverage preferences (Heineken, coffee with extra cream and extra sugar, ice-less water), collections (running shoes, ties with little tessellation patterns, Cornell t-shirts), quirks (left-handedness, doing math in his head, incredible parallel parking), and sleeping habits (on his side, one arm curled under his pillow, one hand on my ass).

We didn't know each other at all. Our version of 'getting to know you' was distinctly carnal, and we made little time for anything beyond the basics. He was a cool guy, but I didn't *know* him. I knew more about the barista I chatted up while my latte was brewing this morning. Hell, I knew more about the woman who sat down beside me on the Green Line this afternoon.

"Listen," Shannon continued. "He hardly ever dates, and he's never let us meet anyone he's with, so all of this is kind of unprecedented. We didn't realize his client was also his girlfriend."

"Oh no, no no, I'm not—I mean, we're not—no," I stammered. Drinking? Yes. Fucking? Yes. Dating? Absolutely not. "No. Not at all."

"Huh," she murmured. She stared at me, her purple pen tapping against her palm, and it was clear she was waiting for more. "I didn't mean to make it weird. I just got the impression," she gestured to her phone, and I didn't have to know what Riley said in that group text to know it supported Shannon's argument. "Whatever. I've made it weird."

"No," I said. "It's not weird. Just a big misunderstanding."

Right, because there was something unclear about Matthew announcing he wanted to fuck me on his desk.

"I hope I didn't scare you away. I'm sitting here with my

disgusting hobbit feet hanging out, and that fact alone is probably terrifying."

The self-deprecating comment overshadowed her aggressive exterior, and I suddenly realized her intrusive questions weren't meant to rattle me. This was her version of affable, though it more closely resembled a cross-examination. She wanted to befriend the woman her brother was seeing.

Her assumptions about Matthew and me were all wrong, and I couldn't get in any deeper with him or his family. At the same time, I didn't have the heart to leave her hanging, regardless of whether my fizzle out plan was set to launch in a matter of hours.

"If you want to talk about disgusting hobbit feet, I haven't had a pedicure since July. Boot season couldn't have come soon enough for me."

At Shannon's murmur of solidarity, I laughed.

"I can't even get my hair cut on a regular basis, either. Hobbit feet plus split ends, and that's at least part of the reason I can't meet normal guys. You wouldn't believe the assclowns out there these days." She inspected a few strands of hair between her fingers and impatiently tossed them over her shoulder. Looking up, she frowned at me. "But maybe none of it matters. Maybe it just happens when you're not looking. Or tending to your toes."

AFTER NEARLY FOUR hours of negotiations and counteroffers, Shannon handed me a stack of papers with an earnest nod. "This is a steal."

Flipping through the pages of legalese, I smiled at the

bottom line. She drove a hard bargain and fought to get the best possible price while saddling the sellers with all of the inspection fees and forgoing her commission.

The waiting between counteroffers gave us time to chat, and I discovered Shannon was my kind of lady. When she wasn't riding herd on her brothers, she trolled for shoe sales and cozy wine bars, but never found herself a tight group of girlfriends, and beneath her take-charge bluster, she was lonely. She filled her free moments with spin classes and online dating, but neither held her attention for long.

She was ambitious and audacious, and wore sensational shoes, and I didn't have the first clue how I'd end things with Matthew and still be her friend, but I wanted to make that happen.

"If you really want a button mill—and really, Lauren, what girl doesn't?—sign here, and here, and on all of these other flags, too."

"Not a button mill for long," I said.

Inhaling deeply, I followed Shannon's finger and signed. When the paperwork was finished and her assistant was on his way to file the documents, I sensed Matthew behind me. It was as if his body broadcast a frequency only mine could receive.

"I hear we're in possession of a building?" Turning, my smile summed it up. "I told you Shan would knock it out of the park. My favorite general contractor is ready to roll, and we're pulling permits the minute we get that title. Riley is in the basement printing the bluelines now."

"One giant priority off my to-do list," I said. "Thank you both, so much."

"Hey, it's what we do," Shannon said. "And when you're

back in town, text me. We'll get that pedicure. And some cupcakes and wine and other things boys don't like."

"Boys don't have objections to wine or cupcakes," Matthew muttered. "Boys like them very much. Boys want to be invited for cupcakes and wine, and boys will get your drunk asses home."

"Definitely," I said and wrapped her in a tight hug. "Thank you again, Shannon."

"Safe travels," she called as Matthew guided me out the door and back to his office. His touch was urgent and familiar, and I was letting myself savor this. Twenty-four hours from now, I'd be thousands of miles away and my iPhone would be serving as my primary companion.

"Happy?" Matthew asked.

"Yes. Everything is falling into place. This was the most productive day in a year, no exaggeration, and it's because you dragged me to the bar on Friday night."

Matthew smiled and backed me against his office door, his fingers skimming up my neck to cradle my face. "That's the nicest thing you've ever said to me. And it involved forced drunkenness."

"I've said plenty of highly complimentary things about your cock. I think I described your reboot time as remarkable."

"You said impressive, but I'll also allow remarkable," he said, his lips brushing over mine. "Let's go to your place. It's closer, and you need to pack, and we'll have drinks."

I nodded, not willing to entertain a futile debate about doing anything else. His lips captured mine, and my fingers moved from his chest to the erection pressing against my belly.

"Is your desk out of the question?" I asked against his mouth.

"For what I have in mind? Yes, but if you ask one more time, I won't be able to say no."

A laptop clicked shut. "I'm still here."

"Fuck me," Matthew sighed. He dropped his forehead to my shoulder and released a ragged breath.

"Sorry, Riley," I laughed. "I didn't see you over there."

"Whatever," Riley muttered while he jammed his laptop into his backpack and unraveled a set of earbuds. "I think you want to get caught. Fuckin' exhibitionists. I need my own goddamn office."

"Three other conference rooms," Matthew said under his breath.

We stepped apart, and Matthew headed for his desk to shut down his laptop. Riley shouldered his backpack and inserted his earbuds, offering me a brisk nod and closing the door behind him as he exited.

"Let's also pretend that didn't happen." Matthew propped himself on the edge of his desk and pulled me between his legs. "What'll it be, Miss Halsted?"

I smiled and nuzzled my face into his chest. "I'm hungry. I'd like some wine. And I'd be happier if I got out of these shoes. The suit, too. And you've invited yourself to my apartment again, as any good creeper would."

"If I didn't invite myself over, how else would you get out of the suit?" he laughed. He reached back and grabbed his phone. "I'll go pick up, you go pack." He handed it to me, and I glanced at the take-out menu on the screen. "Decide what you want."

"Yeah," I managed. "Sounds good."

I stayed pressed against Matthew, scanning the take-out menu while his words echoed in my head.

Decide what you want.

They were brutal, haunting reminders that, regardless of what I kept telling myself, I had no idea what I wanted.

Fourteen

MATTHEW

TAKING in the mix of charmingly mismatched furniture and eclectic typography prints accented with piles upon piles of books, I felt the warmth of Lauren's apartment surrounding me. Her home was wonderfully lived-in, a comfortable level of organized chaos, and nothing like mine.

I expected the rigid, military order I saw in her work, and guessed the lack of structure and precision in her home mirrored her more accurately. I didn't know which versions of Lauren she wanted me to embrace—the pin-up with the dirty mouth, the unrelenting workaholic who kicked and screamed every time she was separated from her smartphone, the quirky girl who filled her home with a rainbow of velvet pillows and funky art, or the sweet, innocent teacher who offered everyone kind smiles whether they deserved them or not—but then I remembered she wasn't thrilled about me embracing her at all. She liked her workaholic ways, and though I was kicked back on her sofa, she wasn't keeping me around for my sparkling conversation.

She just wanted me fucking those contradictions right out of her. But at least she was keeping me around.

Clearing off her coffee table was an interesting challenge. Every book was propped open with index cards, paper clips, ribbons, or pens, one layered over another, and they appeared to live in an ecosystem I was helpless to understand.

She needed some fucking shelves.

Eventually, I carved out space for the Spanish take-out and stationed several oddly-shaped velvet pillows on the floor while she finished packing. Her kitchen was crammed with a random collection of colorful tools and appliances, and she would have benefitted from decent cabinetry. I popped the cork on a bottle of Rioja as she emerged from the bedroom in black yoga pants and a camisole.

I stared at the bottle in my hand, desperate to remember whether Lauren liked red wine, let alone this variety, and came up empty. "I picked up a Spanish red. Is that okay?"

She stared at the glass for a moment, her lip caught between her teeth and she shrugged. "Uh, sure."

In other words: no, it wasn't okay.

I handed her the glass and gestured to the tapas. "Any strategy here?"

"Little of this. Little of that." She snatched up a stuffed Medjool date and groaned in delight when it hit her tongue. My new favorite sound.

I dug into the shrimp with cascabel chiles while Lauren scooped paella onto her plate. "I didn't expect everyone to show up in my office today."

At least Angus hadn't made an appearance.

"You work together. I'd assume they stop by all the

time," she said around another date. "We don't have to talk about it."

Twisting the stem of my wine glass between my fingers, I polished off the contents before going in for a refill. "Yeah, but it's always like that with them. My siblings, they aren't even remotely normal. To be honest, Lauren, it shocks the shit out of me that you haven't kicked me to the curb yet."

"So you want to talk about it?"

I turned to face Lauren and stroked her thigh. "Why aren't you furious? Why aren't you inventing new reasons to disappear on me?"

She was focused on composing the right distribution of paella flavors on her fork, and for all I knew, ignoring my question and devising ways to sneak out of her own apartment in the middle of the night. I downed another glass and watched her paella-eating technique for several bites. The wine was turning down the volume on my annoyance with Sam and Riley. Lauren in a tissue-thin camisole—braless—was helping, too.

I shook my head. "I'm sorry about Riley. And Sam. I should have thrown them both out."

I refilled my wine. Emptied it in two gulps.

Lauren plucked the glass from my fingers and set it aside before straddling my lap. She grabbed a fork and the container of paella from the table, and bit into a chunk of chorizo. She hummed and bobbed her head from side to side, and I watched her debating with herself.

"I could tell you a story about my brothers, and how they decided to interrogate my high school spring formal date. I mean rendition-level interrogation while surrounded by my dad's gun collection. But I'm leaving tomorrow and we moved mountains today so I want copious amounts of wine, tapas, and nakedness, and very little serious story-telling."

"Let me tell you what I heard just now: your brothers are manically protective of you and they have guns."

It was a reminder that, in everything we shared over the weekend, Lauren told me hardly anything about herself. I knew her body—every last inch of it—and her specifications for Trench Mills, and some other offhand personal details, but I never stopped to ask whether her brothers were going to pull a black hood over my head, hogtie me, and toss me in the ocean after finding out what I did to their baby sister.

These seemed like important questions.

"So yeah, Riley's even more of a creeper than you, but when you think about these things, these little annoying things, they don't matter because they're the people we have, and we don't get them for very long. We need to take them as they come and accept the crazy ways they show their love."

My brows lifted and I trailed my fingers up and down her thigh. "You're not scarred for life because Riley watched me grope you, *and* he heard me narrate the whole thing? Twice?"

"Not scarred for life," she laughed. "And Sam is comedy, right down to the weird socks that don't really go with the look, but work because they're weird."

The wine was obscuring her words. Had to be. That was the only way she'd say she was good with Sam skeeving all over her. "Just to be clear, you tear into me when I text you to make sure you're alive but you have no problem with my douche canoe brother staring at your tits for five solid minutes? You're okay with that?"

"It's good for my ego for beautiful boys like Sam to stare at my tits, but if you want to talk about this for even one more minute," she stood, inching her camisole up her torso and over her head, "you have to talk about it while I sit here naked."

Her shirt sailed to the floor, and though I wanted to ask about all these velvet pillows and the girly, feel-good determination quotes plastered on her fridge, and the probability of her brothers snapping off my testicles and feeding them to sea otters, it could wait.

It was time for me to lick my naughty schoolteacher until she screamed.

───────

I BACKED Lauren into her bedroom, my hands on her waist and my mouth on her neck, and we tumbled onto the bed, sprawling over each other and laughing. The wine was saturating my brain, and it didn't matter whether I brought any finesse to this moment. I had my filthy girl and I was going to do terrible things to her.

"Get undressed and get over here," she said.

After toeing off my shoes and leaving my unbuttoned shirt hanging from my shoulders, my hand settled on my belt buckle while Lauren's tongue darted out to lick her lips.

"Keep looking at me like that, Lauren," I said, fully aware of my sharp, stern tone. "And we might not get very far."

"I don't even know what that means."

"How can you not know?" I froze in place, exasperated that she still didn't recognize what she did to me, that we still didn't understand each other. Or I'd forgotten about her inexperience again.

Lauren crawled to the edge of the bed and reached out to grasp my belt, looking up at me with a virginal smile. "I need you to explain it to me." Sitting back on her heels, she unlatched the buckle and drew my zipper down. She jerked my shirt from my shoulders and pushed my trousers over my hips, leaving them pooled at my feet.

"It means I know you've been thinking about me fucking you all day. It means I can't wait to hear the filthy things you want. It means you have me so worked up right now, and all I need is one of your hot little looks and I'll be coming all over you."

Pushing her to the bed, I leaned down, my eyes fixed on her while my mouth covered her nipple, and she responded with a low whisper of approval. Smiling, I kissed and licked my way down her body until my lips traced the flesh between her hips.

"Tell me what you want," I growled into her skin.

"Lick my pussy. I want to know how good it tastes."

Her words—those dirty, electric words—were everything I needed and they did something to me I couldn't explain. And I didn't want to waste a minute on explanations when I could have my mouth on her clit.

My fingers brushed over her folds while I kissed from one hip bone to the other, and then down, lower, to where her arousal perfumed the air. I parted her, holding her open to feather my tongue over her, then dipping inside to taste her.

Pushing up on her elbows, Lauren gazed at me between her thighs while my lips fastened around her throbbing nub. She allowed an occasional moan or hum of satisfaction, but said nothing else while I drew her clit between my teeth, sucking and teasing, and filling her with my fingers.

She drove a hand through my hair and shifted my head to hit a different angle. "I want to hear it," she said, her tone domineering. I fucking loved it. "I want to hear how good it tastes."

I shifted my hand, pressing my thumb to her ass and adoring the flood of arousal it triggered. She didn't know how to ask for it yet, but she liked it.

"You are fucking delicious. Sweet and salty and perfect," I said against her mound, and I meant it. Not all pussy was created equal, and though I rarely made enough oral offerings to the beasts for adequate points of comparison, Lauren was my favorite. "I don't know what I'm going to do without this pussy for three whole weeks."

I looked up, following that golden skin over her belly, past those full, beautiful breasts, and up to her mouth. Our eyes met and my thumb pressed harder, and I saw the tremor move through her body as she came apart. Her head fell back, calling out for *there, there, right there*, and *oh, yes, don't stop*, and her thighs tensed around my head. She held me in place while she rode through her spasms, and I kept my tongue fixed to her.

Remembering Friday night was like calling up a distant memory, one gilded and soft around the edges. Four days stretched between that night and this moment, but inside the warp-speed incubator of those ninety-six hours, I was lost, overwhelmed, confused. But I didn't want it to stop.

"I licked it and now it's mine," I said, my tongue sweeping from her clit to her core, and laughter rolled through Lauren.

Fifteen

LAUREN

SPITTING the toothpaste into the sink, I rinsed out my mouth a few more times. My knowledge of oral sex was pathetically limited, and though I savored the way Matthew surrendered when my tongue was wrapped around his shaft, and I even liked swallowing when he exploded in my mouth, there was nothing wrong with disliking the aftertaste.

I stared at myself in the bathroom mirror, trying to recognize the person looking back at me. I was different yet everything was exactly the same, and I wanted to find that thread of newness, that variation, and study it under a microscope. I wanted to know what it was and where it came from, and how I could encapsulate it and hold on to it forever because this night was ending too quickly, and my reality waited for me on the other side.

The hallway floor creaked beneath my feet, and I leaned against the doorframe, gazing at Matthew's bare backside. I didn't think they actually made men like this—strong and defined without being muscle-bound, dark without being excessively hairy, and gorgeous without being too pretty.

And most importantly, he was naked in my bed at three in the morning.

"I'm gonna need a little time after that."

"Hmm?" I stammered, my thoughts stuck on the curve of his ass.

"Need some time to recover. I might be paralyzed."

I collected the twisted heap of sheets and blankets from the floor, shaking them out and spreading them over the bed, over Matthew.

"Your eyes give away all your indecent thoughts, Miss Halsted."

Peeling back the covers, I ran my palm up his leg to his ass. I squeezed, feeling his muscles cording under my hand, and landed a resounding slap.

"All of them?" I challenged.

He shot a heated glance over his shoulder, and I rubbed the pink handprint blooming on his skin before switching sides. He rolled, swinging an arm out to grab me around the waist and pin me beneath him.

"I'd really like to know what you're thinking."

I brushed the hair from my eyes and smiled up at Matthew. "I'm thinking you are an unbelievably hot sample of your species, and I wanted to feel the perfection for myself. Then I was wondering whether you wanted to fuck me in the shower, and if you did maybe you'd want to use the massaging showerhead on my—"

"Holy fuck, Lauren."

A howling groan filled the room, and Matthew balanced on his forearms, kicking the sheets away and rocking into me with one rough motion. That response told me everything I needed to know about the unrefined and frankly shocking requests that kept rolling off my tongue.

I probably wouldn't admit it to anyone, but I was drunk on the power he gave me and my words. I didn't understand where they came from or how he drew them out or why we needed them. But I knew they did something to him, to us both, and I was slowly understanding the depth to which they affected us. They freed me from everything, from my rules, from myself, and they didn't just turn him on, they turned him *up*.

"You always say you need some time," I said. It came out in a stutter, rasping in time with the hammering of his hips. I wrapped a hand around the headboard; we usually found ourselves on the floor after this kind of thrusting, and we'd done this enough to know when to hold on. "And look where you end up."

"Thought I did. But then you spanked me, and opened that filthy mouth of yours." He shook his head, his expression bewildered. "If I knew I'd like you slapping my ass so much, we would have started there."

He lifted my hips a few degrees, and I knew from the concentration on his face and bunched muscles in his shoulders he was close, but that angle hurt like hell.

"Don't stop but please don't keep doing that," I said.

He froze for a moment, then pulled out. "What'd I do? What's wrong?"

I rolled over and settled in his lap, my back to his chest, knowing this position always worked for us. We'd tried them all, and determined our strengths and preferences quickly. I guided him into me, and we sighed when I sank down over him. "You can still be a caveman while being gentle."

We moved together slowly, undulating in a patient rhythm with his arm braced over my breasts and his mouth on my neck and shoulders. This was sleepy, middle-of-the-night sex, quiet and calm and instinctual, with the only sounds coming from hushed moans and skin sliding across skin. I felt Matthew—all of him—swallowing all of me until there was no delineation between us.

We weren't frantic and we weren't primal, and we weren't hiding behind filthy bucket lists, alcohol, or a certain degree of anonymity. We'd needed those things to come together before, to be whatever, whomever we wanted—at least I needed them—but we didn't need them anymore. This was where we knew each other, where we anticipated every sound and shiver, and we didn't need anything else. It was just us, just Matt and Lauren, and we only needed this.

He brought his hand to my pelvis, holding me there and pressing, and we felt my walls closing around him, magnifying the fullness. I laced my fingers with his, guiding him.

"I want your fingers on me, just like…" I demonstrated, my fingers scribbling over my clit while I arched into him. I was right there, so close *so close*, but I wasn't ready to go over yet, and I stiffened, holding back and fighting off the first tickles of release. My clit couldn't take any more stimulation right now, and I moved our fingers lower, to where he moved in me. Our pace slowed to an aching roll, and we moaned in concert when we rubbed the base of his cock.

"Tell me what you need," Matthew said against my throat. His voice was strained, almost gravelly, and it strummed every tightly wound nerve in my body. "There is nothing hotter than watching you touch yourself while I'm fucking you, and I know you're so fucking close and you're just waiting until I let you come."

"Why do I love it when you talk to me like that?"

He rocked against me, his forehead pressed to my shoulder and his rough groans against my skin, and I focused on nothing more than the warmth and wetness where we were joined.

"The same reason I love your filthy mind, so just tell me what you need."

I didn't have to think about it. The words were right there, rising to the top like perverted little bubbles in my champagne, just waiting for him to ask for them, and here's the thing: I wanted everything I asked for. I didn't want him calling me his dirty slut while we ate paella, of course, but I wanted it when the lights and clothes were off. Sex with Matthew was a special type of truth serum for me, and it was the one place I could completely shake off the world and rely only on instinct.

My hips swayed, and through the smooth, round motion I locked our fingers around his base, squeezing while I met his thrusts. And then I turned my head, my lips brushing over Matthew's, and in the most demure voice possible I said, "I want to be your fuck toy. All for you. Only for you. Only ever for you."

A strangled grunt rumbled from Matthew's chest, his arms tightening as he surged into my body. He bit my shoulder hard—harder than ever before, harder than necessary—and I came apart with a shriek, my body liquefying in his arms. The electricity crackling between us went from bright white to starlit darkness, and I felt everything inside me unraveling. Every stitch and seam was sliding loose, and I was undone by him, this, us.

"You're incredible. So fucking incredible," he panted. His muscles sagged with a sigh, and his forehead fell to my back.

Matthew kissed my shoulders, holding me close. I studied him over my shoulder for a heavy moment, my gaze dropping to the purple indentations in my skin before breaking our connection to fall into the pillows. He flopped on his stomach beside me and brought his hand to my ass.

"This is crazy," I whispered.

"I'm starting to think you're right about that." Matthew pressed a kiss to the slope of my breast and stared at it, hopefully reminding himself to take it easy with the biting. "But I like this kind of crazy."

I WAS SORE. *Really* sore.

The idea of sitting on an airplane for six hours sent me searching the terminal shops for ibuprofen because there was no room for the constant, throbbing memory of Matthew and last night's nonstop sex festival on this flight. And it wasn't like we could only blame last night. It had been four straight days of this.

Suggestive taglines on the covers of *Cosmopolitan*, *Allure*, and *Glamour* caught my attention, all professing the secrets to making my man happy in bed, and I scowled back at them. Those stories required a warning label: 'You and your man will be happy in bed, but you won't be able to sit down for three days. And P.S.: he might bite the shit out of your shoulder.'

I knocked back three tablets, pulled on my darkest sunglasses, and wandered the terminal. Once my flight was called, I discovered sitting was exactly as uncomfortable as I expected. Wiggling into a tolerable position, I prayed for smooth skies. I skimmed my emails while passengers boarded, busy clearing issues from my inbox and crossing tiny items from my action plan, and didn't notice the unopened text message icon in the corner of my screen until the flight attendants started their safety procedures.

Matthew: have a good flight sweetness. call me whenever.

I stared at those words, those simple, innocuous words, and heard them as if he was whispering into my ear.

"Miss, you need to turn that off." The flight attendant nodded toward my phone with a steely glare. "Now."

I spared the text one last glance before deleting it.

From: Matthew Walsh
To: Erin Walsh
Date: September 28 at 11:32 EDT
Subject: On the topic of citrus fruit

…Clementines.

Birthday: August 16.

And I need you home at Thanksgiving or Christmas. Get your ass back to Boston. I need you to meet her.

From: Erin Walsh
To: Matthew Walsh
Date: September 29 at 04:30 CEST
Subject: RE: On the topic of citrus fruit

M –

I was going to congratulate you on gathering basic information about your new friend, then I realized how absurd that would be. So. As you were.

And by the way, if architecture doesn't work out for RISD, tell him there's work for him calling the plays at high school football games. I can't tell you how wonderful it was to hear him recap your little in-office molestation, even if his texts are slamming my data plan.

But here's the real question, kid: did you read her in?

- e

From: Matthew Walsh
To: Erin Walsh
Date: October 4 at 22:56 EDT
Subject: History

E –

You know I'd rather talk this out than go back and forth over email, but you can't find five minutes to call me or get on Skype. One of these days, you need to explain to me what it is you do with those volcanoes.

She doesn't know anything about Mom or Angus, and she doesn't know anything about you and Shannon, but hear me out before you tear into me.

She was raised right, with parents and structures and rules, and happiness and Christmas cards, and you know, decent human beings. You should see her mother's travel blog, E. It's like rainbows and puppy dogs and lollipops. That's what Lauren came from. She's not like us. She's good. She might also be a trained assassin, but she's good.

It was bad enough bringing her to the office for one afternoon. She doesn't need the highlights of the past twenty years. Trust me on this.

M

From: Erin Walsh
To: Matthew Walsh
Date: October 5 at 05:09 CEST
Subject: RE: History

M –

Volcanologists study the remains of dead or dormant volcanoes, and analyze copious amounts of data in the monitoring of those volcanoes that are active, and those the data suggest will soon become active. At its heart, volcanology is concerned with tracing the mechanisms and causes of volcanic eruptions, pinpointing data trends in advance of eruptions, and drawing correlation and causality between eruptions, Earth's geological history, and humans and their environments. My work is largely geodesic (studying the correlation between shifts in the planet's geometry and ground deformations following volcanic incidents) and geochemical (studying the chemical structures of the planet and its volcanic products, specifically, emitted gases).

And you're wrong. You're 100% wrong. Are you just hoping she won't stay around long enough to find out, or that you'll be able to bleach that particular asshole?

If she's the fairy princess you'd like to believe she is, she can handle it and you should let her.

- e

From: Matthew Walsh
To: Erin Walsh
Date: October 7 at 03:39 EDT
Subject: RE: History

Hey Little Mermaid –

It appears I've had a few adult beverages tonight. You can I call now?
That's a stupid question. You're probably scuba diving volcano or doing shots of ouzo. don't combine the 2.

I know it's selfish but I you should come home. You've been away for sooooo long. First U-Hawaii, and now Portugal/Spain/Italy/wherever the fuck you are. It's been like 19 years ok not really more like 6 and I know you're pissed at Shannon, and sometimes I'm pissed at her for you, but when are you coming home?

Sometimes I wish I could leave like you did. You're probably petting turtles in the Galapagos and that's really cool.
Like really fucking cool. Turtles are awesome.

Wait. The Galapagos aren't near Spain. Why the fuck are
you in South America now?

Anyway. My life is pretty much a giant bag of dicks. It's 3 in
the morning and I'm cleaning up another one of Sam's
designs that will probably win 9 different awards for and he
wont mention that anyone made sure the goddamn structure stayed up. It's taking a really long time to fix his shit,
but that might be alcohol's fault. Don't tell him. Ill make
sure its all ok. lol. But probably shouldn't do structural
analysis and get blasted on whiskey.

Patrick has me babysitting Riley and I swear to god, E, he
doesn't know how to zip his motherfucking pants. I see his
dick more than I see my own and that's problematic for
many reasons. I started calculating the probability of seeing
his junk on a given day then decided to gag myself instead.

Did we leave him with a pack of wolves or a bucket of lead
paint for a couple of years or something? He is a fratty
brochild and I don't have enough shit together to be a father
right now. side note: did you know he's crashing at sam's
place? I don't think ive ever BEEN to sam's place. I sure as
shit haven't been invited to stay over.

like I said: big bag o'dicks.

Oh, and guess what? Your favorite person won't return my

texts. By favorite person I mean Lauren, the very nice and pretty girl who lives clementines and has a dirty mouth for daysssss and it doesn't make sense that you don't like her. that's why I need you home for Christmas but I think shes over me anyway.

It's probably my fault cuz I told her I wanted drinks but she's always disappearing. But I always find her and that sounds sooo creepy. #muststopcreeping

I like her. A lot. Like a crazy a lot and it sucks that she disappears.

But I still have her pussy necklace so that's got to count for something, yeah?

What country are you in now? Just pick up the phone. It isn't that hard to talk. Tell me how to sort this out.

Ok well bye, erin ailise. Don't swim in volcanoes.

M

From: Erin Walsh
To: Matthew Walsh
Date: October 13 at 10:03 CEST
Subject: Step back from the ledge...

Holy drunk rambles, kid.

If you need to call me, call me. It's morning here. You don't need permission. I have bad reception most of the time but don't get drunk and hate the world alone. And I'm still in Europe. No plans to visit the Galapagos or turtles anytime soon.

And I never said I didn't like Lauren. It just seemed like you did everything backward with her, and that can be awesome or disastrous, but I don't want you getting hurt.

Seventeen

LAUREN

I DECIDED a long time ago that I was finished with diets, and I was going to eat what I wanted by keeping my treats in balance and doing it without guilt. The birthing hips I inherited from my mother meant I tried on at least thirty pairs of jeans before I found a decent one, but they were me, and I was going to love my shape regardless of whether I had to search high and low for the perfect fit.

The decision came after Amanda, Steph, and I all agreed to a pact one semester. We got fired up about bikini season and went low carb—slightly psychotic, by-the-book low carb—and it fell apart one morning before finals when Amanda slapped Steph over her secret cache of English muffins. There was some hair pulling and screaming involved, and when it was over, we sat on the floor of our college apartment, nursing our split lips and scratches.

Unhappy didn't even begin to describe that semester. My hip measurements didn't budge, and any pounds lost came from my boobs, and that was terribly unfair. I never reached that healthy Zen place where I didn't feel starved

and awful, and at a certain point I not only hated the existence of bread, I started hating people who ate bread.

I learned two essential things that semester. First, my
friends were much too disciplined and competitive for any
shared activity. Second, everything was acceptable in
moderation. Eliminating any one thing—carbs, sweets,
alcohol, meat, diet soda, whatever the fads demanded—
wasn't the answer. It would lead to unhinged deprivation
and a small slap-fight over English muffins.

I didn't know what surfaced that memory, but gazing at
the blank page on my screen, I released the breath I didn't
know I was holding. Everything felt wrong—more wrong
than carb deprivation—and nothing was making it right.
Each day was like swimming through pudding, slow and
tedious, and I couldn't snap out of it. Shoes, clothes, cakes—
none of it helped, and I couldn't sit here pretending I was
all right any longer when everything had been so wrong for
the past two weeks.

I bolted from my seat in the back corner of the classroom
and tried to collect my bag and laptop without causing a
major disruption. As with all things requiring me to be
graceful under pressure, I knocked over two diminutive
chairs and every child turned to watch me exit the classroom. I mouthed "sorry" to the teacher as I charged for the
door.

Initially, I had attributed my restlessness to all the travel.

Living out of a suitcase, sleeping in different cities every
few days, eating most of my meals at Starbucks: not for me.
I never wanted to see another yogurt, fruit, and granola cup
again, and it wasn't looking good for the frosted lemon loaf,
either.

I also made the mistake of streaming the entire first

season of *American Horror Story* from Netflix on my first night in California because I napped through the six-hour flight and couldn't get to sleep. Now every creak and noise was keeping me awake, and I kept expecting someone in a latex bodysuit to jump out of the closet.

Then I realized I was completely overwhelmed from the conferences and school visits, and while my meetings were incredibly helpful, they served to highlight the demanding work ahead. I spent most nights trudging through my action plan to keep my head above water.

My flats were soundless in the hallway filled with children's artwork and large class photos, and I was happy to simply escape for a moment. I dropped my things in the small meeting space the school designated for the day's visitors and absently picked at a smashed Lärabar I discovered in the bottom of my tote bag while scanning my messages.

As I thought about the unopened texts from Matthew glaring back at me, I couldn't help but wonder whether putting him in the Off Limits column was at least part of the reason for my misery. I glanced at my phone as pouty, self-centered tears rolled down my face. His texts were funny and sometimes suggestive, and though I wanted to delete them automatically, I read every single one. And then I read them again.

Matthew: good morning.
Matthew: I'm sure you have a busy day. call me whenever.
Matthew: the original stables/garage situation at Trench is coming down today. I'll send you a pic after demo.
Matthew: how's your morning?
Matthew: are you a pumpkin spice latte fan?

Matthew: random question, I know.

Matthew: Shan lost her shit this morning when she saw that they're back at Starbucks.

Matthew: she's sent her boy toy, I mean Tom, to get refills three times already.

Matthew: she's prob going to be rocking in a corner soon and awake until next Wednesday

Matthew: what's your evening looking like? Call me when you're in for the night. preferably when you're in bed.

Matthew: I don't care what time. I'm around.

Matthew: btw, Sam's insisting there's no actual pumpkin in those lattes.

Matthew: and this is how I spend my days: mediating debates about coffee flavoring.

I thought about the unread emails, the missed calls, the to-do lists, the calendar reminders, and the scrumptious man asking for some of my attention, and I wanted to scream. There was enough work on my plate for me and my three clones, my friends were moving on to shiny, new lives with their husbands and babies, and I couldn't schedule time to have sex with my architect even if I wanted to.

Everyone else was marinating in a special blend of late twenty-something wisdom while I tried on every size and style of hot mess. I wanted to hold it all together, but most days I was barely holding myself together.

It was so much easier when I was crying in stairwells over closed offices, so much easier before I knew what I was missing, before I truly understood the sacrifices I was making for my work. I let the tears fall, and tapped out a quick message to Matthew, not caring that I was breaking all my own stupid rules.

Lauren: I'm sorry I haven't been around to talk or respond much. I'm really stressed right now and haven't been getting a ton of sleep. Strange story, I'll tell you later.
Lauren: I do want to hear how it's going at the site. Let me know when you can talk.

PENANCE. That's what I was doing.

Penance for the Back Bay brownstones running more than three months behind schedule and six figures over budget. Penance for letting Riley take a crack at Angus's Bunker Hill properties when I should have been the one jumping in front of those bullets.

Angus pushed the designs across the table and sneered. "That's pathetic."

And penance for minding my own fucking business. I should have yanked Riley out of Patrick's office sooner. He was young and green and needed miles of direction, and Patrick expected everyone to be as brilliant as him. He could barely speak to people unless they existed at his level of architectural genius.

Unlike Patrick, Shannon, Sam and me, Riley never worked in the office as a kid. We used to go there after school, and we could read and write bluelines by the time we were seven or eight. That's where we made our mistakes and learned the basics, but Riley never had that experience, and it showed. By the time he was old enough, Patrick and Shannon were already out of the house, and Angus's projects were limited to small restorations requiring little more than basic designs. He also gave up on being instructive right after my mother died and he elected to view the world from the inside of a scotch bottle.

I tightened the arm across my stomach and pressed my fist to my mouth for a moment, biting into my finger to channel my aggravation. The numbers in my head weren't helping. "Would you like the build on that? Perhaps tell Riley what you don't like?"

Angus folded his hands over his belly with a scowl. "I hope you didn't pay much for that education, because if this is all you got from it"—he gestured to the designs—"it's not worth the paper it was written on. That gutter rat mother of yours didn't pass along too much intelligence, did she?"

Whichever mechanism in my brain that once allowed me to ignore him, the element that switched on while he tore us down and allowed me to sit there, emotionless and detached, was malfunctioning. Angus's comments used to roll right off my back, but today they stuck, and the fury was suffocating.

"Yeah, that's gotta be the most constructive feedback I've ever heard," Riley muttered. "If you have nothing else, I'll just—"

"There are a couple of crews that need laborers. You'd be good at that," Angus said, his chin jutting toward Riley. "Come on now, this work isn't for turnips like you. You barely graduated high school. I always knew you were slow as shit. Just like your cunty sister."

"Do not talk about Shannon that way," I said, my jaw

tight and my teeth grinding together. "You can go. I'll take this from here."

Angus huffed and murmured about my mother being a dumb drunk, Riley being a brain-dead turnip, and me thinking I knew everything there was to know about anything, and eventually clattered his way out. He kept his tirade going as he rotated through each of the offices, and on a different day I would have intervened. I would have talked him down and pushed him in the direction of the nearest pub, but I didn't have it in me right now.

We sat side-by-side at the conference table in my office, listening as he berated Sam for being short and queer, hurled a few ethnic slurs at Patrick's assistant, and suggested Shannon wasn't in her office because she was sucking dicks at City Hall.

Seething with aggravation, I tried to refocus on the ancient bluelines dredged from the depths of the city inspector's office, comparing them to Riley's new designs. The lines on the weathered paper blurred together and my mind wandered to Lauren again. I pitched my triangular scale at the drafting table and stalked to the window, shoving my hands in my pockets to prevent myself from throwing anything else. I didn't want to become the kind of asshole who threw things to express anger. That one trended too close to Angus and his supremely fucked up methods for handling the world around him.

"My guess is that you won't be able to blow up my designs like Alderaan, and they aren't worth starting that kind of war," Riley said, his voice ripe with sarcasm. "Go sit in a corner and call your girl. I'm ordering lunch. What do you want?"

"She's busy."

"Yeah," Riley said. "I think texting might have been invented for that reason. Or making doorbells obsolete."

Her unresponsiveness confounded me, and within days of her departure, that confusion had edged into fury. My siblings gave me a wide berth after several irrational outbursts about version control on project plans and the shortage of lead for my particular brand of mechanical pencils and the tribe's wholesale inability to draft stable structures. I *was* being a dick, but it felt beyond my control.

Lauren would have had some comment handy about cavemen, and she would have been right.

I stared at the cobblestone streets below without seeing. In the two weeks since her departure, we never once managed to talk. Her texts came in random bursts, responding to my updates about her building and firing back questions, though she completely ignored my inquiries about her.

The last time I touched her was at the airport—two hundred and seventy-three hours ago—and every second without her reminded me that I was a sad, sad fool for not realizing this trip was another disappearance.

"Dude, I can't get my ass beaten and then watch your moping. Chicks like to be chased. Like, 'rehab the house where you popped her cherry and wait for her to leave her fiancé then tell her stories about your love when she loses her mind' chased. Get on that. At least sac up and *call* her, but stop your fuckin' moping."

I pivoted, gazing at Riley where he leaned back with his feet outstretched on an adjoining chair. "Did you just paraphrase the plot of *The Notebook*?"

"You should watch it and take notes. Ryan Gosling gets

them panties dropping every time, and he does some fuckin' beautiful work on that old house."

I released a tight, slightly manic laugh and dropped into a seat across from Riley, my phone skating to the center of the table.

"I don't think she wants to be chased." I propped my arms on the table and rested my head against my clasped fingers. "I think she's over it now."

Riley's feet hit the floor and he leaned forward. "Unlikely. Miss Honey was totally in your pocket, and I should know. Almost saw some babies made."

"Yeah, I'm sure that really helped. She's probably dodging my calls now to avoid pervy little shits like you." I looked up and pinned Riley with a glare. "Miss Honey?"

"Yeah," he said. He spoke without tearing his eyes from the phone. "Didn't you read *Matilda*? That sweet little teacher?"

I stared at the table and frowned. "I don't think so."

"Anyway. Your pussyboy mood is bringing down my college football buzz, and that's a problem. How can you go through life like this? All moody and shit? She's out of your league by a couple of pegs. It shouldn't be a surprise to an old man like you that you gotta work for that ass."

"Are you sure you can't bother Sam right now? This seems like a conversation he'd be thrilled to have with you, and if it helps, I'll pick up the tab for lunch. Just leave me the hell alone."

I went back to the design I was sketching in my graphing notebook, the one that had been stuck in my head for weeks. I didn't have time for passion projects—this whole operation was a passion project—but this design was demanding my attention. It kept me up at night, preoccupied my thoughts through traffic, and sent me searching for innovative techniques.

"None of that is going to happen. Just be quiet and I'll take care of this."

My ears didn't register the ringing until Lauren's voice bloomed over the speaker. I dove across the table to grab my phone from him, but he held up a hand and fired a warning look at me.

"Hey, can I call you back in—"

"Hey girl, it's Riley," he said. "How's it going?"

She laughed stiffly and the stress balling in my shoulders multiplied. "Hi, Riley. I'm doing well. Busy, *really* busy, but good. How are you?"

"I'm fuckin' fantastic. October is the most wonderful time of the year, especially when the Sox are leading. You still in Chicago?"

"Yep, until Saturday. Then NOLA. So...what's up? What can I do for you?"

I couldn't decide whether to kick Riley's ass for inserting himself—again—or bow at his feet for getting Lauren talking.

"If you only knew. But, baby, the question is what can I do for you?"

Ass kicking it is.

"I'm going to fucking kill you," I hissed. I sprang across the table and ripped the phone from Riley's hands. Switching off the speaker, I stormed out of my office and into a narrow hallway leading to the fire escape before turning my attention to Lauren. "Sorry about that."

"It's fine, don't worry. He's adorable, in random and bizarre ways."

Heavy tension lingered between us while I searched for

the right response. Our time apart outstripped our time together and I didn't know how to find my way back to her.

"Hey," I said. "How are you?"

Silence greeted my question, and I pulled my phone away from my ear to check the signal strength. I wanted to ask her, right then and there, what the hell was going on. I wanted to know why she was blowing me off and why she wouldn't talk about anything but her project, and I wanted to know which version of Lauren she was showing me now.

I heard doors close and the rustle of wind, and a long exhale. "I know, I know, I owe you so many texts, and I'm so sorry. How's my building coming?"

Within the span of a few words, she knocked me off course, and I slid down the wall until I hit the hardwood floor. I never wanted to talk about architecture again.

"It's on track."

"Just what I wanted to hear. I knew you'd make it happen. I've been crazy busy. And I've been with all these brilliant people who have started schools and I'm just trying to soak up every bit of brilliance while I can. Oh, and I think I met the perfect candidate for my Dean of Students, and if I can convince him to start next month, I might be able to sleep more than three hours a night."

"Good. Good, that's really good. I'm happy you're getting so much out of it," I said.

"I am. But I think I'm going to change my flight next week." I muttered a sound that urged Lauren to go on, but I couldn't find the words to respond. "Originally I was coming in late Saturday morning, but I'm trying to get out on Friday, be back in town that evening."

I cleared my throat. "Okay."

"Would you want to get drinks?"

Drinks. I didn't know how to interpret that—drinks-sex? Or drinks-drinks, like normal adults who weren't fucking and rehabbing a button mill together? Or drinks-I'm-letting-you-down-easy?

"Yeah," I said. "Send me your flight info. I'll pick you up, if that isn't too much of an issue for you."

"Great…?" From the cautious lilt in her voice, it was clear she noticed my clipped tone. "Is everything all right?"

Dozens of harsh answers cycled through my thoughts but they all resembled my drunken ramblings to Erin, and I didn't want to go there.

"Matthew?"

It didn't make sense that my name sounded so right in her voice. It should have sounded exactly the same as anyone else who said it, and not loaded with meaning and memory.

"What? Yeah, nothing." My head landed against the brick wall with a low thunk.

"Really? Okay, well, let me know if anything comes up with my building."

I swore under my breath when my head knocked against the brick again. "Call me this weekend."

"Once I land in New Orleans, I'm all over the place—"

"Call. Me. This. Weekend."

The warm ring of Lauren's laugh only added confusion to my knotted pile of frustration.

"Okay, Matthew. This weekend. But I really need to go. Some people are waiting for me, and they've been so generous with their time already. Bye, for now."

The floor seemed like a safer choice than going back into my office. It was ground zero, filled with memories of Lauren sitting across from me in that red dress while I tried to conceal my erection and burgeoning fascination with her, or the way she melted into me when we thought we were alone. I folded my arms over my bent knees, staring at my phone's black screen.

My office was no comparison to the torture of my loft. Lauren's scent lingered on my sheets and pillows, and the solitary strands of golden blonde hair I found clinging to my clothes and furniture and pillows were mean little tokens from the nights we shared.

I craved her and I missed her, and I was annoyed at myself on both counts. I didn't let women rattle my thoughts, disturb my sleep, or invade my life.

This wasn't what I wanted. I wanted sex with Lauren and I didn't want to care what she did when we weren't having sex. But I also wanted more, maybe a lot more, and I couldn't explain how or when or why that happened, but I wanted it.

And she didn't.

"Are we checkin' jobsites or what? I want to be at the bar at McGreevy's with two beers under my belt before kickoff."

I shifted my attention from the phone to squint at Riley. "You check in on our sites. I'm taking off."

Riley pivoted, looking around the hallway as if I was speaking to someone else. "You're letting *me* do that?"

"Christ, Riley, what the fuck did they teach you in Rhode Island? Just go to a few sites, look around, make sure nothing's crashing down tonight, and get on the GC's ass if you need to. Don't change any plans. Don't talk to any inspectors. Understood?"

"Got it, yeah, all over this." Riley nodded enthusiastically. "Where're you going?"

I popped to my feet and pocketed my phone. "I don't know yet but I need to get the fuck out of here."

I STARTED with a run along the Charles River, crossing over the bridge into Cambridge and through Harvard Square, looping back to follow Storrow Drive, but the miles did nothing to quiet the pounding in my head. Neither did the numbers. I counted everything I saw— parking meters, bridges, women who vaguely resembled Lauren—and created insane equations in my head with those numbers.

I elected to leave my phone in the cup holder of my car. I needed to get away from my father, my siblings, my work for the night, but it felt as if I lost a limb and my only tether to Lauren. I reached for my absent armband nearly every half mile, holding out hope that she would call and explain it all away.

Veering off my original course, I opted to push my limits by jogging to the gym for a grueling hour of burpees, tire flipping, and box jumps. When I dropped to the ground to guzzle water, my muscles burned with exhaustion.

"Whatever you're thinkin' about, you're thinkin' too damn hard."

I slanted my eyes toward the light Texas drawl and allowed a grim smile. Nick Acevedo, the brother I chose, yanked his t-shirt over his head and wiped the sweat from his face before falling beside me. "They let you out for the night?"

"Yeah," Nick said. "They figure I've spent the past eighty-nine hours in surgery, so I get a couple off. I'm free until tomorrow. Or when they page me. Whichever comes first."

"Do you do exorcisms?"

I wasn't sure who needed it more, me or Angus, but I wanted a practitioner at the ready either way.

"No sir, I do not. The American Medical Association frowns upon medieval surgical practices and I like my medical license." Nick tossed his empty water bottle aside and studied me as he braced his head in his hands. "Although my grandmother did have a lot of remedies down on the ranch for batshit crazy. Maybe we can get you some scorpion venom and prickly pear juice. You'll be set. What's ailing you now?"

In which order should I roll out my issues? There was Angus's singular desire to piss all over my sweet mother's memory, plus his focus on destroying my siblings one by one: Patrick was a traitor, Shannon was a cunt, Riley was dumb, Sam was gay, and Erin wasn't his.

None of it was true, but didn't nearly matter.

He never came after me directly, and it was only because I was the referee. He preferred to drown me in his complaints about everyone else, assuming he was gaining me as an ally for his cause, and I supposed it was better that way.

And then there was Miss Halsted and her general refusal to answer text messages within a reasonable timeframe.

Nick stretched his legs straight in front of him, his fingers wrapping around the soles of his sneakers as he dropped his head to his knees and grumbled at the sting of sore muscles. I followed his lead and started stretching as I anticipated the stiffness I would feel in the morning. The steep office stairs would kick my ass worse than any quantity of planks.

"Walsh, I'm not going to drag this shit outta you. I need a shower, a beer, and some red meat. In that order. If you want to unload your problems, you can buy me dinner."

I studied the hard set to Nick's pale hazel eyes before shaking my head. "You need to get laid."

"Right. That way I can spend my time being just as miserable as you."

"HOW DO YOU DRINK THAT?" I held Nick's Hobgoblin brown ale up to the light over the booth and studied the liquid.

"I don't like the fruity, hoppy IPAs out there these days. I like it thick. Real men chew their beers, Walsh." Nick wiped the last of the Russian dressing from his fingers. Burgers at JM Curley's in Downtown Crossing was a satisfying event, though a messy one. "I can't remember the last meal I ate sitting down. Hell, I can't remember an actual meal."

"You make residency sound like a cult."

"It is," Nick said with an emphatic nod. "Gotta be crazy to do it, to stick with it, to put up with all the bullshit. But I pulled a golf-ball-sized tumor out of the top vertebra of a toddler's spine yesterday, and that doesn't suck."

"And the kid's going to live to tell about it?"

"Very funny, dickhead." Nick shook his head and checked his pager. "Everything always goes to shit after midnight. I'm giving you an hour, tops."

"I'm seeing this girl...or not. I don't know." I sighed and tossed a balled up napkin to my plate. "She's building a school in Dorchester. Really cool girl. Funny, smart, gorgeous, bossy. Totally turned my life upside down since I met her."

Nick crossed his arms over his chest, his dark eyebrows raised. "Turned your life upside down how?"

I drained my beer as I contemplated my response. "I spent about four days straight with her." I gestured to the bartender for another.

"And I take it she's redecorating your place and naming your kids?"

I thought about Lauren's presence in my loft more times than I could count, and went so far as to stop into a few shops in search of velvet pillows. Rubbing small pillows in a swanky boutique—alone—felt exactly as weird as it sounded.

"I'd rather that than the cold shoulder I'm getting." I shrugged and sipped the beer when it arrived in front of me. "I think she only wanted help with her project. Or she's blowing me off."

Again.

Nick rolled his eyes, his fingers drumming against the table impatiently. "She's the chillest chick ever. Hot and maybe a little dominant? Do I have that?"

"Yeah. And she drinks tequila like a boss. She's on the road for work right now, and only wants to talk about her project."

"And she's using you for architectural services?"

I shrugged, and Nick continued shaking his head, running his fingers through his dark hair until it pulled in haphazard directions. "Matt, you know I don't get much time for interests beyond surgery and pissing off my attending, and I am rusty in the areas of relationships that don't involve on-call rooms. But everything you've said is fucking nuts. You're a steel trap, man. I don't care how hot she is, I don't see anyone manipulating you—and for architect shit no less. If you could tell this story again, hooked up to an EEG, I might have something for the *New England Journal of Medicine*."

I balanced my arms on the table, gesturing toward Nick with my glass. "By all means, what do you recommend?"

Nick's pager beeped and he frowned at the readout. "Hang on." He punched a few numbers into his phone and waited. The transformation from Nick to Doctor Acevedo always fascinated me, and I tried to decide whether I kept my personal and professional sides separate as seamlessly as Nick did. It probably wasn't possible, not when my work was so intertwined with my family that I could barely tell where one started and the other ended.

"This is Doctor Acevedo."

We had it easy compared to Nick. It probably didn't seem that way, with our sixteen-hour days and working straight through most weekends, but architecture wasn't life and death. We took our work seriously—sometimes too seriously—but it was a challenge we freely accepted. If we took a day off once in a while, we weren't putting the lives of sick children on the line, and we needed to remember that.

"That's early sepsis but I'm most concerned about this kid throwing a clot. Get the on-call pediatric resident, page the attending, and press broad-spectrum antibiotics. I'll be there within the half hour. Get me an OR. Three or five, but not four, definitely not two." Nick disconnected his call and pocketed his phone and pager before turning back to me. "As predicted."

I stretched a hand across the table for a firm shake, and he slipped out of the booth.

"Something I learned about diagnoses," he said, turning back toward me. "Unless you ask the right questions, you will always get the wrong answers. You missed something. Get in front of her. Couldn't be any worse than crying into your beer."

I GULPED, propping my hands on my hips and mentally picking through the passengers streaming through the jetway. This was the definition of a poorly conceived idea, and I was probably going to have my ass handed to me in the middle of the New Orleans airport by a little blonde hurricane.

That was assuming Lauren didn't already see me waiting, and evade. She knew how to tap into that ninja sense when she needed it.

Finally, a crown of golden hair caught my eye. Head lowered, eyes glued to her phone, she was walking past me and would have kept going if I hadn't put myself directly in her path. She bumped into my chest and braced herself on my arm.

"I'm sorry, didn't look where I was...Matthew." Her mouth quirked into a beautiful, stunned smile and she laughed. "You're here."

Her tote bag slid from her shoulder and tumbled to the ground, her phone falling on top of it, and she reached up to wrap her arms around my neck. She struggled without the ass-kicking heels, stretching up and pulling at me, drawing me down to her. Her lips were on me, and I reacted, pushing my tongue into her mouth, tasting her, drowning in her. She was commanding and impatient, and exactly how I wanted her. With my hands comfortably seated in her back pockets, I squeezed her ass, and she met my hungry growl with a laugh.

"What are you doing here? I mean, seriously, why are you here?" Her hands moved down my chest and under my shirt, fingers cool against my skin.

"I wanted to get a drink with you," I said into her mouth.

Every kiss was frenetic, a bit too eager, a bit too aggressive, and our hands were everywhere, touching, pulling, holding. I couldn't keep my mouth off her, not after the weirdness of the past two weeks. Not after the way she jumped into my arms and attacked me.

"Drinks? All this way…for *drinks*?" she said, shaking her head. She was breathing hard, her chest heaving against mine and her cheeks flushed. "Please tell me my building didn't collapse or you found a tyrannosaurus skeleton or some other ridiculous thing."

I rolled my eyes. This wasn't the time to ask her if she was fucking me for architectural advice, and honestly, I couldn't find a way to form those words without sounding like a self-important asshole.

"Would you shut up about your fucking building for a minute and let me kiss you?"

I backed her against the wall, yanking her up on her toes, kissing her like we were alone in this terminal and there was nothing else but her, and I felt wild. It was raw and demanding and urgent, and if it weren't for that tiny, obnoxious corner of my brain and its incessant reminders not to rip her clothes off in an airport, I would have been inside her by now.

Lauren's hand moved, sliding along my torso and past my navel, and her fingers dipped into my boxers. We looked down at the same time, staring at her fingers against my skin, her palm over my belt buckle, and the thick bulge of my erection as it pointed northeast.

"Yeah, I think I'd like some day drinking," she said with a smirk.

Nineteen

LAUREN

OKAY, so the fizzle out wasn't happening.

It was probably better that way. Moderation, right? I was the queen of moderation; it was the only reason my ass wasn't the size of a picnic table.

I leaned against the elevator wall and eyed Matthew. He was the last person I expected to see when my flight from Chicago landed, and I still couldn't wrap my brain around him flying to New Orleans. He said he wanted to be with me, but there was something behind his eyes I couldn't get past. "I see you haven't gotten treatment for that creeping problem yet."

"And why would I?"

He shot a glance at the group of woman alongside us in the elevator, and wrapped his arm around my waist, pulling me in for a quick kiss. It was nothing like the overwhelming moments we shared in the airport, or the borderline indecent ones in the cab, but it reminded me of the immediacy, the automaticity with which I responded to him.

Whether I liked it or not, my body knew Matthew, and knew what to do without my direction.

I tried suppressing a wide yawn when we stepped off the elevator, shielding my mouth to hide my exhaustion, but he noticed with raised eyebrows. Time zones were kicking my ass. That, and *American Horror Story*. "I'm tired. It's a long, bizarre story. Or not so long, but definitely bizarre."

Matthew grasped my hand at the threshold to the room, a sweeping view of the French Quarter stretching before us, and the muddy Mississippi in the distance. He didn't have to tell me he upgraded the suite; there was no way in hell I reserved a room like this when I'd been staying in glorified shoeboxes the past two weeks.

He stood behind me, his arms wrapped around my torso. "Too tired for…drinks? We could just talk."

I pivoted, shaking my head. Talking seemed far too complex right now. "Remember all those times you promised to bend me over your desk? Let's work on a rendition of that."

Walking through the double doors leading to the bedroom, I kicked off my shoes and stripped out of my clothes, and laid against the tall, four-poster king bed, my face to the fluffy down blankets. He edged my feet apart, and made room behind me. Not looking up from the bed, I heard the rustle of fabric and the metallic purr of his zipper, then I felt him, and that was all I needed to rouse that deep spiraling ache in my core. He was hard and hot, and rasping his stubbly chin over the most sensitive parts of my shoulders, and I was never comparing him to bread ever again.

His fingertips trailed up and down my spine, and then

lower, over my ass, slipping inside me, and I knew I'd never been so wet. As much as I told myself I didn't want this, my body wasn't lying about what it wanted. "Miss Halsted," he growled.

He pressed into me, his head sliding through my slit, and I was already there, the early tingles of orgasm crawling up the backs of my legs, around my ribs, through my scalp. His hand spread over my back, pushing me flat against the mattress, and when he finally filled me, we moaned, greedy and hungry and desperate for each other. We didn't move for a long moment, and I savored the weight of him inside me.

"I think your pussy missed me." He moved my hair to one side and kissed my neck. "I think it wants to come all over me right now."

"Mmhmm," I said. "It missed your cock and your fingers and your tongue."

He grabbed my hands, stretching them out over my head, holding them in place, and brought his other hand to my clit. My teeth connected with the blankets, and I groaned against them, knowing I was seconds away from dissolving into a sloppy orgasm puddle.

Matthew started moving, sliding in and out at a leisurely pace while his fingers hovered near—never exactly on—my clit. I sensed him straining, his muscles pulled taut, his breaths coming fast, his control eroding with each measured stroke.

"Did *you* miss me?"

There was a method to his agonizing madness. As if he knew there was one place I couldn't hide from him, one moment when I was wholly unfiltered, his thumb strummed my clit—just as I'd shown him—and I came, screaming, "Oh fuck, Matthew, yes, I'm never leaving you again."

I was too busy shattering to care what I admitted, but I knew I wasn't ready to absorb his reaction, and kept my eyes screwed shut and my face buried in the blankets.

"Good," he growled. "I missed you too."

He didn't relent, the pressure low in my belly building again, and when his words turned into unintelligible pleas and demands, I whispered, "I want to feel you coming inside me."

He pumped into me, his fingers steady on my clit while I exploded again, and then he came with a hoarse roar and his teeth on my back. I expected to find my limbs and vital organs in bits all over the room, obliterated by the force of my climax and the tension between us. We stayed there, panting, basking in the aftershocks, and I wanted this little moment to continue forever.

"Get under the covers," Matthew said. He pulled out, and slapped my ass. "I'll be right back."

I climbed onto the mattress, groaning as my muscles relaxed into the marshmallow bedding. I needed to take notes and do some major redecoration at home. Rolling to my side, I smiled at Matthew's beautiful face when he returned from the bathroom and joined me. So scrumptious.

He drew his finger down my arm, but didn't smile back. "Be honest with me."

I stopped admiring the pillowcases. That sounded cryptic.

"Since you've been traveling, the only thing you've wanted from me is news about your project. I want to know if that's the only thing you're getting out of this."

My lips parted but no sound came out.

"I need to know why you've avoided me for two weeks. You don't even acknowledge my texts most days, and I need to know if you're over this, or I did something to piss you off."

I couldn't lie in our warm glowy bubble anymore. I brought the blankets to my chest and scrambled off the bed. "Did it escape your notice that I just had sex with you? Do you really think I would have done that if I was over it?"

"No, no, no, that's not what I'm saying," he said.

What did I get for being uninhibited with a hot architect? For doing things I'd never done, never dreamed of doing? For breaking all my rules about men and relationships and sex? All of it thrown back at me.

"Did you come here just to ask me that? And then what? You're on the next flight to Boston?" He paused, glancing back and forth between the bed and me. "Or did you come here to fuck me and then tell me I'm a slutty, slutty whore?"

I searched for my clothes, still clutching the sheets, and refused to look at him when he walked across the suite and stepped into his boxers. He handed me his Cornell t-shirt, and I snatched it from his hands without a word, storming to the other side of the room. I couldn't handle this swing, this violent shift from high to low, and I needed space to breathe.

"That's not why I'm here, and that's not what I was implying, and you know that. You know I'd never say anything like that, ever."

"Really? How am I supposed to know that, Matthew?"

"I fucked up, and it came out all wrong." Matthew rubbed the back of his neck and groaned. "I missed you like crazy, and you weren't talking to me, and I didn't know why."

"It's not about the goddamn project, Matthew! How about being busy? I tried to tell you I wouldn't have time for—"

"I know all about busy, sweetness. That one's not working on me."

We gazed at each other across the room, and despite Matthew's intensity, I refused to look away first. He continued staring into me as his long legs ate up the distance between us and his hands gripped my waist.

"Tell me what you want," he begged.

I knew that request so well, but this time, the words weren't there. When we were together with nothing but breaths and kisses between us, I understood—deep, in a tender place I couldn't locate on a map—what we needed and wanted. I *knew*. But now, with him in his unbuttoned jeans and me in his t-shirt and daylight soaking the air around us, I couldn't reach that place. "I don't know."

Matthew stared at me, nodding, and shifted his focus out the window. I stood there, pantless and vibrating with fury—maybe it was hurt or indignation or even whiplash—while his hands drew small circles on my hips and anchored me in place. I understood that his words came out in the wrong combinations, but the thought that I was getting naked with him for architectural work still crossed his mind more than once, and he let it.

"You stopped talking to me, and I don't know why," he murmured. He tucked my hair over my ears, running his fingers through the strands and down my back. "But I do know you should stop pushing me away."

I shouldn't have crept out of his bed that foggy Saturday, and I shouldn't have left town without telling him it was time to fizzle out, but maybe—just maybe—I always wanted to leave those doors slightly ajar. To find out what I was sacrificing. To sample something I shouldn't have. To break some rules.

"Tell me what *you* want, Matthew."

"I want you to let me hang out with you this weekend. I want you to stop disappearing," he said. He squeezed his eyes shut, as if he were trying to withstand a tremendous discomfort or repress a gruesome memory. "And I want to stop calling it drinks. I want you. Just…you. We'll see what happens after that. Okay?"

I didn't want to pretend I could find a way for this to work without my life running off the rails, but I didn't want to say no either. My hands roamed over his chest and shoulders and I nodded. "Fine," I said. "But you suggested I was using you, and I'm not okay with that. I hate that you entertained that thought for more than one hot second, and you entertained it so hard you came down here to ask."

"I never believed it," he murmured. "Never. But when you don't talk to me I invent my own stupid explanations."

"Just to clarify, you're *not* saying I'm a slutty whore?"

"Sweetness, you can be my slutty whore whenever you want, and I'm telling you right now, I'll worship you for it." His thumbs brushed under my eyes and he frowned. "I already worship you. You get that, right?"

"I think so."

"You should." He inclined his head toward the bed. "This was exhausting, and I just want to hold you because I said tremendously douchey shit and you don't deserve that. And I haven't seen your fine ass in two weeks, and that's far too long. Snugglenap?"

"Mmm," I sighed. "Yes please."

We crawled into the bed and curled around each other, our fingers laced together. My body melted into him, and the tension skittering between us seemed to dissipate. It was a struggle to keep my eyes open, but the pressure of Matthew's stiffening shaft against my bottom kept me from falling asleep. "You probably want me naked and telling you all my deep, dark desires."

"I just want you." Matthew pulled a blanket up to my chin and circled his arms around me again. "This is all I need."

"Me too." My head bobbed against Matthew's chin, and I dropped over the edge of sleep.

THE ROOM FELT COOL, and when my eyes peeked open, I noticed darkness pouring through the windows. There was tapping over my shoulder and I yelped, scrambling to my knees and ready to strike. My heart pounded as I stared at Matthew, his laptop open on his thighs and his hands folded in his lap, an inquisitive expression on his face.

"This is new," he said, gesturing to my defensive stance.

My fingers landed on a wet patch on my cheek, and I tried to brush away evidence of drool. I glanced at the clock and combed my fingers through my hair. "You let me sleep for six hours?"

Matthew shrugged and powered down his laptop. "Isn't that the point of the snugglenap?"

I grabbed my toiletry kit and headed to the bathroom to deal with the drool remnants and brush my teeth. "Just figured I'd wake up naked with your cock in my mouth and your head between my legs."

Matthew vaulted off the bed and I saw him braced against the doorframe. "Can I interest you in that now?"

I smiled to myself as I applied a fresh coat of mascara. "Maybe if you woke me up an hour ago, but I'm starving."

I breezed past him to rifle through my bags for clean clothes, which were in short supply after two weeks away from my washing machine. Tossing his t-shirt to a chair, I slipped a gauzy kimono-style shirt over my head and stepped into a pair of jeans. Matthew's chest pressed against my back, his hands skimming under the shirt and cupping my breasts.

"Give me ten minutes," he said, his lips hovering over my ear.

"I could give you ten minutes," I said, my body softening into his. "But it's never ten minutes. And I'm hungry."

Matthew rained kisses along my neck and shoulders, his fingers brushing the soft undersides of my breasts while his hips bumped in a lazy rhythm against my ass. He groaned, squeezing my breasts before walking away. "Hard to believe someone so heavenly could be so fucking evil."

"You love it," I said. I dropped a scarf into my bag and headed toward the door.

"Something like that," he murmured.

As we walked down Chartres Street toward the Jackson Square restaurant, Matthew pointed out the blend of French, Spanish, and Creole influences in each building, and contrasted the architectural styles we saw: Greek revival, Art Nouveau, Art Deco, Renaissance Colonial, Gothic, Victorian, Italianate, Queen Anne, Postmodern, Mid-century Modern. He knew with a glance which predated the Civil War, which survived the Great New Orleans Fire in 1788, which had been restored.

When we settled into the bistro's cozy patio, he described the Pontalba Buildings, the matching block-long red brick apartments flanking two sides of the Square, and explained the four-story structures launched the wrought iron balcony trend in New Orleans. He paused to order drinks, then continued, so charming and animated, about the complex geometry of mansard roofs.

We never talked like this. It was either sex or work or squabbling about who was bossy and who was a caveman, but it was never ordinary conversation about our interests, our passions, our places in the universe. And it was my fault. I spent so much time trying to shut him out, shut *this* out.

The waiter delivered our cocktails and I stirred my glass to study the contents of the New Orleans specialty, the sazerac. "To dinner outside in October."

Matthew murmured in agreement and our glasses clinked together.

I stifled a cough after sipping and my eyes flashed to him. "That is *strong*. Are you trying to get me drunk?"

"Of course not." He smiled, his eyes sparkling and mischievous. "I'd be happy with tipsy."

We opted to share three authentic Creole dishes, and spent the meal talking and laughing. Like everything else with Matthew, it was natural. Was this what he wanted when he asked me to stop calling it drinks? Did he want us sharing meals and stories, and hanging out together without crumbling under the need to rub up against each other? Did I want that?

Then his fingers tightened around my hand, and I realized my foot was sliding over the back of his calf.

So meals, stories, and some light rubbing?

We discovered a mutual love of many restaurants and bars, and realized we'd been daily patrons of the same obscure coffeehouse for nearly two years. Once that peculiar shock wore off, we agreed hands down that autumn was the best season in Boston. Those fools who loved springtime were kidding themselves—Boston in the spring was cold and wet and muddy, save for the odd week or two of perfection around the end of May.

I mentioned an affection for *The Avengers*, *Iron Man*, and the first *Transformers*, and Matthew brought up the origins of his siblings' comic-book-inspired nicknames. They referred to Sam as Tony Stark but never Iron Man—brilliant but a womanizing manwhore in the business of collecting obsessive-compulsive tendencies—and I laughed so hard my drink sprayed out my nose.

We both admitted feeling like we'd accomplished a barrelful of nothing since college, and insisted the other was insane to think so, but that didn't stop us from comparing ourselves to others in our fields. I couldn't understand how he saw his work as anything short of extraordinary—especially after the dissertation I got on New Orleans architecture—and he argued that point right back to me until we accepted each other's compliments.

Matthew divulged a small addiction to running, and for him that was a gateway to biking and swimming, and occasionally doing all three for about one hundred and forty miles.

I told him about my treats: baked goods of all varieties,

shoes, and disgustingly expensive lacy things. I didn't offer explanation other than saying the shoes and the lingerie made me feel stronger, more capable when everything was complicated, and people would be happier if they ate more cake. He feigned disbelief when I mentioned the lacy things, demanding proof even though he had watched me dress and knew plenty about my undies, and I might have slipped my panties into his pocket on my way back from the ladies' room.

Matthew inquired about my fondness for velvet pillows, and I confessed an obsession with wandering through farmers' markets and random little shops, and that my favorite place in the area was Cape Cod. I loved walking along the shore, gazing out over the Atlantic, and feeling like I was teetering over the edge of the earth and absolutely, totally free from everything else in the world, where no one expected anything from me, and I could just *be*. We realized we frequented the same beaches, and quite possibly the same quiet cove at the same time, but never noticed each other until I went ass over elbow down the stairs at Saint Cosmas.

When Matthew's eyes flashed with vulnerability, I shifted closer, and he told me about the hot July day twenty-two years ago when he and his siblings found their pregnant mother on the floor of her bedroom, clutching her belly while blood pooled around her. The memories poured out, and my heart broke for the little boy who watched his mother die.

A heaviness settled between us, and before the waiter could present the dessert menus, I held up a hand and said, "One of everything, and another round."

We sampled the crème brulee, flourless chocolate cake, and pain perdu, and I set the pecan pie aside for the morning. My position on pie for breakfast brought him to the origin of his family's famous butternut squash pie recipe—his mother substituted squash after he and Patrick climbed the roof of their childhood home for a pumpkin-smashing experiment—and that it was the only thing Shannon was allowed to cook, ever.

As a transplant to New England, that was a new one for me, and I filed it away with the frappes and fluffernutters, and whoopee pies and Indian pudding.

With a fresh sazerac in hand, Matthew leaned forward and said, "I actually need to hear this from you, Lauren. I need to understand why you stopped talking to me because I don't. I don't understand any of it."

Licking chocolate from the fork's tines, I shrugged. "I've had a really hectic few weeks."

My words sounded flimsy and hollow, and while we both knew I *was* busy, we also knew there was more to the story.

He folded his arms on the table, his hands circling the tumbler, and I watched his fingertips as they tapped the glass. I liked his hands. Long fingers, light freckles all over, and a dusting of hair near his wrist. His watch was the size of a puppy's head, but on him, it was almost proportional.

"And you thought I wouldn't want to hear about that?"

"I didn't know what you wanted," I said.

Eyebrow lifted, Matthew leveled me with a sharp look. "Yes, you did."

Instead of trying to fill the most awkward silence in the history of humanity with empty babble that certainly wouldn't make him happy, I finished the crème brulee. He signaled for the check, and snatched it up when I reached across the table.

"You're a caveman," I murmured.

"You're bossy."

He didn't look up when he said it, and it wasn't the same loving quip without his usual smirk and sarcastic tone.

Is this what I've been doing all this time? Is this what it feels like to be shut out and pushed away?

The return trip to the hotel was quiet, and he didn't reach for me. The French Quarter was vibrant and pulsating, and I wanted more than anything to feel that way with Matthew right now, to banish the prickly energy between us. He stopped at the corner of Bourbon Street, gesturing to lively venues boasting jazz and bourbon, voodoo and hurricanes, and asked, "Will rum bring you back to me? Or is it just tequila?"

"I don't know what you want me to say," I sighed and wrapped my scarf around my shoulders. Armor. The thin, flowery fabric was the best shield I had, and I needed it to protect me right now.

"Tell me why. That's all I want."

Partiers spilled onto the streets, laughing and singing, and I shrugged. "The past two weeks have been…awful. I mean, I've learned things and met people, but awful. It's been ridiculous and shameful and appalling how much I've missed you. We had an incredible weekend, and that should've been the end of it. But I can't get you out of my head. Okay? Was that what you wanted?"

"Yeah," he said, brushing my hair over my shoulder. "Keep going."

"I never sleep and all of this travel is kicking my ass. And it's really obvious I only have half a clue of what I've gotten myself into with opening this school. I'm pretty sure I'm failing at life."

"And if you'd mentioned any of that to me, I would've told you it was bullshit. I would've said dirty things over the phone to make you feel better because I missed you too and I want to solve these things for you."

"Matthew," I laughed impatiently. "I can't find room in my life to breathe right now. I thought if I kept my distance, if I only talked about the project...I thought it would be easier."

"Was it?"

We both knew the answer. We knew it the second we kissed at the airport. We knew it every time our eyes locked. We knew it when he was so deep inside me that he took my breath. Finally I shook my head, and said, "No, but I didn't see any other way."

"Let me find one, Lauren. Just let me in and I'll find one."

I studied the brain throughout grad school: how it worked, how it stored and organized information, and how teachers could make instruction more accessible for all kids. While my focus was classroom-centric, I also learned how the brain perceived experiences and engaged the senses to form emotions and memories.

I knew the brain decided what it wanted to see. The rods and cones within the eye's structure transferred images, but in the process, the brain morphed them, shifting and shaping and shading until they aligned with each person's unique cognitive structures. The hard-wired neural pathways made eyewitness accounts unreliable, and meant we didn't notice our keys were in their usual spot all along. Sight was belief's most subjective, manipulative source.

I'd known this yet ranked myself above it. I thought I was the ultimate seer. I thought I could look beneath the layers, understand more than I saw, and read between the lines, but I couldn't see what was right in front of me.

When had it stopped being just for fun, just for now? When had Matthew and I transitioned from drinking buddies to an *us*, an entity requiring care and communication? I paged through memories of Matthew while the humid air and rich fragrances of the Quarter rose around us, and realized it had never been casual. Not even once.

It was controlled chaos, and I needed to embrace it. Or running screaming.

Maybe it was the whiskey or the anise-flavored Herbsaint, or maybe just the sharp and sudden realization that I wasn't in charge now, and perhaps I never was, but I wanted to close the distance between us. I wanted to get back to the place where I knew him, and with my head against his chest and his arms around me, I was close enough.

He pressed his lips to my hair and murmured, "I didn't fly here for drinks. I flew here for you."

He tipped my face up, his lips hovering over the corner of my mouth, and in that split second, life was perfect. I was perfect. There were no overdue action plans, no epic strangeness, no failing at entry-level life. Right now, with his hands in my back pockets and his lips on my mouth and those gazelles storming across my lungs, *we* were perfect.

And that was all it was—*now*.

I wanted to step outside of myself and snap a photo of us, and then I'd always be able to find that perfection when everything else fell apart.

Lauren: flight officially changed to Fri night.

Matthew: good. I want you back in my time zone

Matthew: and bed

Lauren: your bed misses me now?

Matthew: every piece of furniture in my loft. shower. dick. hand.

Matthew: they all miss you

Matthew: the next time I'm jerking off in the shower, I'd really like your tits there so I can come all over them

Lauren: that's very specific

Matthew: you're all about specific requests, sweetness. I learn from the best

Matthew: …where'd you go?

Matthew: I thought you'd be into that. it's cool if you're not, it's fine

Matthew: I want what you want.

Lauren: just clearing my weekend schedule. wanted to block time on my calendar for these little shower adventures you've described

Matthew: can I ask what you've titled that event?
Lauren: hydraulics inspection
Matthew: YES

IT SHOULDN'T HAVE BEEN that easy—a flight to New Orleans, a spicy meal, and two days buried in my hot blonde—but that was all it took to unwind the deep knot of tension in my neck and the numbers in my head.

"Look at this: clean-shaven, sharp clothes, no bitter scowl. What a difference a weekend makes. Speaking on behalf of the tribe, it's delightful to see you've dislodged the steel I-beam that was in your ass, Matt," Sam said as I took my seat around the attic conference table. "Even if you are ten minutes late."

"Hells yeah," Riley said. "Did you say hi to Miss Honey for me?"

"For everyone's safety and sanity, it's fair to say that Lauren isn't allowed to leave town without you anymore," Patrick said.

I indulged their ribbing with a self-deprecating shrug, busying myself with testing the temperature of my coffee and adjusting the volume settings on my phone. I knew her conference would keep her tied up through the evening, but I wanted to know immediately if she messaged, and I didn't care if Patrick lost his shit over it either.

For once, the firm and this job weren't coming first. Lauren was.

"So it went well?" Shannon asked.

I studied my screen as I formulated a response. I wanted to keep my weekend with Lauren in a private place far from the ravenous purview of my siblings. At times, I regretted holding Shannon at an arm's length when I shared so much with Erin, but Shannon required more explanation, and she wanted to analyze everything beyond recognition. I knew last night's quick text when I landed at Logan was inadequate, but it was the best I could give her then, and probably the only thing I could give her now.

Looking up, I met her glare with an even expression. "Yeah."

"Christ almighty, you are impossible! What happened? What's the deal with you two?"

"Not during my meeting, Shan," Patrick said. "Today's agenda is packed and I have a nine o'clock consult. We need to get moving."

"Okay people, let's get high-level updates on projects, whiz bang fast," she said with a snap of her fingers. "Sammy, you start."

I half listened as Sam walked through his current work, turning my attention to my weekend emails. I'd plowed through several hundred at the airport and during my flight last night, but many more appeared early this morning. All of my masonry contractors were working straight through the weekends wherever city regulations and building permits allowed, getting in as much time as possible before snow and frozen earth made their craft substantially more difficult. Famously unpredictable, Boston winter weather could bring my stonework to a grinding halt, and I needed to wrap up several projects before the first major snowstorm.

My thoughts turned to Lauren and I pictured her curled up next to the fireplace at my loft, watching a storm blow in off the water. The idea of being snowed in with Lauren landed in my chest, and my heart beat harder, heavier. I barely noticed when Riley leaned toward me and tapped my arm.

"Dude."

I refocused on my siblings, quickly realizing that four pairs of eyes were staring at me. Sam pressed his fist to his mouth, a poor attempt at concealing his smirk, and said, "We need to take a minute to observe this. Many moons will pass before anyone else at this table shows up looking quite this love-drunk."

"Updates?" Shannon prompted, her knowing smile a stark contrast to Patrick's bland scowl.

"Back Bay properties are down to punch lists, and I'm going to spend most of the day sitting on the GC to get them knocked out," I said. "Shan, plan to list them in a week or two. HVAC and flooring upgrades are finished at Trench, and framing and drywall are on track for this week. Newton is a mess because the homeowner has requested a fifth floor plan overhaul. North End needs a foundation rebuild, as I predicted two months ago, and we're pouring concrete tomorrow."

"Add an extra twenty percent to Newton. Call it the dicking around fee," Patrick said, his eyes focused on his master spreadsheet of projects, timelines, and budgets. I envied no part of that. "What about Angus's Bunker Hill buys?"

"RISD, you got this?" I glanced over to Riley, waiting for a confident response. I spent weeks coaching Riley through the process and overseeing the development of his proposal, and despite Angus's pissing and moaning, I knew he had some strong, unique ideas for the four properties no one wanted to touch.

"Yeah," he stammered. "I drafted a few different scenarios. Depending upon whether we're going for single-family, multi-family, or mixed use." He spread his designs over the center of the table, pausing while Patrick, Shannon, and Sam studied his work.

"That's interesting," Sam mused, pointing to one of the designs. Patrick nodded in agreement, and I sensed Riley's anxiety multiplying as the minutes passed. He still couldn't manage to zip his fly or make it to the office without spilling coffee on his perennially wrinkled clothes, and it didn't appear he owned any socks, but I was starting to see some potential. His work clearly reflected a different approach than the one Sam, Patrick, and I shared, but after some fine-tuning, I liked it.

"What's your recommendation?" Patrick asked.

Riley turned expectant eyes to me, and I nodded in encouragement. "That area's coming up fast, but it's mostly triple deckers and apartments. Not a lot of single-family. The data seems to indicate that the few single-family properties listed sell in days."

Patrick studied the designs again. "Have you approved these?" he asked, pointing the papers at me.

"Yeah. Everything checks out."

Patrick nodded and pushed the papers back toward Riley. "RISD, you're still Matt's shadow. Do this, do this well, do everything Matt says, and we'll talk. Shan, look into the Charlestown market to be sure about the SFH demand and get some conservative sales estimates by midweek. Let's look at bottom lines before we lift a hammer. And someone get Angus to decide how much we're investing without letting him in the office, please."

"I can do that." Riley shrugged indifferently, but I noticed him biting back a proud smile.

"That's all I got," I said.

"Good," Patrick murmured. "Nothing to report on the intern front. Shannon is meeting with accounting and payroll providers to get that off her plate, and we're looking at candidates for another assistant for her. Someone to support marketing and publicity, and all that shit."

"Nothing to report on the intern front because Patrick is literally impossible to please," she said. "We've met nine perfectly pleasant candidates."

"We've met nine morons," Patrick said, scowling. "Bring me someone who can spell sustainable preservation, and I'll consider it. We're not talking about this right now, Shannon."

"Wow. Shit just got real," Riley said.

"You have a decent design. Now you have to stop with the quippy catchphrases," Sam said. "Expand your lexicon."

"Hate the game, not the player," he scolded with a wink.

From: Matthew Walsh
To: Erin Walsh
Date: October 13 at 11:25 EDT
Subject: answer your phone

E –
I need you sorting me out right now. Call me. Whenever.
M

"IF WE BLOW out this wall, we get all the natural light from the front windows, and the flow of the space completely changes." Riley gestured to the dusty parlor windows with one hand and pointed to the adjacent wall with the other. "I think natural light is the best asset of this one."

I paced from the windows to the back of the Bunker Hill property, mentally calling up the blueprints and scanning the space for load-bearing walls. "While I agree with that, I'm concerned about structural support without that wall. Original plans seem to indicate it supports the second and third floors."

"Which is why we need to move the staircase. Here, look." Riley spread his latest draft on the window seat and pointed to several new arteries of steel. "Struts here, here, and here."

"That's a lot of steel," I murmured. "What's Angus thinking for a budget on these properties?"

Riley cleared his throat and rolled up his drafts, tucking them into his cylindrical canister. "Half million, all in. He's not talking about where that kind of scratch came from. I'd rather not be implicated in the affairs between him and his bookie, so I'm not about to ask."

I whistled, my palm running along the recently discovered carvings in the arched doorway to the parlor. I couldn't understand the logic behind covering such fine craftsmanship with shitty composite wood paneling, hiding it for decades, but underneath it all, these properties were hidden gems waiting for someone to understand their structures, put in the work, peel back the layers, and honor their original beauty. As much as I hated giving Angus credit for anything beyond taking up space, these were incredible finds.

"By all means, load up the steel. That's going to double the timeline, though. We'll want to save a lot of this." I waved my hand at the exposed brick walls and plaster detailing around the windows. "Let's get White's crew in here next week. They're the best at gentle demo. We'll want to supervise, too. I'm thinking we're going to find more when we start tearing out walls."

"These plans, they're good? You'd tell me if I needed to fix something, right?"

"I would tell you." I gestured toward the door. "Let's get out of here. It's freezing."

Riley followed me to the Range Rover. "Does it make sense to get rid of the parlor if we're restoring this property? Wouldn't a restoration preserve the original design? Sometimes I don't think I understand what we do and if I'm doing it right."

I swiped my phone to life and waited for the airline's app to load while I considered Riley's question. I typed in Lauren's flight information and stifled a groan when I saw it delayed by ninety minutes. At the same moment, she texted.

Lauren: hey. Not getting in until 1015 now. crazy day getting crazier.
Matthew: yeah, I just saw that. Are you ok?
Lauren: yes. hold on tight for this: woke up late. put on the wrong suit coat and I'm rocking black pants and a navy jacket. got salad dressing on my silk shirt. tripped because I'm wearing the wrong shoes with these pants and grabbed some lady's boob to break my fall.

Lauren: karma's kicking my ass over something today.
Lauren: So...I might spend the next hour and a half in the bar. introduce myself to nola's other specialty: the hurricane.
Matthew: pace yourself, sweetness.
Lauren: we're going to miss dinner. gah...hate that.
Matthew: tomorrow.
Lauren: but I had a plan.
Matthew: you always have a plan, sweetness. sometimes you just need to roll with it.

"Dude." Smiling brightly, I looked up from my phone and realized Riley was still waiting on my response. "I was talking."

"Yeah, sorry. Let me just send this. Lauren's flight's delayed. You want a beer or something?"

"Sure. That'll make up for you sexting right in front of me." He shook his head and stared out the window. "I put up with a lot of shit from you guys."

Lauren: :)
Matthew: I'm getting a beer with Riley. Text me when you board.
Matthew: Or when TSA picks you up for drunk and disorderly conduct, whichever comes first.
Lauren: say hi to RISD for me.

"Lauren says hi." I pulled away from the curb and negotiated my way through traffic, crossing the Charlestown Bridge into the North End.

"She's getting in tonight?"

"Not until after ten." I zigzagged through narrow

cobblestone streets toward my building. "How about the Sail Loft?"

Riley snickered. "If you're buying and you don't mind yachty bros."

"How could I? I spend all day with you, and your sock-less boat shoe situation."

We parked at my building and walked down Atlantic Avenue. Cold, wintry wind mixed with sleet was gusting off the water, and I felt the chill in my bones. Definitely time for warmer layers and snow gear. We found two open stools at the corner of the long bar and ordered Oktoberfest beers.

"As I was saying," he started. "I think it makes sense to blow out the parlor because it wrecks the entire flow and cuts off the natural light. But if we're restoring this joint, wouldn't I keep the parlor and *restore* it? Isn't that the deal?"

I sipped my beer and shrugged. "Not always. Heritage restoration is all about preserving the effects of age and decay, and that's usually removing elements that were added after the original build. Like linoleum and popcorn ceilings and that fucking wood paneling. We also do a lot of heritage restoration on structural issues, and that's okay because most of the engineering techniques didn't exist until recently."

Riley signaled to the bartender. "Sweetheart, can I get a fisherman's platter?" He glanced to me. "I don't share. If you want something, speak up."

"Steamed mussels." I figured I wouldn't get Lauren back to my place until after eleven. I doubted we'd spend much time eating although I didn't expect the cupcakes in my fridge to go untouched tonight. The naughty schoolteacher had one hell of a sweet tooth.

"And a basket of onion rings," Riley called. He looked back to me. "You said you're buying, right?"

"Yeah, whatever." I glanced to my phone and saw no new messages. "While opening up the original parlor is not a strict restoration, we're saving everything that can reasonably be restored, and upgrading all the structures and systems. We're not winning any National Trust for Historic Preservation awards—okay, Sam will, but that's Sam. At least we'll prevent that property from being torn down."

"And you're good with that?"

I nodded, and checked my phone again, estimating that Lauren would be boarding in the next fifteen minutes if her flight wasn't delayed further.

An overflowing plate of fried shrimp, scallops, calamari, cod, and clams landed in front of Riley, and he bit into a clam with a low groan. "Hot plate," the waiter warned as he dropped the bubbling mussels to the bar.

"I don't get why we're basically flipping houses."

"We're not," I said. "When the market turned a few years back, we ended up with a few abandoned projects on our hands. Owners couldn't afford to continue and walked away. Knowing we weren't getting paid, Shannon said we had too much invested to blow them off. She wrote lowball offers and we bought the properties, sold them high, and cleaned up. Angus likes to pretend he invented that strategy, because he's doing the same thing now."

"Dude, I'm not trying to tell you your business, but that sounds like flipping to me."

"Flipping is putting in granite countertops and stainless steel appliances. Slapping on some builder beige paint. The market downturn came at a time when we were taking over the business from Angus, and it showed us that some people don't want to buy fixer-uppers anymore. Especially not the kind of fragile, restriction-heavy multimillion dollar properties we work on."

I lifted my phone when it alerted, dropping my fork into the dish of mussels. "Instead, we buy, fix, and sell. And make a killing, and that's why we couldn't do this without Shannon. And we still take on plenty of non-investment properties."

"If you say so, dude. I always thought we drew up blue-lines and handed them over to GCs and walked away. Easy peasy. This is…not even close to that."

"It isn't exactly what we expected when we planned to take over the business, but it's working for us." I glanced at my message from Lauren with a chuckle.

Lauren: I'll have you know I'm on the flight. No incidents to report.
Matthew: how many hurricanes?
Lauren: just 2.
Matthew: and you're standing?
Lauren: sitting but pleasantly intoxicated and holding it together just fine.
Matthew: you'll be able to make it out of the terminal?
Lauren: you really underestimate me, Matthew.
Lauren: my brothers used to take me out drinking and then try kidnapping me
Lauren: they'd time how long it took me to escape
Matthew: 1. that's incredibly weird
Matthew: 2. they are going to beat the shit out of me some-day, aren't they?
Lauren: I'm ignoring all that nonsense you just spouted. I will see you at the curb in 3 hrs.

Matthew: text me when you land. I'll come inside if you want.

Lauren: oh I bet you'll come inside.

I laughed out loud, my eyes widening as I read her message. Not so innocent anymore. Dismissing Riley's inquisitive look, I shook my head.

"You're really whipped," he said, watching my fingers as they flew over the screen.

"No," I said. "I don't think that's the right term. I just like talking to her."

"I'd rather chicks not speak at all," he said with a mouthful of scallop.

"Maybe you haven't found the right one."

Matthew: only if you let me.

Lauren: you know I will.

Lauren: evil death stare from the flight attendant. gtg.

"And you have?" Riley asked.

He was too busy watching the Celtics game to notice the irrepressible smile on my face.

Lauren wasn't just the right one.

She was the *only* one.

SLIDING my finger over the tiny rosettes adorning a pretty pair of panties, I knew I was in dangerous territory. A late afternoon meeting with a team of education researchers in Cambridge left me only a few blocks from my favorite lingerie shop, Forty Winks, and it was my Friday treat. I promised myself one sweet purchase, yet a mountain of silky, frilly, scandalously delicious items now sat beside the cash register.

And the rosette panties were going on top.

Lingerie was one of my most beloved splurges, but I didn't like thongs—I didn't equate sexy with basically bare —and garters were altogether too complex for me. A simple bikini or boy short in the right fabrics, styles, and colors was adequately devastating for me.

And Matthew.

Not long ago, I wore fancy panties because they made *me* happy, but if it was possible, I now gained more satisfaction from his reaction than anything else. The perfect pair left him speechless, and I loved possessing that power.

He knew my days started winding down around six or seven, and that was when he usually texted to inquire about my skivvies—guessing the color and cut, asking when he'd be able to rip them off, debating whether he'd want to carry them around for a day or two after dragging them off.

It was hilarious and delightful, and despite Steph's commentary on this topic, not at all perverted or fetishy.

The best part was he understood there wasn't much space in my head for more than a couple flirty texts each day, never mind properly scheduled dates or plans exclusive of take-out and Netflix. This was our version of *more than drinks*, and I appreciated his low key approach. It was fun and easy, and we weren't busy overthinking it.

Last Friday was a great example. He texted in the late afternoon, curious about my underthings, and decided we needed dinner in the North End. He was taking care of reservations and I was to meet him at the restaurant. It was one of those extraordinary planetary alignments where we weren't too exhausted for a night out, we didn't have any work crises to manage, and we were free to sleep in the next morning.

Matthew and I indulged in pasta and people watching and wine, and under the table I let him slide his hand all the way up my thigh and over my new panties. We shared innuendos and inside jokes, and we stumbled all the way back to his place, clinging to each other in laughter as we reveled in our private stories. My dress was on the floor seconds after he closed the door, and I stood there in only my bra, panties, and heels.

"I think I understand now," Matthew said, his hands on his hips, "why they're called unmentionables."

With that thought, I tossed the rosette panties on the heap, and headed toward the bras. Soon cradling an armful, I closed the dressing room door behind me and felt my phone ringing in my back pocket.

"Where are you?" Matthew asked, breathless.

"Um...I'm out."

"Where?" he said, the word bursting out in a whoosh.

Looking around the room, I considered how much to tell him. The slightest mention of lingerie was known to turn him into quite the caveman. "Cambridge. I'm doing some errands. Why? What's up? Everything okay?"

"Everything is awesome," he said. "We sold those brownstones, the ones in the Back Bay. All of them. Out of my hands, finally, and off the books. And it was a *big* sale."

"Matthew, I am so thrilled for you. That's incredible!"

I knew he'd been dedicating long hours to that project and dealing with all manner of problems.

"Hey, so, whenever we have huge wins like this, we go out and celebrate. And I want you with us tonight."

I was about to say no—it seemed like something Matthew should enjoy with his business partners and I had a ton of work to plow through this weekend—but I caught my reflection in the mirror and paused. I looked the same as always, but I was different now, somehow more *me* than I was before. With my phone tucked between my shoulder and head, and a half dozen bras under my arm, I decided planetary alignment wasn't the only reason for a night out.

"Okay. Let me finish these errands, and meet me at my place in an hour."

"Does that mean you'll let me stay over when you get hammered and I have to carry you home?" Matthew asked.

"If anyone's getting hammered—"

"Just say yes, sweetness. I'm happy and I want to spend the night with you and not everything needs to be a debate."

"Fine. You can stay over. But I'll definitely want croissants for breakfast tomorrow morning," I said.

"And I'll definitely want you sucking my cock for breakfast. Let's see who wins."

"Such a caveman," I groaned.

"You're bossy. You leave me no choice."

MATTHEW'S mischievous grin caught my eye as we walked toward the tiny bistro on Park Street. Almost an hour late to meet his siblings, my skirt was on sideways and there were very distinct teeth marks on my collarbone. We could safely add sex hair to the list, too.

He had been waiting at my door, zeroing in on the Forty Winks bag the moment I rounded the corner, and we barely made it to the bed.

"Good thing you have so many scarves," he chuckled.

"Yeah, so you can be a little vampire."

He smirked, and I was tempted to drag him back to my place and beg for his teeth all over again.

"Your brothers and Shannon are going to take one look at us and know," I murmured.

"No, they're not. They're busy getting drunk and talking about how many times I fucked up this build. Far bigger issues than whether I spent the past hour owning your pussy."

He grabbed my hand, kissing my palm then lacing our

fingers together as we joined the group inside the restaurant.

I'd seen plenty of Shannon since returning from my conference travel. We went so far as to calendar drinks and pedicures, and spent the weeks before our appointments harassing each other to get shit done and not cancel at the last minute. So far, it was working.

Riley often accompanied Matthew to Trench Mills, and he occasionally led the progress-monitoring walk-throughs. He was charming and sarcastic, and if my parents had ever given me the younger sibling I requested on multiple Christmas lists, I would have wanted him to be exactly like Riley.

Sam and Patrick were still question marks for me, and Matthew didn't share much about either. He jogged with Patrick, which was to say Matthew jogged and Patrick— allegedly—complained about it for the duration.

We sat, and after a round of greetings and brotherly ball-busting, the table fell quiet and all eyes were on me. It was painfully obvious I was the only outsider, the non-architect, the plus-one, and it felt oddly similar to sneaking into my brothers' tree house when I was four.

"Why the fuck did you kick me?" Sam yelled, his glare leveled on Matthew.

"Consider it a warning shot," he mouthed.

"If I may," Riley said from beside me, his hand raised for silence. "You shouldn't be staring at Miss Honey's tits, Sam. She's a nice lady, not one of your party girls, and I would've kicked you, too."

"Is that a thing now?" Shannon asked. She passed the white wine to me, the red to Matthew. "'Miss Honey?'"

Nicknames were a rite of passage for this group. Initially

I found them rude and rather cruel—how else can you explain referring to Sam as 'the runt'?—but I came to see them as part of the Walsh DNA. They were tough on each other, yelling and criticizing and insulting each other easily, and swearing with impunity, but it was how they showed their love. I figured their name-calling was roughly equivalent to the elaborate training operations Wes and Will staged with the Commodore.

"Yeah, I'm taking credit for this one," Riley said. "I think we should adopt her."

I felt Matthew's gaze on me but I couldn't interpret his preoccupied stare, his slow, measured sips, or the way his eyes lingered on my face.

"Do you adopt many people?" I asked.

"So far? Just Nick," Patrick said.

Nick was the one person apt to show up at Matthew's door at six on a Sunday morning and drag him out for a bike ride, or invite himself in for breakfast. The pediatric neurosurgeon and I got to talking several weeks ago, and discovered a shared nostalgia for the West. We missed In-N-Out Burger and street grids that made sense, and admitted to love-hate relationships with New England winters. My Commodore Halsted stories could go toe-to-toe with stories from his superstitious grandmother. We were both the babies—he had two older sisters—and to the dismay of our families, we both ended up staying on the east coast after college.

"What's his nickname?" I asked.

"Doctor," Patrick said. "And we aren't entirely sure he's earned that one."

"And what's yours?" I asked Matthew. Still watching me with his wine glass in hand, a curious expression moved across his face, as if he was trying to understand something complex.

He shook his head. "Never found one that stuck."

"That is *not* true," Shannon said. "More like you squirmed out of everything we tried."

"The Flash," Sam offered. "He is a brisk runner."

"Jugger," Riley said. "For that hard head."

"None of them worked," Patrick said.

"We even tried Mitt, you know, for MIT." Sam shrugged. "I prefer Mitzy, but that one didn't last."

"Thankfully," Matthew muttered.

Dinner was fun, and chock-full of ridiculous stories about the brownstone restorations. The one about the flooded basement. The one about the nest of bats in the linen closet. The one about the frozen grout. The one about the small pet cemetery in the backyard. The one about the ghost because why else would the plumbing materials mysteriously relocate themselves every night?

"You live around here, right?" Sam asked, gesturing toward me and—finally—keeping his eyes above my chest. "Matt said you're in an awesome building. Good light?"

"Yeah, just over on Chestnut and River. I have really big windows, and these cool ones in the bathroom with little, um—"

"Muntins," Matthew supplied. His hand was on my upper thigh, and it had been there since he finished eating. I figured he was six seconds away from licking my neck and peeing a circle around me, and if that weren't tragically gross, it would be endearing. "A diagonal diamond casing, just like the ones we saw in the West End last week, Patrick."

"Those were old." Patrick considered this, nodding and

staring into his glass. He was a chatty drinker, and I liked it. Much of that cool exterior warmed with the alcohol. "Have you been there long?"

"And can we buy the building because I really want some garden-side restoration action," Sam added.

"Can we let the cash sit in the bank for twenty minutes, Samuel? God help me," Shannon muttered.

"I've been there about three years, and I don't know whether it's for sale, but I will be moving in a few months. The guy I sublet from is finishing a tour in Afghanistan soon."

I felt it again, Matthew's gaze on me, weighty and potent. As he watched me, I sensed pieces of me shifting and realigning, my muscles and bones and organs making space inside me to accommodate the immense pressure of his stare.

Sipping my wine, I cut my eyes in his direction, trying to translate the unspoken currents between us.

"When?" he asked. It came out as a whisper, hoarse and pleading, and now I sensed four more pairs of eyes on me.

On *us*.

"In the new year. January or February, but knowing the military, maybe later."

"And what are you looking for?" Nodding, he added, "I know what you need and I think I know what you want, but I'd like to hear you say it."

Discussing my apartment search with Matthew's entire family seemed strange, especially tonight, but I knew they loved talking real estate, and he was responsible for finding my other home: Trench Mills.

"I'd love to stay in this area, and size doesn't matter to me—"

"It should," Sam snickered, though he was summarily ignored.

"—and I'd love a bigger kitchen, something open and maybe an island. Lots of windows and natural light. Definitely a tub. I can't live without one." I shrugged. "But that's it. I can be flexible, and I'm not too picky."

"I'll see what I can do," he murmured.

Shannon launched into an analysis of every neighborhood in town, and she forwarded me listings from her phone while Matthew sat beside me, his hand on my thigh and his eyes never wavering.

Maybe that odd sensation was just me making space for *him*.

Twenty-Two

MATTHEW

Matthew: I'm in bunker hill for a few hours and then heading out around 7
Matthew: want to grab dinner?
Matthew: I can get take-out?

THIS WAS the game we played, the battle of wills we fought every day. Lauren was busy being busy and just once, I wanted her to come to me, and I wanted her to stay with me. We were closer after New Orleans, and slipping further into messy, complicated intimacy with each passing day. But for every obstacle we bested, two more stood in our path.

I stared at my phone, knowing it was fully charged and the reception in this part of town was impeccable, and flicked a glance at my watch. *Twenty-five minutes.* Sometimes I thought she read my texts but waited, letting some indiscernible amount of time pass before responding.

I told myself I could live with it, I could handle the need for distance that I knew she saw as self-preservation, but I was greedy and I wanted all of her. Especially today. After another run-in with my favorite inspector and Angus's most recent renditions of batshit crazy, I wanted an easy night with Lauren. But nothing was as easy as I wanted it, and Angus was making a lot of appearances these days. None of them pleasant.

He threw a crystal paperweight at Shannon three weeks ago, narrowly missing her and bringing down the glass wall separating her office from the interior workspaces. He didn't give a reason, and more than likely didn't have one.

There was surprise visit from state auditors the next week. They were following up on a tip about undocumented workers, and needed to see five years' worth of filings.

News of the lucrative brownstone sales finally made it his way, a month after the fact, and Angus showed up at the bank last week, requesting twenty grand in cash from our business account. He had his own account from back in the day, but bitched out a bank manager for access to our funds. He didn't get it, thankfully, but Shannon spent the following day smoothing things over with the bank.

We got word from a small-run community newspaper that the original Wellesley headquarters for Walsh Associates cleared escrow this week. They wanted us to comment on centralizing our operations at the Beacon Hill office, and Shannon managed a decent sound bite despite being blindsided by the news.

These were uncommonly public shows of the division within our family. He cared enough about his reputation and the firm's prominence to keep his assholery at home and under the radar, but between the bank and the office sale, things were taking a markedly external turn.

We later convened in her office, the five of us staring at each other, shrugging and shaking our heads in response to this turn of events. There were plenty of theories about why he sold the office and what he did with the cash and why his stunts were occurring with such frequency, but we attributed it to a new level of bastardhood and went back to work.

I wish I could say this wasn't typical Angus. I wish I could say his antics were the product of hitting the bottle too hard by all standards, but this was who he decided to be after my mother died: a violently angry man who seized every opportunity to share his rage.

Angus didn't break windows when we were younger, but in some ways he was worse then. One day while we were at school, not even six months after she died, he destroyed everything with any glimmer of my mother attached to it—pictures, clothes, even the little blankets she knit for Erin's crib. In his fucked-up, diluted world, we were to blame for her death, and though I hated hearing those words now, it didn't compare to the way they sounded when I was eight.

Another glance at my phone told me Lauren hadn't responded, and though I wanted to throw it across the fucking room, I tapped out a message. I was strung too tightly to play the game today.

Matthew: we've spent every one of the past 33 nights together. let's stop pretending I won't see you tonight. my place.

STANDING BETWEEN PATRICK AND SAM, I watched as Riley described his plan for the third of the four Bunker Hill restorations. His technical vocabulary wasn't precise and even his most detailed ideas sounded vague, but he was making progress and I needed my brothers to recognize that. Riley worked unbelievably hard at giving everyone the impression he didn't care, but I knew he did, and I knew he needed this walk-through to go well.

And thankfully, his fly was zipped.

"So we're moving this staircase," Riley said.

Sam paged through the designs and studied the exterior elevations. "Any thoughts on rain catchment? Have you considered a roof garden?"

"Would you shut up with the roof gardens? No. End of discussion," Patrick said.

Sam muttered something about Patrick needing mood-altering drugs and inspected the exposed studs and duct-work. "Can someone walk me through the insulation plan? I have less drafty tents than this structure, and this wall?" He pointed over his shoulder. "This wall is from the fifties or sixties. It's fucking criminal that we're not upgrading this. There's nothing special about it, and it's flimsy as fuck."

Riley flipped back several pages of design plans spread over a makeshift sawhorse desk and said, "This is what I'm thinking—"

"No one gives a shit what you're thinking, turnip. Don't waste my time with your stupid bullshit," Angus roared from the doorway. He stormed to the desk and slammed a two-by-four against the plans, missing Riley's fingers by an inch.

Patrick and I groaned in harmony, and I met his eyes

with an exasperated headshake, my arms crossing over my chest as I assessed Angus. His formal wool coat and old-fashioned hat were out of place at the Bunker Hill construction site, and he looked small, bloated, and hunched. His silver hair poked out from his hat, disheveled, and his face red. He looked every one of his sixty-eight years, and if I had to guess, I'd say he spent the morning reminiscing with his old friend Johnnie Walker.

"This needs to stop," Patrick murmured.

No amount of new office space or glossy magazine spreads was changing Angus, or his sick fixation with fucking us over. Whether it was replacing windows or him stirring up trouble at job sites, we couldn't run a business like this much longer. Hell, I couldn't protect Lauren from it much longer.

Angus advanced on Sam. "What the fuck do you think you're doing here? You're not involved in this project, princess. I saw to it myself that you stayed as far away from this as possible."

I saw him for what he was—an abuser hungry for a fight—and unless we left right now, we weren't walking out of this house unscathed. I gestured to Patrick, and caught Riley by the elbow, but Sam was already in it.

"I know it's difficult for you to understand, Angus, but we work together on most builds."

"That's what they tell you?" Angus swung a glance at me and Patrick. "That's because they don't want to hurt your little feelings. They know you're selling snake oil. They know sustainability is for hippie queers who think slapping some solar panels on a roof makes you an architect."

We did not have time for this today. I stepped forward. "Angus—"

"Don't fuckin' Angus me. Not in the mood for your shit today, boy," he yelled, the lumber wagging in his hand. "You know he's an impostor. Tell the princess how you and Patrick have final say over his designs. Tell him how the contractors go to you with their problems because they know the princess can't answer them. Tell him that all he does is pick out fancy window dressings while everyone else covers for him."

Regardless of whether I handled all of Sam's structural analysis, I wasn't selling him out to Angus.

"No, he's not, and you have to—"

"Matt comes to your rescue now, princess? Always did need someone to rescue you. That whore never wanted you, but she spoiled you, turned you into one ripe mama's boy, and then your cunty sister picked up where the whore left off. Is that what did it? All those women, they turned you into this."

Angus waved the two-by-four at Sam's slim navy suit and sneered at his pink plaid Oxford, paisley tie, and pocket square.

"Or is it because you look like a little girl? And you dress up in faggoty colors because you like pretending you're a girl? Does your boyfriend like this? I bet he likes hearing all about the window dressings and solar panels, too."

"While this soliloquy is truly impressive, I don't see a point in listening much longer. Your information is inaccurate, and I've told you a hundred times, I'm not gay, and claiming I am is not an insult."

Angus stalked Sam. With every step he pushed one end

of the two-by-four into Sam's chest until he hit a wall. Even hunched, Angus was still a bit bigger than Sam and the look in his eyes was pure hatred. Sam was in decent shape but he struggled with more medical issues than I could count—childhood diabetes, asthma, anxiety attacks, digestion problems—and I wasn't watching while Angus exacerbated any of it.

"You've never been good enough for my name, and you never will be. You're a liar, and an abomination, and hell's too kind for filth like you. You never should have been born. All these problems," Angus gripped Sam's wrist and twisted his medical alert bracelets, "were God's way of trying to erase his mistake."

Dropping Riley's elbow, I advanced on Angus. I grabbed the lumber, but he was stronger than I expected, and it smashed into my jaw. I staggered backward and heat rushed to my skin, the coppery flavor of blood spraying over my tongue.

"Who the fuck do you think you are? You, Mr. Massachusetts Institute of Technology, Mr. Big Shot Engineer. You're a fuckin' joke, just as bad as that faggotty-ass princess. You don't know the first thing about art or preserving history. You just know steel and concrete."

I cocked my head and rolled my eyes, ignoring the pain radiating from my jaw. I reminded myself to stay detached, and ignore the bait Angus dangled. "As always, it's great to see you too, but we have other properties to check today."

Gesturing to Sam and Riley, I stuffed the plans back in their canister and we moved toward the door where I could only hope to find some ice and plenty of beer.

"I hear you got yourself a girl. A pretty little blonde thing. Better watch yourself," he warned. "They're all whores. They lie and they cheat and they spread their legs the second you turn your back. Maybe I'll introduce myself to her."

The canister slipped from my fingers, bouncing against the plywood floor as I crossed the room in three strides and yanked Angus up by his lapels. Bile teased the back of my throat, and panic warred with rage in my veins.

"Don't you dare say a word about her. You don't know what the fuck you're talking about," I whispered, my words icy and quiet.

A disgusted scowl pulled at Angus's lips. "You gonna hit me? You beat up senior citizens?"

Narrowing my eyes at Angus, I crossed my arms over my chest and leaned back. "You aren't worth the energy." Glancing up and down at my father, I searched for a reason why my mother would have wanted anything to do with the sniveling, derisive man in front of me. She was recently immigrated to this country when they married, and only nineteen, sixteen years younger than my father. I wanted to believe she saw something good in him. "What would Mom say if she could see you today?"

"This is over," Patrick hissed. He pointed at Angus. "You're drunk, and one more bullshit stunt from you and I'm putting you in a seventy-two-hour psych hold."

"You and that cunt of a sister of yours, you think you're so fucking smart. You'd be nothing without me. This business, everything, you owe it to me."

Angus clasped the front of his coat together and picked up the two-by-four. He sidestepped me, and I let him go. He stopped at the door, his back to us. He sighed, and his shoulders slumped, his head hanging forward. For a split second, I thought my father heard me—truly *heard* me after all these years. Then he pivoted and speared me with his cold, empty eyes. "She'd say that's what you get for being the rotten pieces of garbage who let her die."

The door slammed behind him.

Rationally, I knew Angus was a vindictive, angry drunk who needlessly blamed us for Mom's death, and he was hell-bent on getting his pounds of flesh from each of us.

Emotionally, I couldn't claim the same level of objectivity. It was all too easy to drown in Angus's loathing, and I knew Sam already spent the better parts of most evenings doing some version of that. I found myself struggling to tread water, and as I looked around the room, I knew I wasn't alone.

For a few minutes, we were silent. I saw Patrick's fingers flying over his phone, and I knew he was either updating Shannon or calling his buddy at the State Police to make good on that psych hold. Riley's hands dug deep in his pockets, and he kept his eyes trained on the ground. Rubbing a hand against his chest, Sam stared out the window.

"All right," Patrick muttered as he gestured toward me. "Broken or bruised?"

"Bruised."

Patrick glanced around the room, confused. "Who drove?"

"I did," Sam whispered. "We are not going back to the office tonight."

"I have beer," Patrick offered. "And whiskey." He glanced at my face. "And ice."

Considering we grew up under the same roof and then lived together at Cornell and now we worked together all goddamn week, I didn't make a habit of spending time at

Patrick's apartment, but I went along anyway. True to form, he put Riley to work stowing his outdoor furniture in preparation for the snowstorms expected in the coming weeks while I rinsed the blood out of my mouth.

I found Riley flipping through the stack of industry journals and magazines on Patrick's kitchen table. "Do you actually read all of this?"

Patrick locked his fingers around four beer bottles and shook his head. "Asking that tells me you don't."

I didn't know how they could nag each other right now.

"Can someone tell me what we're going to do about this?" I snapped. "This is fucking insane. *He* is fucking insane. How am I supposed to have a life when he's whacking people with two-by-fours and throwing paperweights and trying to hijack the business accounts and threatening to go find my fucking girlfriend?"

Patrick busied himself with the bottle opener, and I waited, hoping he'd have the answer. He always had the answer.

"That's just it, Matt," Sam said. "You don't. We just need him to hurry up and die."

LAUREN DIDN'T RESPOND to my text, and after rereading it forty-one times while holding a bag of frozen peas to my face and mainlining whiskey, I remembered she hated being told what to do. This was her method of teaching me a lesson about my caveman tendencies.

So I went to her. The walk from Patrick's place in the North End to her Beacon Hill apartment burned off most of the alcohol but it did nothing for the waves of anger and frustration in my system.

"Miss Halsted," I said when she opened the door. She was wearing the clingy yoga pants that did terrible things to my imagination and that little UCSD t-shirt that stretched across her chest in the best possible way, and I forgot most of my argument.

"Mr. Walsh, you should know you're only allowed to tell me what to do when I'm naked," she said, her eyebrow arched. The stern expression stayed in place just long enough for her to notice the contusion. "Oh my God, what happened to you?"

Her fingers passed over my jaw, and she frowned at the bruise. Flinching, I pushed her hands away and stepped back, trying to locate my anger.

"It's nothing, I don't want to talk about it." She peered at me, incredulous, and I knew if she showed up at my door with a big-ass bruise on her face, I'd freak the fuck out too. Of course, that would require her showing up at my door of her own accord, and that seemed rather unlikely. "You didn't return my text."

"I wish you'd tell me what happened." I shook my head, and she muttered something about cavemen. "If you wanted to see me, you could have asked, Matthew."

I reached out, stroking my finger down her cheek, over her lips, and we stared at each other. It was clear I was on the prowl, but I didn't think either of us knew what I wanted.

Her face in my hands, I kissed her, my tongue moving between her teeth, begging her for all the things she held back. I didn't care how much my jaw hurt; I just wanted to feel her, to own her tonight. She wrapped her hands around my coat, pulled me inside, and slammed the door. My hands were under her clothes within a heartbeat, and her skin, her sighs, her scent—they were the balm I required to feel whole again.

"I love that you're naked under this," I murmured against her mouth.

"If that's what you like, I'll stop buying fancy panties," she whispered. She unfastened my belt, drew my zipper down, and pressed her palm over my cock, and if she asked me right then whether I liked her daily game of Make Matt Beg, I would have said yes. It was so simple, her hand on my body, but it leveled me every time.

"Don't...don't do that," I said. "Fancy panties are nice, too."

No need to mention I considered arriving at her door with a pair in my hand. This probably wasn't the time to discuss the pussy necklace in my pocket either. I didn't leave the house without it.

Clothes landed in piles around us, and I pulled her to the velvet sofa, settling her on my lap. She was damp and ready, and I couldn't keep my mouth away from her nipples and I wanted her like this—always. I wanted this place we created where she stopped caring about everything else, where the only thing that mattered was how we fit together, where we could get lost in each other. This was what I wanted.

Burying my face in her hair, I murmured filthy words about her ass, her tits, her pussy, about wanting my fuck toy, my dirty little slut. And the tension riding my nerves subsided as I breathed her in.

She responded, I knew she did, but I couldn't hear it, couldn't interpret anything she said. I knew only the rhythm of her body, her skin against mine. Her nails scratched along my scalp and shoulders, and I was there, pressing into her, and I couldn't think past the frenzied hunger in my head. I filled her with one thrust, groaning her name as I bottomed out.

I closed my eyes, focusing on Lauren's musical sighs and reminding myself to be gentle. My hands clamped on her hips, my fingers digging grooves into her skin, and we crashed into each other. Her mouth mapped my chest and arms and jaw, and I wanted more than the warm, wet sensations she left behind. Bites and scratches weren't enough; I wanted her fingerprints tattooed on my skin. I wanted something that would be there tomorrow.

"Tell me what you want," I panted.

"What you're doing. That. More. Harder."

Grasping Lauren's free hand, I placed it between us. "Touch yourself."

I watched as her fingers skittered over her clit. I felt the difference immediately, her tissues turning molten, her skin flushing, and her breaths coming rapidly.

Nothing separated us but it wasn't enough for me. I needed more, a type of *more* I didn't believe I'd be able to quantify, and I lifted Lauren's hand to my mouth. I gazed into her emerald eyes, searching for the flecks of gold while I sucked her arousal from her fingers.

"Tell me what you want," I whispered.

"I want you to come on my—"

"No," I said. "No. Tell me what you *want*."

She dropped her head to my shoulder, evading, rocking faster and faster until the pulses of her orgasm rolled over my shaft, her walls clamped around me, and she cried out against my neck. I lived for the soft whimpers and moans that heralded her orgasms, and I wanted them to exist in a secret place that only I knew.

"Tell me," I repeated, and it sounded all wrong—demanding, yet desperate.

"I don't know," she said. "I just want you."

Pumping into her, my orgasm barreled down my spine, snapping my corded muscles and wiping every thought from my mind but one: Lauren. I spoke mindless obscenities into her lips and neck and hair, stopping just before I revealed everything else I wanted.

Lauren lifted her head, and before her lips brushed over my battered jaw, her eyes flashed to mine, anxious and confused and so fucking beautiful. She was all sweet kisses and tiny purring whimpers, and as I sensed myself hardening again, I led her to the bedroom and buried myself in her until we fell asleep.

I woke up around four-thirty, and I stared at her in the blue morning darkness, seeing everything she wouldn't say. She slept with her head on my chest, her legs twisted between mine, and her hand over my heart, and I wanted it to be enough.

I knew it wasn't.

Twenty-Three
LAUREN

"YOU THINK I could pull off this look?" Shannon's elbow grazed my arm, and she handed off the magazine featuring an assortment of long skirts. "I can rock pencil skirts every day of the week, but those are tough for me." She gestured to her frame. "This height doesn't work with everything."

Too lost in my own thoughts and pedicure-induced bliss to think critically about her question, I nodded and handed the magazine back. "Yeah, definitely try."

"Are you crazy? Those skirts are the exclusive domain of nuns and peasants," Sam snapped. He tore the magazine from Shannon's hands and sent me an irritable glare. "And if there's one thing you're not, Shan, it's a nun."

"What about weekends?" she asked. "I could wear one of those jersey skirts to brunch or the market, or," she gestured to the nail salon, "out for a Saturday afternoon pedi."

Sam shifted in his massage chair and rolled his eyes. "Who do you think you are? Stevie Nicks? Stop it with the long skirts, short girl."

They continued arguing about skirts while I paged through a dated copy of *Real Simple*.

Our regular pedicure program usually focused on the important stuff: Shannon's disasters in dating, new fashion trends never intended for petite women, and whether high heels were actually screwing up our feet. We'd touch on the friends of our twenties who were flocking toward marriage, babies, and suburbia, and our refusal to live beyond the reach of the T subway lines, and the infrequency with which we truly unplugged from our hectic careers.

Shannon and I were built alike. We shared a bone-deep dedication to our work, the belief we'd each be unstoppable if we put in enough hours, and the fuzzy faith that we'd be able to postpone our lives—that was, the actual living portions—for a few more years.

Sam joined us occasionally, and when he wasn't busy crafting that manwhore façade, he was comical and fascinatingly neurotic, and on his way to becoming one of my new best friends.

Shannon considered the skirts again and snapped a photo of the page with her phone. "It's not like I have time for shopping anyway," she mumbled.

"You're not too busy," Sam said. "No one is ever too busy for anything. It's a matter of priorities."

The world through his eyes was linear and ordered, and everything fit into proper, square compartments. It was only a matter of moving those little boxes around and making it all fit. He worked long hours but when he left the office, the office left him. Calls went to voicemail, emails waited until the next morning. It was that easy for Sam.

There was even a tidy compartment for women. He wasn't especially forthcoming with details, but it was clear he subscribed to the 'you sucking my dick in a bathroom stall doesn't require me to learn your name' dogma. Seeing him here, his jeans rolled up to his knees, an oatmeal skin treatment painted on his calves, and a heated argument about skirts underway, I couldn't imagine the same man as a cavalier player.

He went out most nights, hitting all the see-and-be-seen spots. He received invites to the swankiest events and sipped whiskey from the comfort of VIP lounges, and his name appeared in Boston's gossip and society pages along-side socialites and local celebrities. And yet I knew he was more insecure than most tween girls.

Shannon turned toward me with a grin. "I'm reprioritiz-ing. Want to go shopping? No, better idea: let's shop and then hit Bin 26 for wine. I've been lusting over a new white blend."

"I am not interested in any of that," he muttered.

I tugged my scarf over my chest at the memory of Matthew's teeth on my breasts early this morning, his voice hoarse after hours of growling when he said, "Nick and I are biking to the Vermont border and back, and I want to see you tonight. I want you in this bed, all naked and fuck-able, all night. Tell me you'll be right here when I get home."

I glanced up at Shannon. "Maybe for a bit. I have some work to do, and I have plans with Matthew."

Of course I agreed to his demands. Growly, bitey Matthew was irresistible, and despite my attempts at moderation, at taking care of me, at focusing on work, we always ended up together, night after night.

"Why do you call him that?" Sam asked. "Matthew. We only call him that when he's in trouble."

"Well..." I started, rewinding to those first moments we

shared. I'd always called him Matthew. I didn't think much about the structure and definition of us, but calling him Matthew was part of our foundation. It went hand-in-hand with my obscene requests and his cavemanning, and it wasn't something we could explain to anyone else. "I like it, and so does he."

Sam shrugged, considering my response for a moment, and then returned to the latest edition of *Dwell*.

Things were changing, that I knew. The days were shorter, air crisper, trees barer, but it wasn't only the slide of autumn into winter. There was something inside me— something elemental—and it was shifting at a pace I couldn't comprehend. At first I thought it was immediate, and quite possibly attributable to hiring Drew the Dean and off-loading a chunk of my overdue action items to him. I then realized it was most likely a gradual change, quiet yet invasive, like vines crawling around the slats of a fence, twisting and knotting and spreading until the two were indistinguishable, inseparable, indivisible.

I didn't know whether I was the vine or the fence.

In the hushed moments when his head was nestled between my breasts or on my belly or just a breath from my center, we revealed softly spoken truths about everything before *us*. He seemed glee-filled to know I could count my lovers on one hand, not including the thumb or pinkie. It was his brand of cavemanish pride, something tangled up with possession and purity, and I accepted it without further analysis. He nudged me for some explanation of why my number was so low, but I offered few details and he didn't push further.

I harbored a spoonful of silly triumph after discovering Matthew's past relationships were cut from the friends-with-benefits cloth. When I pried, he mentioned never liking anyone enough to want more than basic fucking. He also referenced how, ahem, *vocal* I was in the bedroom, saying, "The minute I saw you, I thought 'naughty school-teacher.' Turns out, I really dig the naughty part."

We called it casual, we told our friends and families it was casual, we carried on with our lives as if it was casual, but it was powerful—*magnetic*—and the language necessary to describe what was happening to us hadn't been invented yet.

And I wanted Matthew. I wanted to claim the notches and grooves around his collarbones and throat as my private hideaway, and I wanted the growls, bites, and sweat, and the tender heart he so diligently worked at hiding. But as much as I wanted to tell him everything, those words didn't flow like my obscene demands. The only adequate method of communication was rough, profane sex, and I had to believe he knew what I was thinking and feeling.

WE HUDDLED against the bone-chilling wind, too cold to talk, hurrying through the narrow Boston streets, our shopping bags slapping against our legs, until we arrived at the wine bar. We settled into a narrow table looking out onto Boston Common, and a waiter delivered menus and a small bowl of olives.

"There's a bottle I really want to try. Is that okay with you?" Shannon asked.

"I do not discriminate. You know what I like, and you know the wine in my glass is my favorite kind."

Shannon ordered an Australian white blend, and it wasn't long before it was empty and we were sampling something new.

"So I invited Matt's friend Nick to dinner next week," Shannon said. "Those eyes. Swoons. I'd like to bite his ass. At least lick it."

I wanted to ask why the Walshes were such biters, but exploring that path with Shannon seemed unwise. My brothers' sex lives were not one of my preferred discussion topics, and I had to believe Shannon shared that position. "Does he know that?"

"I've been forthcoming with those interests. He's less excited about the ass biting than I am."

"You're sure I can't bring anything?"

I was looking forward to Thanksgiving at Shannon's next week. It was a new chapter for me, and I liked hanging out with the Walshes. I doubted I'd encounter any vegan green bean casseroles with this crew, but I was excited about the butternut squash pie. A strange new sentimental part of me recognized this as my first coupled holiday, and that knowledge filled me with a twinge of giddy anxiety.

This wasn't how I expected things to happen for me, but I kept reminding myself to embrace the controlled chaos. It wasn't the polite series of dates leading to precise relationship milestones, and that left my rule-following good girl rather twitchy.

My holiday enthusiasm didn't transfer to drinks with Elsie and Kent. Her cheerful email last week reminded me that I promised an appearance at her champagne luncheon, and Steph and Amanda insisted via group text that a pop-in wouldn't kill me.

It took them two days to respond to my original text

("would it be wrong for me to tell her I have malaria and skip?"), and in those two days, I devised several ways to break the news of my malaria to Elsie. They didn't respond to my follow-up ("would it be wrong to send fancy champagne and skip? seems like a win for all...?"), and I found that more unpleasant the prospect of brunch with Elsie.

Rather than waiting for approval from my friends, I sent champagne and a quick note omitting all mention of malaria. With my karmic luck, she'd organize a mosquito net benefit event in my honor, and then I'd be screwed. Yeah, it would be a win for malaria prevention, but I couldn't handle that much time in Elsie's company.

I expected geography would alter my relationships with Steph and Amanda, but I was stunned how quickly our old patterns faded. Where we once maintained a religious adherence to group texts on Monday mornings, we rarely shared inspiring memes, amusing weekend stories, or photos of heinously-expensive-yet-necessary-for-survival shoes anymore. Most weeks, it was like talking to an empty room, usually waiting hours and sometimes days for a standard "omg we have to talk soon! heart you" response.

Steph was pregnant, and surprised didn't begin to capture my reaction. I couldn't imagine her going through that again—the bed rest, the c-section, the post-partum anxiety—and I had only watched from the sidelines when she was pregnant with Madison. But she and Dan wanted a big family, and they wanted their kids close in age, and this time around she didn't even mention they had been trying until after she missed her period.

Amanda had been promoted to managing partner at her finance firm, and was busy interviewing candidates for the squadron of nannies and housekeepers she would need when the baby arrived this spring. She wanted my opinions on gender neutral toys and intentionally diverse story-books, and when she realized I knew plenty about school-children but nothing about babies, she announced she needed a nursery consultant, and advised me to start plan-ning the birth of my yet-to-be-conceived child while I had the time.

Their lives were different now, I understood that, but things with Matthew were too intricate to manage alone. And after nearly ten years of sharing most major decisions in my life with Steph and Amanda, they weren't available when I needed them. Realizing the relationships that served us through college and our twenties were dwindling away hurt. I knew we'd always have memories of Williams College and The Dungeon, but it was another form of chaos I wasn't prepared to navigate.

None of my other friends knew enough about my inner workings—my hot mess, my control freak, my crazy Commodore Halsted stories, my good girl, my rebel with good causes—to serve as proper sounding boards, and I didn't want to start from scratch with them.

My mother offered some well-intentioned advice about following my heart, but bringing her in required intensive editing because Mom and I did *not* talk about sexytimes. In the end, my mother realized what I was doing, and her all-knowing chuckle gave it away.

"All right, Lolo," she laughed. "I don't need the whole story. But you have a lot of love to give, and you should let yourself give it."

When I stepped back to think about my relationship with Matthew, every turning point was inextricably linked to those sexytimes. We communicated through dirty talk and touch and need, and every time I tried to convince myself that was crazy, I realized it was also perfectly right. Everything I needed to know and everything I needed to say were offered between the sheets—and against walls, in showers, and on the desk in his office—and nothing more was necessary. Not now, not yet.

Shannon and I were tight, and though we often talked about everything and nothing, she was altogether too close to this situation. We weren't talking about biting and we weren't talking about whether I was falling for her brother.

I was on my own with this one, fumbling around in the dark.

"Don't worry about Thanksgiving, Lauren. I order the meal from an organic farm, cooked and everything, and my assistant, Tom, will drive out to Boxboro to pick it all up on Wednesday. Less of a salmonella risk that way." Shannon rolled her eyes. "Besides, it's not like the boys ever bring anything."

"Exactly. So what I can do? Wine? Flowers?"

She leveled a serious gaze at me. "This is not a classy event, Lauren. The Walsh children do not do classy. My brothers are well-educated, well-dressed brutes, and don't let anyone tell you otherwise. I'll be happy if the cranberry sauce stays out of the rugs. Did Matt ever tell you how this all started? The 'let's raid Shan's place on Thanksgiving' tradition?"

I refilled our glasses and shook my head.

Shannon dropped her gaze. "We basically stopped doing holidays when my mother died. Sometimes my father's sisters would have us over, but not always, and my father turned it into a shit show. He does that a lot."

Where Matthew never mentioned his father, Shannon

and Sam often talked around the issues with him, and his tenuous role in the business, and I knew things were getting worse. The bruise on Matthew's face was the work of his father, though the exact turn of events was still unclear. Matthew wouldn't discuss it, and Sam struggled to talk about the most recent incident without lapsing into incoherent swearing rampages. It all made the Commodore's quirks that much more tolerable.

"Thanksgiving at my place started the year Patrick finished college. The rest of the tribe was either still in school or at home with my father." She paused to sample the olives, and turned back to me. "Erin had a huge fight with my father and the situation was shambles—which is how she leaves most things—so she was staying with me. Somehow everyone else ended up camping in my five hundred square foot apartment. Patrick and his stiff upper lip convinced me that we needed a family holiday. Just once I'd like to see these events in his pristine apartment."

I nibbled an olive, waiting for Shannon to continue. I couldn't imagine a childhood without holiday celebrations and the traditional trappings of family. Mine might be scattered and engaged in our own pursuits now, but my best memories and everything I knew about family came from holidays and trips.

"Riley convinced me to cook, and there are more exaggerated stories about me giving everyone food poisoning that year than I care to recount. But it was the first time we actually had Thanksgiving together since my mom died. And aside from everyone puking all over my apartment, it was nice."

I covered my face with my hands and leaned away from the table, trying and failing to conceal my laughter. "That's a terrible story, Shannon! 'Aside from the puking it was nice'? Oh my friend, what are we going to do with you?"

She smiled and glanced around the wine bar. "We've done it every year since, but with far less food poisoning."

"We need to stop talking about this." No wonder this girl was starting to prefer Soul Cycle to connecting with the opposite sex. Ball-busting was her national pastime, and she couldn't find a polite topic of conversation with two hands and a flashlight. "New topic: getting Shannon some action. Last week you were meeting Charlie for coffee. How'd that turn out?"

"Oh my God," Shannon groaned.

"That bad?"

The number of men who could go up against Shannon and hold their own was woefully limited—Matthew could probably construct an equation and give us an exact number—and it was no surprise her online dating endeavors met with little success. She required an unshakable alpha male who could handle every ounce of her alpha girl without expecting her to yield in the least.

"He had this white phlegmy thing on his lips. I spent the entire time staring at his mouth, silently willing him to wipe it off. I even started wiping my own mouth excessively as a hint. Nothing." She groaned. "And he lacked the most basic social skills, in addition to zero awareness of white phlegmy stuff."

"How'd you leave it?"

"Eh, you know. 'Maybe we'll grab coffee or a drink after the holidays.'" Shannon rolled her eyes. "Remind me to stop seeing club guys outside of clubs. They're like trolls: they need to stay under their bridges."

From: Erin Walsh
To: Matthew Walsh
Date: November 16 at 01:51 CEST
Subject: RE: answer your phone

M –
Sorry, kid. I've been way off the grid. I'm in Germany, btw, right on the border of the Czech Republic and working in the Vogtland region. I think this might be the place where Hansel and Gretel went missing. A couple nights ago, some of us followed a path through the woods and ended up in the CR, and after the weird shit we saw, I can easily write scary children's stories now. Photos attached.

The thermal springs around the Kammerbühl volcano are wild, but I speak no Deutsche and some of the people in this village think I'm a witch. It's like, cool, whatever, but stop throwing holy water at me, you know?

I'm headed back to Spain soon, and we can talk then. Any
urgent/Matt's-on-the-ledge-again issues?
- e

From: Matthew Walsh
To: Erin Walsh
Date: November 16 at 09:12 EDT
Subject: RE: answer your phone

E –
Whenever I think my life is complex, I get an email from
you about sneaking into foreign countries and holy water. It
reminds me that I need to put aside bail money for when
you get arrested.

And no, I'm not on the ledge. Things are good. Let me
know when you're back in Spain.

M

From: Erin Walsh
To: Matthew Walsh
Date: November 16 at 23:09 CEST
Subject: vague much?

M –
Not trying to get all psychiatric on your ass, but I'm pretty

sure saying "things are good" is your way of telling me
things aren't exactly good.

- e

From: Matthew Walsh
To: Erin Walsh
Date: November 17 at 06:41 EDT
Subject: things ARE good

E –

The sun isn't up yet and I've been in my office for almost an
hour.

I'm registered for a triathlon this weekend and I haven't
swam for more than ten minutes since Labor Day.

Patrick fired another assistant. The current total for the year
is now four fired assistants, and we're placing bets on
whether he makes it to a clean five.

Sam wants to add roof gardens to every single project that
comes through the door, and he doesn't actually know
enough about landscaping or horticulture or anything that
might qualify him to put gardens on top of roofs, but no
one wants to tell him that.

Riley still can't zip his pants and I had to explain to him
why we ALWAYS double check that we've turned off the
main water line before doing any demo. And yes, I had to
explain it while standing in two feet of water.

But yeah, things are good. Where are you?
M

From: Erin Walsh
To: Matthew Walsh
Date: November 18 at 11:29 CEST
Subject: RE: things ARE good

M –
I notice you didn't mention a word about chica. Is that done?
- e

From: Matthew Walsh
To: Erin Walsh
Date: November 18 at 19:31 EDT
Subject: RE: things ARE good

E –
Things with Lauren are good. Different. Complex. But good.

Where are you?
M

From: Erin Walsh

To: Matthew Walsh
Date: November 19 at 01:09 CEST
Subject: Italy

M –

I'm in Naples. Spending time in the lab and then rubbing Vesuvius's belly for a bit. No travel on my calendar for a week or two, not unless someone wants to sneak into the CR with me again. And I'm totally game for that.

Expand on "different but good." Let it out, kid. Just let it out.

- e

From: Matthew Walsh
To: Erin Walsh
Date: November 19 at 22:17 EDT
Subject: RE: Italy

E –

Come home for Thanksgiving or Christmas or whatever. You can stay at my place and you don't have to see Shannon. Let me know when you want to come, and I'll order a ticket for you, but I can't talk about this shit over email anymore. Meet her and you'll get it. You'll love her. Come home. Even for a few days.

M

From: Erin Walsh
To: Matthew Walsh
Date: November 20 at 20:02 CEST
Subject: RE: Italy

M –
Will I love her as much as you do?
- e

From: Matthew Walsh
To: Erin Walsh
Date: November 21 at 05:49 EDT
Subject: RE: Italy

I hope so.

Twenty-Five

WITH ONLY NINE months until the doors of my school opened, I was rounding the curve and finally seeing the end of this marathon. As the first day neared, my confidence grew. I understood the role I'd fill when it was time for teaching and learning, and I loved everything about it. I needed kids and classrooms, and the craziness of running the building was nothing compared to chasing down vendors, board members, state officials, and researchers. The preparation, the non-kid, non-classroom stuff I could do without.

Lifting my head from my hands, I groaned at the forty-four emails suddenly clogging my inbox, and that groan stretched into a full-blown whine when my phone started vibrating with an incoming call. My number one draft pick teacher declined my offer earlier in the day, and as if the phone were to blame for that turn of events, I wasn't taking any calls until this day perked up.

The call went to voicemail, but another quickly followed. Peeking an eye open, I saw my father's picture flashing across the screen. Two options sat before me: answer, or expect a member of the armed forces to come find me.

I really did not want a SEAL fast-roping down the exterior of my building right now.

"Hi, Dad."

"There's my girl!" he boomed.

"So where are you today?" I was several weeks behind in my travel blog readings.

"Outside Rosarito, but that's not the purpose of this call," he said. "I heard from one of my sailors last week, Paraza. He's in private contracting now, and doing well for himself. He asked about you, and I updated him on the progress of your endeavor, and he wants to provide funding for your operation. He'll have someone in his office call you to establish the agreement."

"Wow, Dad, that's wonderful. I don't know what to say."

"Nothing to say. Teach those kids, put them on the right path; that's all you can do," he said. "Is the work going well? You're staying focused on the targets?"

I laughed. "Yeah, as much as possible. Some of these days are challenging, though, and it's hard—"

"Only easy day was yesterday, Lolo. Remember that."

"I know, and I do. That doesn't mean it's any less frustrating when I spend three months cultivating a candidate and she backs out at the last minute."

"Give in, give up, or—"

"—give it all I've got, I know. I know, Dad. I don't need that reminder."

And I didn't. I repeated that mantra until it pounded through my body, beating in time with my heart. It kept me centered when the work was exhausting and aggravating, and detached from everything I loved about schools. It kept me going when I debated how many more brick walls I could safely demolish with sweet talk and pastries. It kept me driven when I wanted to spend my mornings wrapped in Matthew's arms, avoiding the world beyond his touch.

Dad didn't deserve my sharp tone or my impatience, but a small part of me wanted to wallow in defeated misery for a moment, and he wasn't having it.

"Make it through the mission, Lolo. It's a long one, but you knew that going in. You knew the stakes, and you knew the score. Get your head in the game, and don't let the scenery slow you down. You'll regret it."

I'd heard this speech before, as had countless Navy SEALs. There was a gravity to his words, a weight that pelted my skin like the driving rain, chasing me toward my destination. It worked; this speech had pushed me through my toughest college courses and the most difficult days in the classroom. It made my issues feel insignificant, irrelevant, and surmountable. Nothing stood in my way after one of the Commodore's 'leave nothing on the road' speeches.

"I know, Dad. I'm on it."

"Excellent. Now let's talk about you coming to Cabo for Christmas. It's the only thing your mother wants, and you know what happens when I don't get her the right gift."

MATTHEW'S HEAD rested between my breasts, his arms wrapped tight around my body, and we stared out his bedroom windows while I ran my fingers through his hair. It was the kind of drowsy euphoria I adored, the languid place where we were sticky and sweaty, and staying entwined was the only option. We dug in, clinging to each other, pulling and squeezing, and just wanting more contact because there was no other way to express the fiery, desperate desire between us.

"I like being with you at night," he murmured.

His words vibrated against my nipple, and I squirmed beneath him. "Me too."

"And I like waking up with you." He shifted, suddenly fascinated with my nipples and inspecting them with his tongue.

"Mmhmm."

"And I like fucking you in the middle of the night."

"Also good," I sighed, my hands fisting in his hair. His fingers traveled down my belly and toward my center while his teeth scraped over my nipple, and I closed my eyes, enjoying this orchestrated attack on my body.

"And you need to find a new place, right?"

"Mmhmm." Didn't want to think about that right now. At my price point, apartment hunting aligned with the college calendars, and I missed the critical September move-in window. The options this time of year were woefully anemic, but Shannon was lining up tours after the holiday and she promised to find something spectacular. Moving and packing and figuring out how to get all of my shoes into tiny city closets weren't my favorite discussion topics.

"So why don't you move in with me? You can live here, and we can do this every night." He was hard against my side, and I knew he was a breath away from levering up and fitting himself inside me.

"Don't we already do this every night?"

Matthew's fingers retreated and he released my nipple without ceremony, leaving me aching and on the verge of incoherent begging. Sitting back on his heels, he stared at me, seemingly unconcerned with the erection pointing in my direction. I tried not looking it in the eye, but it was hard to miss.

"No, Lauren, we don't. I wait all day for an opening from you. Then I persuade you to have dinner with me. Then I convince you to spend the night with me. And that's what we do every day."

I didn't see it that way. To me, there was no doubt we'd see each other but we didn't figure out the where or when until later. Our days were hectic and often took us in unpredictable directions. Why not wait until the evening to make plans? And it wasn't like we hadn't been together every night for the past two months.

"Sometimes I think you're still looking for exits," he said. He stood, pulling on pajama pants and pacing in front of the windows. This was the side of him I rarely saw: angry Matthew. He typically operated within degrees of seriousness, all piercing stares and hipshot stances, and I knew he didn't get all the way up to angry very easily. "I always feel like you're five minutes away from blowing me off."

"I'm not, I'm just—"

"—busy, I know. I've heard all about your schedule and the demands of your work."

There were only two ways to have this discussion: as mature adults, talking it out over coffee and pastries, or as lovers, intoxicated from happy sex hormones, and free to be totally honest and bare with each other.

Coffee and pastries made the most sense for a normal couple, but I was more interested in the naked option. If he dropped those pants and came back to bed, we'd be able to sort this out the only way we knew how.

"That's not what I was going to say." I sighed and ran my hands through my hair. I reached for his t-shirt and pulled it over my head.

"I want to be with you. Here, a new place, I don't care, but let's do it. Think about it. We basically live together. Nomadically, of course. The only thing that would change would be figuring out where to go and staying there."

"Matthew, I don't think I can do something like that right now."

He arched an eyebrow at me. "I work all the time, too, and that's not about to change. I want you with me, every day. We'll sleep together every night, and I know you need that as much as I do, and you won't have a tantrum the next time you forget to pack the shoes you want."

"It wasn't a tantrum, I was simply expressing some frustration… Nevermind. This is ridiculous."

He shot me a bland look. "Give me one good reason why not."

"I have a great little apartment that I love, at least for a few more months, and I like things a certain way. I've lived alone for a couple years now, since Steph got married. I don't know how to coexist anymore. And please come back to bed."

"Let me tell you what I think about that." Matthew ticked off his responses on his fingers. "First. I'll move in with you until your sublet ends. And you've been coexisting with me since October. Face facts, sweetness."

Perhaps my favorite Walshism—biting and growling aside—was the way he and his siblings made lists everywhere, all the time. They couldn't run to Dunkin Donuts for an afternoon coffee without a neatly written list, and they talked that way, too. Though I never admitted it to Matthew, I adored Riley's idiosyncratic lists. They always went something like, "first of all...and B...moving on to point numero quatro," and I couldn't keep a straight face when he lapsed into Spanish.

"Second. If you want to stay here, I want this to be our place. However you want it. I'll get a storage unit for Erin's junk, and you can have an office. I'll build you some bookshelves. You need bookshelves, and I need you. Or we'll get a new place. You tell me what you want, and I'll give it to you."

"Matthew, please stop. Your reasons are lovely, but they don't change—"

"I'm not finished, and I know I'm interrupting you, but hear me out. Third. I've lived alone even longer, but I'm willing to compromise on just about anything. I'm not willing to compromise on you."

"This is just really fast, Matthew, and it's been—"

"None of that matters. I want you and I've known it for a long time, and I don't want to wait. I can't. I can't wait anymore."

Whenever my students misbehaved or did something inappropriate in my classroom, my emotional constancy held strong. I was ready with the stern glances and pursed lips, and they never knew I was boiling with aggravation, or cracking up when a kid read the word *tentacles* but said *testicles*. But I couldn't access that muscle when it came to Matthew. I knew my stunned, stupid reaction was all over my face, and I was helpless to hide it.

"The way you're looking at me right now," he said, his voice turning thick, his words plucked one by one. "It tells me you have no idea that I'm lost to you, that I'm in love with you, that I can't fucking *breathe* without you."

He stared at me, his hands propped on his hips and his gaze solemn, and I focused on that expression because I couldn't handle his words. He was used to getting what he wanted with that look. At least three occasions sprang to mind where that look was all it took to get me on my knees.

I approached Matthew, my fingers walking along the fine trail of hair, past his navel, and beneath his pants. "And *that* look tells me you want your cock in my mouth."

Groaning, he shook his head and gripped my wrist. "Stop," he snapped. "I want to talk to you, I don't want to fuck you right now."

He reached for me, trying to pull me into his grasp, but I crossed my arms over my chest and backed away. "It's ludicrous that we're having this conversation. I've known you for three months," I said.

"And you feel exactly the same way, and it's bullshit that you're pretending you don't."

I sensed my beautifully crafted existence, with all my rules and rebellions, and treats and cheats, was crashing down around me, dissolving into something I didn't understand.

"This isn't how it's supposed to be, Matthew. You can't tell me you want to move in together, then tell me you love me. I didn't want it this way."

"How did you want it?" he asked. He tucked my hair over my ears, waiting. "Tell me, and I'll make it right."

And he would, if it were possible. I studied the room, remembering our first night together when we fell off the bed, and the hours we spent caressing and exploring and learning each other. I liked to pretend I could have washed that one night from memory, but his kisses, his sounds, his touches—they were too perfect to forget. And now, months later, forgetting was out of the question.

"Tell me," he whispered.

The only easy day was yesterday.

"I had a plan," I said, staring into the harbor.

"Sweetness, you have a plan for everything. We can make a new plan, a better plan."

"I was going to wait. Until my school was successful, and I had more time, and I was ready, and I knew I could do everything really well. I wanted to wait for my husband, and now I can't, I've screwed it all up, and you probably think that's weird or naïve or something."

"Not weird. Not naïve. You, precisely you. It's all of your adorable control freakishness." He shook his head, his fingers whispering over my shoulders. I surrendered, wanting the affection he so freely offered, and dropped my head to his chest. He pressed his lips to my neck, a chaste kiss in place of his hungry bites and suction. "But now we can make a new plan. Stay this week. Or we go to your place, whatever you want. But let's figure out how to do this."

Don't let the scenery slow you down.

Why couldn't we go back to drinks? Or whatever this was before he offered love and bookshelves and cohabitation.

"I need to think about it." I felt his mouth curve into a smile as he kissed my neck and shoulders, and I stopped trying to untangle everything he said when he led me back to bed.

He wrapped me in his arms, rubbing my back and kissing my neck. A paralyzing terror climbed up my spine and curled around my belly, and though I wanted to embrace the offer of bookshelves, of everything he offered, one word stuck in my throat: scenery. This was nothing more than scenery, and I was losing sight of the mission.

I'd been kidding myself these past months, thinking I could walk the line between dedicating myself to opening my school and seeing Matthew. I didn't belong to the coupled world, not now, and a new plan wasn't changing that.

He fell asleep quickly, but I lay there for hours, vibrating with that suffocating panic, replaying this conversation and every minute of our time together.

I knew the score, and I knew the stakes.

Leave nothing on the road.

Twenty-Six

MATTHEW

ONE OF THESE DAYS, I was going to figure out Lauren, but I could bet my ass it wasn't going to be today. She stewed in her stress, tucking it aside and plastering fake smiles on to keep everyone away, but she let it linger and fester. I saw past the smiles and the bullshit, but I couldn't see the source of that stress.

It went downhill last week, that I knew. It was risky asking her to move in, but we couldn't keep wandering between her place and mine. I was nearly thirty-one, and living out of a backpack for days on end was altogether too undergrad-esque for my tastes. But instead of agreeing to make our arrangement slightly more permanent, Lauren started plotting her escape.

I always figured she had a tidy plan for selecting the right guy and engaging in a fair amount of relationship due diligence. It wasn't surprising to hear she wanted to wait, either. Part of her loved military precision, and her desire for thorough rigidity made sense when I thought about it long enough.

But what confounded me was that she *wasn't* waiting and she *wasn't* following the tidy plan, and it was only problematic when I suggested officially moving in together. Why didn't she see that we were following her plan, but in a slightly modified order?

Or was I not husband material?

She responded to some texts but ignored most others, and for the first time in months, we were sleeping apart. She blamed her period, but that never barred me from her bed before. I would have gone to her, banging on her door with panties in hand—and maybe her favorite cupcakes, too—but the atmosphere shifted when I told her I loved her and asked her to live with me. She was disappearing, and I was watching it happen.

And now, parked outside Shannon's apartment building, I felt her drifting out of my reach.

"We don't have to go in," I said. Lauren glanced at me with a raised eyebrow and I continued. "That Thai place on Cambridge Street is open today. The one you like. They have good sake."

She shifted to face me, her eyes narrowed. "This seems really important to Shannon, and it's one of your only family traditions. Why would you skip out on that?"

How was it possible? After all this time, how could she not see how much I adored her?

Drumming my fingers on the steering wheel, I forced myself to count to ten in my head to reign in my percolating frustration. "For you. I'd skip it for you. I see them," I gestured toward the building, "every day."

"You're being ridiculous," she muttered, turning her attention out the window.

"No, Lauren, you're being ridiculous. I want you, whatever it takes, but I need you to stop pushing me away."

"You say that, Matthew, but you don't think about anything. You just say the first thing that comes into your head because it feels good in the moment."

I ran my hands through my hair, fisting the strands and hating that she interpreted my love as an offhand remark. "I don't obsess about what I think I'm supposed to do, or when I'm supposed to do it, or what anyone will think of my choices, and I don't make myself miserable about any of it."

And now I was treating *her* admissions like offhand remarks.

"I'm sorry, I have to overthink things. I have too much going on right now to do whatever I want."

"Does this usually work for you, Lauren? Pushing people away and hiding behind the whole workaholic thing because it's easier than figuring out what you really want?"

"How can you say that? How can you even say that to me?"

I shifted to face Lauren, my expression grim and chilled. "Let me repeat myself: you'd rather close yourself off to everyone than figure out what you want." I sat back in my seat and bit my tongue before I let this spiral any further out of control.

"I'm not interested in arguing with you right now."

"Fine," I murmured. "Let's go."

I led the way into Shannon's building and wasn't surprised when Lauren positioned herself on the opposite side of the elevator, staring at the fire escape map. She waited for me to exit the elevator despite me gesturing for her to go first, and stayed several paces behind me in the hall.

Riley opened the door, a bottle of Heineken between his fingers and an amused smirk on his face as he eyed us. "Look at these happy people," he murmured. "Is it erectile dysfunction? That's common in old men like you. I'd never let you down, Miss Honey, literally."

"Shut up, Riley," I hissed.

"Hey!" Shannon called from the kitchen. Lauren edged past us and marched toward her.

"What the fuck did you do?" Riley asked.

I shook my head as my sister and Lauren embraced like long-lost twins. "Why do you assume I did something?"

Riley smacked my back and laughed. "Lesson number one: even when it's her fault, it's your fault."

I grunted in response and headed for the refrigerator in search of a beer. Lauren and Shannon were bent over a colander filled with grape tomatoes, baby carrots, and snap peas, and they murmured in collaboration as they arranged them on a tray. I glanced at the stockings peeking out between the tops of Lauren's boots and the hem of her skirt. They screamed naughty schoolteacher, and if I hadn't just yelled at her about being an emotionally unavailable workaholic while avoiding the one question I really wanted to ask, I would have whispered something in her ear about getting her out of those stockings when we arrived home.

"Matt, Nick is supposed to be stopping by later today," Shannon said.

"What?" I mumbled, my eyes focused on Lauren's legs.

"Nick? Your brother from another mother? I invited him," she said, taking care to enunciate each word.

"Why?" Lauren's lips pursed when I slanted a look at

her, and I wondered whether some angry sex would help. It might not solve anything, but we'd be in far better moods. And maybe I could spank some honest answers out of her.

"Plenty of reasons, but primarily because he's really hot."

Lauren chuckled. It seemed like a normal Lauren laugh, a normal Lauren smile, and I couldn't tell whether she was still angry with me. I wasn't even sure I knew what she was pissed about in the first place.

Was it the moving in together? The confessions of love and general hysteria for her? Or something else entirely?

"Your sister would like to bite his ass."

"I would," Shannon sighed, her voice husky as she gazed at the tomatoes.

"I'd be good without that information," I murmured, backing out of the kitchen.

Parking myself beside Patrick and Sam on the leather sectional in Shannon's den, I stared at the football game without seeing.

My initial clue should have been waking up alone after that first night together. She made her intentions pretty clear by walking out on me then. There were plenty of other clues along the way—her uncommunicativeness while traveling, all her pushing and my pulling. The signs were there. I should have known this wasn't shaking out the way I wanted.

"Get you another?" Sam asked. I nodded and handed him the empty bottle, ignoring the curious glances around me.

Sam handed fresh beers to my brothers. "Who's planning tomorrow's pub crawl?"

We didn't have many traditions, but the ones we did

have—Thanksgiving at Shannon's, drinking ourselves sick on the anniversary of Mom's death, and pub crawls on Black Friday and the day before Christmas Eve—were special.

They were also heavily reliant on alcohol, but we'd address that some other day.

Patrick scowled at Sam. "They're forecasting a blizzard."

"Let's do it anyway," Riley said to Sam. "We'll get snowshoes."

"Would you shut up and watch the goddamn game?" I snapped.

I nursed my second and third and fourth beers, my thoughts deep in Lauren while my brothers swapped tales of bachelorhood. All I wanted was to find my way back to her but there was something about the rapid shift—the walls that went up, the defenses she deployed. Those gestures were bright, flashing signs that I was trespassing in forbidden territory.

"Food's hot," Shannon called, and my brothers scrambled into the dining room. I continued staring at the game until Riley flopped down beside me with an overflowing plate.

"Go talk to your girl," he said under his breath.

"I don't think that's a good idea," I said.

"Trust me. She's about forty seconds away from deciding to pack her knives and go."

I groaned and got up from my slouch. A heated conversation between Shannon and Patrick filled the dining room, and he gestured for me to join.

"You're free to talk to Erin all you want," Shannon hissed. "I will not be making any calls today, tomorrow, or any other day."

Patrick dropped a hand to my shoulder and squeezed, a clear indication I was expected to wade into the debate. "She's your sister, Shan, and you need to drop your stupid fucking bullshit and call her. It's Thanksgiving."

I held up my hands in surrender when they turned eager gazes on me. I didn't have any strength or patience for the Shannon-Erin Smackdown today, and I wasn't sure she was even on the grid. Last I heard, Erin was holed up in some remote location in the Canary Islands listening for volcano gurgles. Or something equally unusual.

"She can call *me* if she wants to talk," Shannon snapped.

"It has been years, Shan," Patrick said. "When are you going to grow the fuck up?"

I twisted out of his hold while their argument continued. I spotted Lauren in the kitchen, her back to me as she mixed vodka into a tumbler of ice and cranberry juice. I watched her stare out the window, sipping her drink for several minutes, and her rigid body language communicated everything I needed to know.

"Hey."

Startled, she spun around to face me. "I didn't hear you come in."

"Can we talk?"

She raised her eyebrows but reserved comment, instead draining her glass and setting it in the sink.

"Please. I think we need to."

She lifted her shoulder with a questioning gaze. "I think you said everything already."

I wanted to kick my own ass for going off on her in the car. I exhaled and fisted my hands inside my pockets, twisting the necklace I carried with me every day. I held the cool rose quartz pendant between my fingers, and flashes of that first night passed behind my eyes.

"I can assure you that I have not said anything I need to say…not even close. Let's get out of here. The Thai place?"

"No, Matthew, no," she sighed. She shook her head, the motion slow and resigned.

"What's happening right now?"

I watched her approach, though I wasn't sure if she was inching toward me or time was grinding to a halt. She pressed her palm to my chest, frowning, and met my eyes. "No. You said what you needed to say. We can't force it anymore. I have my priorities, and I can't let you be one of them."

She retreated, her hand falling away, and I felt rooted in place in Shannon's dark kitchen. The pressure in my chest doubled, and I gasped at the pain of her rejection. Not husband material, not hook-up material.

Not even for now, not even for fun.

She never wanted me the way I wanted her.

SPRAWLED ON THE COLD FLOOR, I pillowed my head on my arm and hugged Lauren's scarf to my chest, breathing in the remains of her delicate scent while I watched snow accumulating on my terrace.

My legs and lungs ached from an eighteen-mile run—suicide sprint, if I was being honest with myself—in white-out, blizzard conditions around the Chestnut Hill Reservoir and back. I couldn't remember ever seeing Beacon Street as desolate, the deserted city mirroring the hollow feeling in my gut. My only companions were snowplows and salt trucks, and even they surrendered to the storm around midnight. I jogged a circuit through the slippery streets of the North End until two in the morning, my body consumed with a sick mix of dread and anger and hurt, and I needed to get it out before I could go home. I needed to collapse into a dreamless sleep that would rewind time or wipe the memory of Lauren entirely.

Coughing, I yanked my phone from its protective shield on my bicep, snickering at the messages from my siblings and Nick, all inquiring about my whereabouts and mental status, and nothing from the only person I wanted.

I shouldn't have expected to hear from her, but that didn't change the fact I *wanted* it. She wasn't the door slamming, all caps text message type. She shrank, folding in on herself, and shrouding her emotions in hard, defensive layers.

She liked to think her shoes and her panties were armor, but she had no idea how many layers she really wore, how much space she put between herself and the world.

A shiver racked my body, and I knew it was time to change out of my wet clothes but I couldn't muster the strength to move. If I contracted pneumonia, suffered, and died in this spot, it wouldn't be nearly as awful as Lauren walking away. The outstretched arms of grim death were more favorable than reliving the moment when her hand left my chest.

Uncapping the bottle of Jameson I snagged from the pantry when I returned home, I guzzled the liquid, my throat burning.

This time, *I* was over it. *I* was disappearing.

For hours, I watched Coast Guard boats as they patrolled the waters off the harbor, sipping Irish whiskey and shivering while I kept my fingers wrapped around her scarf. In the distance, I heard my phone ringing over and over until the throbbing in my head synchronized with the obnoxious chime, but I knew it wasn't Lauren. Turning away from the sound, I dropped into dark, fitful sleep.

Later, I barely registered the footsteps around me. Brightness filled the room, and Riley's voice was in my ear. "Gotta get up, buddy. We have a problem on our hands."

"IF YOU VOMIT ON ME, I will be punching you in the throat," Sam said. I grunted in acknowledgement and angled away from him, only to feel the hard plastic armrest gouging my leg.

Bracing my arms on my thighs, I leaned forward and held my head between my hands to dodge the overhead lights. My stomach swayed and pitched like it was on the high seas, and the scent of hospital disinfectant was not helping. I watched Patrick's feet as he paced the silent corridor, and for a minute, the rhythm of his steps lulled me to sleep.

It was quiet there, in my dreams, and I had a long, uninterrupted stretch of jogging trail ahead of me and engineering problems popping up every few feet. It was the perfect place to hide until my sister yanked me up by the ear and dragged me across the hall.

"Shan-*nonnnn*," I wailed.

"Would you shut up?" she hissed. "Get your shit together and shut the fuck up."

Resting against a wall, I rubbed my eyes and watched a blurry version of Nick stride toward us. He looked different in scrubs, his breast pocket filled with pens and instruments, his lighthearted smirk replaced with a sober expression. He was Dr. Acevedo now.

He stopped in front of us, his hands fisted on his hips, and said, "I want you to prepare yourselves. Your father experienced an ischemic stroke. His brain was deprived of oxygen for a period of time, and the longer the oxygen is cut off, the more brain cells die. We're still running tests to determine how the stroke impacted his brain, and will know more in a few hours. We have him sedated right now, in a medically-induced coma."

Standing required too much energy, and I slid down the wall to the floor. My ass hit the ground, and I discovered I was still wearing soggy track pants. They continued talking about Angus and his issues—the old bastard was kind enough to have his stroke in the main hallway, front and center, so the poor cleaning lady could find his miserable ass when she scaled the snow banks this morning—but I didn't care. There wasn't a shred of concern in my cells for Angus, and even in the darkest corners of my mind, I recognized that as one of the cornerstones of major fucked-uppedness.

"What is your deal?" Nick kicked my foot, squatted in front of me, and studied the eggplant-sized bruise on my jaw. It had faded to a gross palette of yellow and purple in the weeks since our last interaction with Angus, and I slapped Nick away.

"He's still drunk," Riley said. "I found him with an empty bottle of whiskey."

"Why is he wet?" Nick grabbed my wrist and pressed his fingers over my pulse. "Please tell me you didn't piss yourself."

"I did a couple miles last night," I said. "There was some snow."

He angled my chin and beamed his penlight in my eyes, and I was ready to rip that hand off and beat him with it. "You're being a little bitch," he whispered, and stood to face the group. "Let's bring y'all up to ICU. You can go in for five or ten—"

"Won't be necessary," Patrick said.

Nick studied us, waiting for someone to show a glimmer of sadness over Angus's condition, and when he finally found none, he nodded to himself. "You need to know this is serious. He might not come out of it, and if he does, he could have extensive complications. Loss of speech, paralysis, memory loss."

"I might prefer those options," I said.

"That sounds sensational to me. He's said everything he needs to say," Sam added.

"You don't have to see him, but you should," Nick said. "At the very least, we're getting some fluids into Matt, so sit tight."

"That's fine," Patrick said. "Let's run through the properties. I want status reports, and I want to figure out where we need crews this morning. Be ready in five minutes."

From: Matthew Walsh
To: Erin Walsh
Date: November 26 at 13:01 EDT
Subject: Angus had a stroke

Call me when you get this.

From: Erin Walsh
To: Matthew Walsh
Date: November 26 at 21:05 CEST
Subject: RE: Angus had a stroke

Ummmmmmm no.
But good luck with that.

From: Matthew Walsh
To: Erin Walsh
Date: November 26 at 13:16 EDT
Subject: RE: Angus had a stroke

Cut the shit, E. Answer your fucking phone.

From: Erin Walsh
To: Matthew Walsh
Date: November 26 at 21:22 CEST
Subject: RE: Angus had a stroke

Let's get a few things straight, kid. He's made it perfectly clear that he's not my father. I don't think this is my concern.

Oh, and I'll be unreachable for a few weeks. No need to send further updates.

From: Matthew Walsh
To: Erin Walsh
Date: November 26 at 14:04 EDT
Subject: RE: Angus had a stroke

No one is disputing that he's an evil cocksucker. We all agree on that. You don't have to keep defending that proof.

Look, I get that you're angry. He shouldn't have thrown you out of the house. He shouldn't have said Mom slept around. He shouldn't have done any of it and we all know that, but you know as well as I do that he's your father. He sees Mom when he looks at you, and Shannon, too. That's why he hates you, and you know that.

None of it should have happened, but he's in a coma right now and we're all here dealing with it. You don't have to care about him, but it would be nice if you cared about us.

You could start small and care about me for a minute. At this moment, my knee feels about three times its normal size, I'm pretty sure I've caused another round of shin splints, and my liver will most likely stop functioning before the calendar year ends.

You'll probably love hearing that Lauren broke up with me and the universe as I know it has imploded. We had a stupid fight and I said stupid shit, and it's over. You called it from the start, and I probably should have listened.

So thanks for that, e.

M

NICK RETURNED with a yellow IV bag, a pissy scowl, and a nurse who probably wasn't old enough to vote. It took her five tries to get the needle in my vein and she left a puddle of my blood behind as a reminder.

"Well this is delightful," I said, wiping a bloody hand over my pants.

"Would this be a good time to talk about Miss Honey?" Riley asked.

This was a good time for curling into the fetal position and sleeping for nineteen hours.

"Riley, do not doubt that I'll reach down your throat and pull out your fucking intestines if you say another word. I don't need your shit right now."

"I think we should talk about what happened with Miss Honey," he said.

Pressing my fists to my eyes, I groaned. I was ready to vomit. Another word, another breath in the wrong direction, and I was spewing that wretched night all over the shiny linoleum floor. "Don't fucking call her that—"

"Actually, I'd like to know the answer, Matt," Patrick interrupted, crossing his arms over his chest. Few were the days when we weren't talking over each other. "Did you call her?"

"Why do you care?" I asked.

"Because she's nice, and she makes you happy," Riley

said. "You're a dick with an attitude problem when she's not around."

"I can't believe you fucked this up," Sam said.

I was definitely vomiting. The jackhammers in my head coupled with the disinfectant that I could fucking taste on the air and the siblings who knew all about poking the rough spots left me choking back bile.

"You need to call her, Matt. She would want to know what happened, and she'd be pissed you're sitting on the floor in wet clothes being all grumpy," Shannon said.

Riley, Sam, and Patrick nodded in agreement, and I gulped back another wave of nausea rocking my stomach. God, I was never drinking again.

"Is it possible I'm *not* the one who fucked it up?"

"Sam's right. Riley, too," Patrick murmured.

"Not really sure why I'm the douche canoe here, or why you're all tearing my ass up right now. She's no angel, you know."

"Yeah, Matt. Keep sitting there, thinking about how perfect you are," Shannon said. "But if you don't call her, I will. Believe it."

Perfect I was not, but I wasn't interested in listening to them bitching at me anymore, and I slumped against the wall.

"Do whatever the fuck you want, Shannon. It's not like anyone gives a damn what I think anyway," I said.

"Could you give it a rest, Matt? I don't feel like listening to your pissing and moaning about us ignoring you and your precious opinions," Patrick said.

"It's not pissing and moaning, Patrick. I told her I loved her and asked her to live with me, and she basically told me to shove it up my ass because she didn't see this going anywhere. Why don't you geniuses enlighten me: what did I do wrong?"

Maybe that was a slight oversimplification, but the one thing I knew to be true was that Lauren wanted something else, someone else.

"Oh," Shannon said, the word stretched and contorted to contain a dozen different reactions. "That's not what I expected to hear."

"Yeah," I snapped. "So either tell me how to fix it, or shut the hell up."

Unable to endure another minute of this debate, I closed my eyes. I sensed their wordless reactions pinging over my head, but I was too exhausted for another round.

Shannon spent the afternoon on the phone with Angus's lawyer, who couldn't get to his office to determine whether Angus wrote any medical directives into his will, because last night's storm dropped a little over two feet of snow and most residential streets were blocked. Patrick went to work getting snow removal crews deployed to our jobsites, and Riley and Sam prioritized the properties at risk for roof leaks and collapse. All in all, a regular day at the office, with the minor exception of the office being an ICU waiting room and my fucking soul was shattered.

As I fell asleep in the corner, I wondered about the roof at Saint Cosmas. This was the kind of snow that would bring it all down, and part of me wanted to see the wreckage. I couldn't be the only thing destroyed right now.

Shannon: I know my brother's on your shit list but I need my friend right now.
Lauren: of course. what's wrong?
Shannon: My father had a stroke this morning, and I'm keeping it together but just barely.
Lauren: where are you? I'm on my way.

SHANNON'S DIRECTIONS pointed me toward the waiting room, but she didn't mention it resembled a miniature Walsh Associates command post. Power adapters shot out from every outlet and tangled in the middle of the room. Shannon and Patrick huddled around a laminate table-turned-desk where they were furiously typing. Sam and Riley were busy writing all over the windows with dry erase markers, and Matthew was nestled on the floor, asleep in the corner.

How was it supposed to be now? How was I supposed

to see him without dissolving into a mopey puddle of regret?

It was awful to admit but I considered ignoring Shannon's initial text today. She sent several last night, but I turned off my phone on the walk between her apartment and mine, and didn't power up until after an hour-long bath this afternoon. She wanted to know what went down —I did scramble out of her place like my hair was on fire— but I couldn't explain the words Matthew and I shared in that kitchen. Or the car. Or his bedroom last week.

And now, with everything in ruins around me, I knew there was no point in trying.

Where Shannon sent her share of texts while I was unplugged, I received none from Matthew. For all my pushing, I hoped for just a bit more pulling from him, just this once. I hoped he'd find a way to make it work, a way that didn't force me to choose.

Shannon's friendship was important to me, but I didn't know how to balance it with the wreckage of Matthew and me. Seeing him now, his long legs extended before him and his arms locked over his chest, the recognition that he wasn't a treat, an occasional indulgence on par with expensive underwear and decadent cupcakes, settled in the pit of my stomach. I couldn't lull myself into believing I could manage any amount of moderation, and I couldn't prevent myself from falling for him.

My head belonged in the mission, and not sidetracked with fanciful activities or growly, bitey boys.

He looked terrible, a gray cast to his skin and an IV in his hand. I knew touching him was a gateway to so much more, but I couldn't help it. He was frigid, his cheeks ice cold. "Oh, Matthew."

"Get out of my dreams, woman," he rasped, and his eyes inched open.

"Not a dream," I said. "You're freezing."

Groaning as he stood up, he braced his hand on my shoulder, and took a wobbly, limping step. "Jesus, Mary, and Joseph," he grunted.

"What happened to you?"

Flattening his hands on the wall, he shook his head, and dropped his chin to his chest. "I don't know, Lauren. You tell me. You're the one who walked out."

Okay, so that was how it was going to be. "I mean why are you limping?"

"Went for a long run last night."

"Last *night*?" I cried. "In the *blizzard*?"

"Yeah, if you want to yell at me, get in line behind the rest of them." He nodded toward his siblings, and shuffled down the hall, his IV bag tucked under his arm.

"He's fine," Sam said, jerking a thumb at Matthew and motioning for me to follow him in the opposite direction. "Just dehydrated. And temperamental. How did you hear?"

In worn jeans and a Cornell hoodie, he looked young and unassuming. Gone was Sam's smooth charm and composure, and in its place was the vulnerable, neurotic man I knew. "Shannon texted me. How's your dad?"

"*Angus*," he corrected, "is in a coma, but he's had a few seizures since we've been here. They think he's been having little strokes for weeks, maybe months. They're worried about..." He wrapped his hands around the back of his neck and shrugged. "There's a lot to worry about."

"And how are you?"

He pushed his glasses up his nose and frowned. "I don't know yet."

"Oh thank God you're here," Shannon called as she rounded the corner. She ran up, pushing Sam away and folding her arms around me. She squeezed hard before pulling back. "Can we get some coffee?"

We walked the hospital halls, and Shannon was silent for several minutes before the dam broke. For as close as she was with her brothers, she was also stoic. It was up to her to hold it together for them, and after all these years, I doubted she knew how to face them with anything less than complete composure.

"It doesn't even bother me anymore when he calls me a cunt," she laughed as she wiped tears from her chin. "It's like nothing."

Sitting face to face on the floor of a quiet stairwell—really, they were the best places for semi-private tears—we cried together as the story of her father's reign of terror poured out in a ragged, sobbing mess.

"You know what I thought when I got the call this morning? I thought, thank God. I thought, I hope it was quick and I hope it was painless, but please let that miserable bastard die." She sniffled, and wiped the edge of her sleeve over her tear-stained face. "I guess that probably makes me just as much of a miserable bastard."

"No," I said. "I think it makes you human. You make mistakes and you hurt people, and you try to survive, and that's what makes you human."

MY RED HUNTER boots squeaked against the gleaming new floors, and despite my thorough inspections, there was no slant to be found. Even though I didn't have the first idea of what I'd say to him if our paths crossed, I had been lurking at Trench Mills most of this week, just hoping to see Matthew again.

When I wasn't here, I was crying over every random memory of him, and the universe was blasting them all in my direction. A tie he left in my closet. A lonely Heineken in my refrigerator. The take-out menu from our favorite Spanish restaurant shoved into my mailbox.

But in reality, he was everywhere, all over my apartment, all over this city, all over my school, and all over me.

The raccoons and water heaters were gone, broken windows replaced, and it didn't feel like the same button mill anymore. I had to look closely to see the places where Matthew and I had been, to call the memories of that September day to the surface. In the gray December light, those moments seemed foreign, distant, unimaginable.

But I remembered the wanting—wanting to touch him, be close to him, taste him—and I remembered denying myself. And I'd denied myself so much of Matthew these past months. Too much.

"It's looking good," Riley boomed over my shoulder. His deep voice echoed through the space and I startled, my hand flying to my mouth to conceal a yelp. "Just another couple of months, and you'll be ready to roll."

"Yeah," I murmured, rising on my toes to look over his shoulder.

"He's not here," Riley said. "It's his turn on deathbed duty."

Their glib treatment of Angus's condition made sense as a coping mechanism when considered alongside their personalities and his heinous nature, but it wasn't my favorite Walshism.

"Oh, okay. I mean, I wasn't—"

"Here's what you need to know about my brother," Riley said. "Even if something isn't broken, he likes to take it apart, figure out how it works, and then break it. He's not a sadist, he just likes trying to put it back together better than it was built. Don't give up on him, even if he broke it and doesn't know how to fix it yet. He won't stop until he finds the solution. He doesn't know how to give up."

Inside my head, something new started forming, a link between all these words and thoughts and emotions, and I nodded, speechless. Synapses fired, neural pathways connected, and I felt the pieces pivoting, aligning, snapping into place.

Riley wandered off with a comment about checking on the heating and ventilation progress while I stared out the window, the mechanics in my mind sapping all of my cognitive processes while this hot ball of awareness pushed up and out, spreading through my cells.

If I had known four months ago that I'd be in love with Matthew, I would have fought for him, for us, and like every other challenge I accepted, I wouldn't have surrendered until there was nothing left on the road.

Hindsight was a bitch.

In a burst of jagged, blurry consciousness, I understood it all. *Finally*.

I never gave up, never gave in, and always gave everything I had, and I'd always fought on the side of right.

Until now.

I gave up on Matthew—on us—the moment I crawled out of his bed in the middle of the night. I bunkered down, conceding everything to my work, and neglecting myself, my relationship, my Matthew. And it wasn't just neglect, it was a refusal to acknowledge the challenge of living my life while simultaneously kicking ass in my career. The two were never mutually exclusive.

Sometimes I cried in stairwells and smothered my stress in chocolate, but I was standing in the middle of my school, the one I dreamed up and formed into reality. And I loved Matthew. Those words lived inside me all along, and I should have said them every time my heart ached to reach out and squeeze him. And none of that required a neat, sequential plan.

In a frenzy, my squeaky boots carried me down the stairs and to the curb where I found Riley talking with the crew.

"Are you headed to the hospital?" I asked.

"I can be," he said. "Let's go."

I BOLTED THROUGH THE HALLS, half running, half stomping, and never determining what I intended to say. Rounding the corner to the waiting room, I found Matthew hunched over his laptop, deep grooves of irritation carved into his face. It was the same expression he wore that day at Saint Cosmas, as if he was annoyed to find a building that didn't live up to his exacting specifications.

"Hi," I said, breathless and flustered.

It had been six days since seeing him last, and if the scowl, thick beard growth, and dark bags under his eyes were any indication, he was about as miserable as I was.

"Shannon's not here," he said, his eyes meeting mine over his laptop's lid for a moment, and then refocusing on the screen.

I wasn't sure what I expected from Matthew, but it certainly wasn't dismissive indifference.

"I'm not looking for Shannon. I'm looking for you."

He glanced up, his expression turning pinched, bitter. "What can I do for you now, Lauren?"

Okay, so he was pissed off at me. That was fair. We weren't going to throw our arms around each other and let kisses speak all the apologies necessary and promise to work it out, and I probably deserved every sour scowl he tossed my way.

"I'm here because we have things to talk about," I said.

"As you've pointed out already, it's all been said."

Why couldn't he sit still, shut up, and let me tell him I felt the same things?

"It hasn't, and I want to talk to you now," I said, irritation creeping into my voice.

He closed his laptop and crossed his arms over his chest, his gaze cool and appraising. "Really, Lauren? What is there to say? Maybe you could tell me about your busy schedule again, or how your life is too complicated to make plans more than three hours in advance? Why don't you tell me how we're forcing this, and I don't meet your—"

"I fucking love you, Matthew!" I dropped my bag and advanced on him, and he shot up, sending his chair tumbling to the ground. "That's what I'm here to say," I said. "That I screwed up and I convinced myself it was one or the other, you or my school, and I was wrong. I can have as much as I want, whenever I want it, and I can make up the plan as I go. I just need you, and I finally understand now."

We stood in the center of the small waiting room, his agitated glare burning memories of this moment into my skin. His breath, his heat, his scent—they surrounded me. I was trapped and confined, and exactly where I wanted to be.

But he wouldn't say it back to me. He wouldn't give me the three little words I craved, and this—*this* was karma.

"It scares me," I said, my voice steady and strong while every cell in my body flew into fits of panic. "It scares me to want you like this, to need you, to be responsible for more than me when I can barely manage myself." Staring at his tie, the green one with tiny pink tessellations, I debated whether I could wait much longer for his touch.

And then I remembered I didn't need to wait for anything.

"It scares the hell out of me," I said, my hand pressing against his tie, and up, over his chest and shoulder, around his neck. Knotty, corded muscles met my fingers. "But here I am."

Matthew narrowed his eyes, his head inclined while I soothed the tension in his neck, and he stared at me for several heavy moments. "Is this because you want my cock in your mouth? I mean, it's been a few weeks now. You must miss it."

Laughing, I dropped my head to his chest and basked in the warmth of his arms when they closed around me.

But he still wasn't saying it.

"I can't force you to want this," he whispered into my hair. "And I can't wait for it to be convenient for you. I've tried, and I've failed, and I can't do it again."

Nodding I pulled back and met his gaze. "You understand how focused I am, how committed I am to my school, even if it drives you crazy, and you understand it because you're the same way."

"Committed is one word for it."

"That's not changing, for either of us, and if you're okay with take-out and Netflix as our primary source of entertainment, I know I can do better at committing to *us*."

"Do better as in...?" He bent to meet my eyes, his brows furrowed. "You're going to stop waiting half an hour to respond to my texts? Or you're going to make plans before sunset? Or you'd consider moving in together?"

He was tentative, and that irritated scowl still haunted his features, but he was making his way back to me.

"I was thinking your place, but I want to bring a lot of my furniture. And art. And pillows. You need more color, and personality. And I don't understand why everything in your kitchen is white."

Matthew's kiss drained the darkness lingering from the past weeks out of my body. I urged him forward, wanting to feel him pressed against me.

"So bossy," he murmured against my lips.

"You're a caveman," I laughed. "I have to keep up."

Okay, so I'd wait until he was ready to say it again. I knew a few things about waiting for what I wanted.

From: Erin Walsh
To: Matthew Walsh
Date: December 14 at 01:51 CEST
Subject: RE: Angus had a stroke

Okay, a couple things.

First, I actually have been off the grid since that last email. I mean, I read it, wrote a really nasty response, deleted the whole thing, and then went off the grid.

Second, you're right about all of it. I know why he's a dick but I'm not ready to let it go yet. You don't see how easy you had it, Matt. You've never been the subject of his hatred. You've just been the one who mediated when he went thermonuclear. We wouldn't have survived without you, but you have to see that it's different from being the one who was tossed to the curb. I can't just get over it right now. I care about you. About all of you guys. I hope you're okay, but me flying to Boston won't solve any of this.

Third, I'm not happy to hear about Lauren. I didn't want that. Yeah, I gave you a hard time, but I was on your side, Matt. I really want it to work out, if that's what you want. When it does work out, maybe instead of me going to Boston, you can bring Lauren to me.

I'm sorry about everything. I hope you're okay.

NO ONE NEEDED to tell us how bad it was, but they kept doing it anyway.

The seizures came and went, and then there were a few relatively uneventful days where Angus lingered in his coma. He mixed it up when a vessel in his brain blew out, and spent the better part of a day in surgery.

Nick offered a complicated story about intracranial pressure and brain swelling and removing part of his skull, but it might as well have been the weather report for northwestern Siberia because I didn't give a damn. He also warned us about the drain pumping extra fluid out of Angus's brain, and that being a freakish sight, though his caution was pointless: we weren't going in that room any time soon.

Then again, strokes and dying fathers were bad news for normal people, and we stopped being normal people ages ago.

After two additional comatose weeks, Nick scheduled a meeting and put the hospital's chief neurosurgeons in front of us. It was a dreary Monday morning the week before Christmas, and a full house in the ICU conference room. It seemed like the type of room designed for bad news. Awkward window angles, odd door placement, unnecessarily bright overhead lights. The table was too big and the chairs didn't match, and nothing good could possibly come from a room like this.

Riley and I filled in the far end while Patrick and Shannon sat in the center, directly across from the surgeons. Sam hovered on the edge, looking like he wanted the floor to open up and eat him. He vacillated between indifference, and the locked and loaded rage he carried for Angus.

The doctors introduced themselves—Chatterjee and Britton, plus their residents—and discussed the complications and intricacies of Angus's case while Nick leaned against the door. They had all manner of scans and tests, and discussed a handful of treatment plans and care facilities, but one statement stood out: no evidence of brain activity.

Britton glanced between Patrick and Shannon when she finished with the prognosis. "Did you father ever discuss end-of-life care?"

She directed her questions to Patrick because it was obvious to everyone who was in charge, but he shifted toward Shannon and gestured for her to respond.

"No," Shannon said. "Not with us, that is. And he didn't leave any advance care directives."

"Patients don't come back from these complications. A recovery would be an exceptionality, Miss Walsh. We can make him comfortable, and provide him some peace." Britton nodded to her team and stood. "Please reach out with any questions. Myself, Dr. Chatterjee, Dr. Acevedo—we're all available for you and your family."

The team left and we spent a few minutes staring at each other until I said, "He's brain dead. It's over, and I know you're all thinking the same thing."

"The life support measures are the only things keeping him alive," Nick said. "If we discontinued those measures, it could be a matter of minutes or hours, and in some cases days."

Patrick looked up from the information about long-term care facilities. "Is that the right decision, Nick?"

He lifted his hands, weighing the invisible options. "It wouldn't be wrong. It would be humane."

"Then we'll sign whatever we need to sign," Shannon said. Her voice cracked, and she put her head in her hands. I hadn't seen my sister cry in years, maybe even decades, and I couldn't stay in that room any longer.

Blindly jogging down the stairs and through the halls, I searched for a quiet corner or empty room, something, somewhere to clear my head. I stumbled into a small, dim room and it took a moment for my eyes to adjust, my brain to process. It was a chapel, and though I didn't believe I belonged there, I couldn't make myself leave. I sank into the last pew and expelled a ragged breath.

When my mother was alive, she went to church daily. There were always candles to light and prayers to offer, and my father used to say she was there more often than most of the saints. The last time I visited a church was my mother's funeral. I never thought I'd go back, and after that, why should I?

My mother had loved us unconditionally, of that I had

no doubt, but it wasn't because she said it often. It was because I felt it everywhere, all the time.

Lauren was like that, too. Her love was wrapped in every glance, every movement, every touch. Some were loud and insistent, and others were barely a whisper, but each one burrowed inside me, making me whole. She said it when the moment felt right, and though I wanted her saying it all day, every day, I wasn't ready to reciprocate.

The place where she tore away from me in Shannon's kitchen still stung, and regardless of how much I wanted to tell her I loved her, we needed to find our footing first. It wasn't easy picking up where we left off, and given the state of affairs with Angus, we hadn't had much time to talk through the important pieces.

But talking—real, clothed conversations—had never been our strength, and we communicated most effectively through touch.

The best part of my day was crawling into bed with her, lying together in the darkness. We spent most nights at her apartment because it was closer to my office and the hospital, where my siblings and I were still rotating through shifts.

On the odd evening when we weren't busy tearing each other's clothes off, we determined all of her furniture was coming to my loft but we were still debating some of her bright prints. I was secretly looking forward to her velvet pillows and colorful kitchen accessories.

But I wasn't excited about her Christmas trip to Mexico next week. Old habits died hard, and I worried she'd decide to disappear again, or her father would lock her in a Mexican convent. Both seemed somewhat plausible, and I was bitter about losing my naughty schoolteacher. I didn't know how to sleep without her.

I stared at my phone, wishing I could sum up the present situation with some combination of emoticons.

Matthew: we're taking Angus off life support.
Lauren: I'm so sorry. what do you need?
Lauren: have you said goodbye?
Matthew: no
Lauren: you need to, all of you do.
Matthew: you.
Matthew: i need you.
Lauren: give me 15 mins.

WHEN LAUREN ARRIVED, it was clear she understood the task at hand. Nick looked on with his tense neurosurgeon glare to back her up, and one by one, she marched us down the hall for a final conversation with Angus.

Riley went first, and I watched as she reached out for his hand when they stepped through the doorway. They stayed for nine minutes—I needed a distraction, and counting the seconds gave me one—and I couldn't imagine what took so long, but when they emerged, all six foot three of Riley engulfed my little Lauren, and he cried in her arms. Sam, Patrick, and I shared confused glances and 'I don't know what just happened to him' shrugs.

Patrick went next, and though he only spent two minutes inside, nearly twenty minutes were spent embracing Lauren outside.

Shannon stared down the hallway for a long time before

nodding at Lauren. They held on to each other—Shannon's arm around Lauren's waist, Lauren's arm squeezing Shannon's shoulders—and I noticed tears rolling down their faces. I didn't track how long Shannon and Lauren were with Angus, but they clung to each other, crying, when they left.

Sam clutched her hand as they walked into the room, but he was yelling within minutes and it took two nurses and a security guard to remove him.

And then she came for me.

She held out her hand and I accepted it, though I never intended to step foot in that room. I looked away when we reached the door, but she wasn't having it.

"Come on, Matthew. It's time."

I looked at our joined hands, her fingers tiny against mine, but knew size spoke nothing to strength. "I don't have anything to say."

"I think you do, and I think you want to, but more importantly, you have to."

I stared at the floor, the clock, the walls—anything but the man on the gurney—but the insistent circle of Lauren's thumb on my wrist drew the words from my depths. "You were a terrible person, Angus. You did awful, unforgiveable things, and I'll never understand…" I sighed and turned to Lauren. "Why am I doing this? That's not even him anymore. What's the point of standing here and doing this? What did everyone else say that took so long?"

"You know what my father always says?"

"'I'm going to tear the testicles off any man who has so much as an impure thought about my daughter'?"

She laughed in spite of her best efforts. "Yes, but he also says 'the only easy day was yesterday.'" Her hand passed back and forth between my shoulder blades as she shook her head. "Today's a difficult day, but you're going to make it through. You need to let him go."

Looking up, I studied Angus under the tangle of tubes and cables. "No, you know what I need to say to him? I need to say thank you. Thank you for being such an evil bastard. Thank you for leaving us to fend for ourselves. Thank you for destroying every good thing we ever knew because Mom's death destroyed you. And you want to know why we took over the business? Because fuck you. Fuck you, for all of it. I'll never understand how it was so easy for you to hate us, or why we were the enemy."

Lauren squeezed my hand, and when she led me out, the rush of emotion that must have hit the others hit me. At once I felt relief, sorrow, hope, but not an ounce of loss. I may have always known we lost Angus along with my mother, but I didn't realize it until stepping out of that room. We had been orphaned with a living ghost, and that haunting was finally over.

I glanced at Lauren—my force of nature. The warmth from her hand in mine only took the edge off the chill riding my bones, and I fell into her open arms.

"You can hold onto me as long as you need, Matthew. I'm not going anywhere."

ANGUS DIED thirteen hours later with Nick and Lauren by his side.

It wasn't more than twenty minutes after they insisted we leave for rest, fresh clothes, and food, and I imagine that was how Angus preferred it. There was a time when he loved us and looked upon us fondly, but that time ended decades ago, and even in death, I doubted he could see past his anger to remember it. He needed to be free of us to die, but I hated that he went with Lauren's goodness surrounding him. She never said it but I knew she held his hand and spoke kind words as he passed, and stayed beside him until the orderlies wheeled him away, and he didn't deserve that.

Somewhere in my foggy consciousness, I knew she did it for me—and Sam and Shannon, and Patrick and Riley, and even Erin—as much as she did it for Angus. She knew that, in a place far beneath our resentment and hurt, tiny slivers of us still cared about him, and she was taking this one for us.

I dropped to the sofa with a tumbler of whiskey and watched the Coast Guard boats patrolling the harbor. I shouldn't have felt relief, but knowing Angus was gone left me lighter, and I could relax for the first time in years. The grief I experienced after saying goodbye—or fuck off, depending upon your interpretation—was brief and cathartic.

The wreckage he left in his wake was substantial, and I knew it would take years to put us back together but we knew all about restoration. We knew about picking up the pieces, brushing away the effects of time, and seeing things as they should be.

Lauren came to me, curled herself around me, and we watched in the hazy darkness between night and morning as the storm rolled in from the sea. I didn't have to request her presence, she just knew I needed it. She didn't say anything, and there was nothing to say that her loving touch didn't already express.

There were versions of Lauren, probably too many to count, but she showed me every one without hesitation, and I knew her. I knew her heart and her mind and her love, and I knew that night at The Red Hat that she was rare and precious. And she knew me, all of me.

Despite every mathematical improbability, we had been waiting for each other. Passing each other in coffeehouses, on the streets of Beacon Hill, and on beaches of Cape Cod, waiting for the moment when our universes collided. Until she fell into my arms.

We belonged to each other.

We sat there for hours—maybe it was minutes, I couldn't tell anymore—and she whispered, "Tell me what you need."

Five words we knew so well, and right now they meant something else entirely.

I studied her eyes, looking for the flares of gold in the seas of green, and said, "Can I show you a few things?"

She nodded, and I grabbed the items I needed from my home office without giving myself a second of doubt.

"I've been drawing this house," I said, settling onto the sofa with her on my lap and paging through my graphing notebook. "I started it a couple of months ago, and I have some variations here, but it's the same house at its core. Here's the great room and the kitchen. The library, the master bedroom."

"This is remarkable, Matthew." She touched her fingers to the paper, tracing the lines. "I thought you did this in a computer program. I didn't know you did it by hand like this."

"It's how I learned. This was the one thing my father taught me: how to let the design move from my mind to my hand to the page." The thought slammed into my chest, more as an unanticipated reminder than stunning grief, and I decided I was all right. Lauren was filling the empty space where Angus usually unloaded his venom, and I knew she'd get me through this. "I took it apart and rebuilt it a couple of times, and I put in a little roof garden, just because they make Sam happy."

Lauren turned the pages, studying each design and feeling my pencil's indentations on the paper. "Is this a project you're working on?"

"No," I said, resting my chin on her shoulder and letting my lips brush against her neck. "But I kept going back to it, over and over these past few months. Every time I made it a little different, adjustments here and there, but it was always the same house."

She nodded thoughtfully, and I knew she was entertaining my ramblings with extreme patience. I hadn't seen a single eye roll from her yet, and I wanted her to stop worrying that my father died tonight and argue with me again. I was finally free to live, and I wanted her alongside me for the journey.

"I realized this morning I'd been drawing it for you," I said. "This is for you, and part of me has known that for months because it's all the little things you like, the things you need. Built-in bookshelves, a claw-foot tub, a big kitchen island, plenty of windows in the master bedroom. This is yours. And mine, I hope. Some day." Her eyebrows winged up, and I laughed, my first genuine laugh today. "It's our house. The one I want to build you."

She stared at the design for long, excruciating minutes, and when she finally glanced up, I saw that familiar grin, that naughty schoolteacher smile, and I could breathe again. "Is that all? I recall there being multiple items on your punch list, Mr. Walsh."

"Do you remember how you came home with me after one kiss, Miss Halsted?"

And then she gave it to me: the eye roll I'd been craving for days. "I think there was more to the story than that, and I think it had something to do with your growls and panty-dropping stares."

"So that's a yes," I laughed. "Do you remember how I asked you to marry me the next day?"

"Yeah, after all my friends rubbed up on you like desperate, skanky housewives. It was lovely to watch."

"You said no that night." Plucking the ring from my pocket, I slipped it over her finger, and placed her hand on the drawing of our home. "Say yes."

Lauren stared at the diamond solitaire, and there wasn't much I wouldn't have given to crawl inside her head and hear her thoughts.

"How can you be sure?" she whispered.

"You take me as I come, ugly parts and rough patches and my insane family and everything. I love you, and you own me. Completely. You have since that first night."

"I love you," she said, her hands flying to my face, her thumb brushing back and forth over my lip.

"Oh yeah?" I whispered.

She nodded, and sucked my lip into her mouth, biting. I pounced, crowding her against the sofa and savoring her. Her scent saturated my senses, and I could think of nothing other than sinking into her wet center and losing myself in her. She rubbed her cheek against the stubble on my chin and pressed a biting kiss to the corner of my mouth.

Pulling back, she cupped my face and arched an

eyebrow. "Why do you have an engagement ring lying around your apartment?"

I leaned into her embrace and my eyes drifted shut. "Because I picked it out after we sold the brownstones," I said against her lips. I inhaled her scent, laced our fingers together, and wrapped our entwined arms around her waist. "Don't freak out. Before you say no—"

"Yes," she sighed.

She dragged her teeth over my lips, and I needed her soft and pliable beneath me. I needed her yielding to me. I just needed *her*. Clothes started flying off around us, and soon I felt the heat of her skin.

"Yes? I don't even know what that means, Miss Halsted. I've only heard you saying yes when my head's between your legs. Yes *yes*, as in…*yes*?"

"Yes." She smiled up at me, and my brain was on an infinite loop of *mine, mine, mine*. I wanted to devour her. "But I need you to meet my parents first. Maybe…you could come with me next week, after the funeral, and we spend Christmas with them in Mexico. Wouldn't that be a nice break from all of this?"

I dropped my head between her breasts—my favorite place in the universe—and groaned. "Your father is going to murder me."

"I'll protect you," she whispered. "He talks a tough game, but never says no to me."

"I can sympathize with that sentiment."

My tongue surged into her mouth while my hands gripped her hips, my erection rocking into her with enough force to shift our bodies across the sofa and onto the floor.

"You're such a fucking caveman," she laughed.

I felt the cool metal of my ring on her finger as her hand

trailed over my shoulder and up the nape of my neck. The primitive sensation of knowing she was mine far outstripped anything I ever experienced, and I brought her hand back to my chest.

"I love you," I panted. "And you did wait for your husband."

"I know, I know, I know," she replied, her words drawn into a moan as I wrapped her legs around my waist and drove in deeper. "I think I've always known. It's always been you."

I was lost in her. But on nights like tonight, it felt a lot like being found.

Christmas Eve
Cabo San Lucas, Mexico

THE COMMODORE HELD Lauren's hand and studied the ring on her finger. He cut a sharp glance to me, then Lauren, and back to me. She didn't notice. She went right on guzzling her margarita as if the Commodore wasn't trying to vaporize me with his glare.

"That's quite the rock," he said. "Only two reasons a man buys something like that: he's making up for shortcomings or asking forgiveness."

The unspoken question lingered over the table while a mariachi band played holiday tunes, circulating through the resort's restaurant.

"My sister, Erin, helped me pick it out," I said, reaching for my water glass. "She's a geologist. She actually talked me out of a larger stone. Erin said this one," I nodded to

Lauren's hand, still in the Commodore's grip. "Was flawless. Perfect. Rare. And I knew it was the one for Lauren."

The Commodore stared at me, his expression clearly articulating his contempt for my response. And as much as I disliked this exercise, I expected it. Lauren had told me more than a few stories about her absurdly protective father and brothers, and I was the guy they'd never met.

The guy who intended to marry his daughter.

Lauren twisted her hand free to intercept another margarita. "Gracias," she said.

"Well I think it's beautiful," Judy, my future mother-in-law, said. She patted my arm and offered a bright smile. It was nice knowing I had an ally at the table. "What are you thinking for the wedding? Any ideas? Wouldn't San Diego be wonderful?"

Lauren turned to me with a sweet, bewildered look on her face, and she shrugged. "We haven't talked about that yet."

Between burying my father and making the last-minute trip to Mexico, there hadn't been time for much of anything. Boston was getting hit with one blizzard after another, and that made the business of restoring homes almost impossible. Half of Lauren's apartment was packed and ready to relocate to my loft, but we didn't know what to do about the rest of it. And we were stepping around the topics of weddings and marriage, as if this trip to Mexico was necessary to finalize our engagement.

"That's not much of a surprise," the Commodore barked. "Did he get you pregnant?"

"Oh, my God," Lauren said. "Give me a little credit!"

I expected that, too. At least there wasn't a shotgun pointed at my head.

"Goddamn it, Bill!" Judy cried. "It's Christmas Eve. Be a civilized person or go back to the room."

Over the rim of her glass, Lauren's gaze pinged between me and her father. His eyebrows lifted before focusing on the pilsner glass to his right.

"You're in architecture," Bill said. "You're successful in that field."

It was a statement, a comment delivered with the cool authority of well-researched fact.

"We've done well for ourselves," I said.

"That's an understatement," Lauren snorted. Her words ran together, slurring just a bit at the end. She waved a hand in my direction and dropped it on my thigh, and I figured I'd be carrying her back to our casita. "Matthew is brilliant. He and his family, they have a client waiting list five pages long. They're in all the architecture and design magazines; they're featured at all these prestigious events. They're beyond successful, Dad. You should see what he's done with my school."

Lauren kneaded my leg, squeezing my hamstring through my trousers. Her thumb, that sweet little thumb, passed back and forth over my inner thigh, and I swallowed a growl.

She was such a handsy drunk, and I loved that about her. But right now, at this moment, in this restaurant, I didn't need to think about Lauren crawling under the table and sucking my cock. Or my hand sliding beneath her gauzy red sundress. Or clumsy, drunk sex on the floor of our beachfront casita.

Not with Commodore Halsted staring at me as if he could read all my perverted thoughts about his daughter.

"I called in a few favors at the Agency," he said.

Oh God, please tell me we are not talking about the Central Intelligence Agency.

"Ran an extensive background check on you."

Yep, that agency.

"Dad!" Lauren said, slapping my leg in concert with her shout.

"William," Judy groaned. "We talked about this. You're being a weirdo!"

What would that produce? Tax returns, parking tickets, college transcripts? I wasn't associated with the mafia. I'd never texted pictures of my dick to anyone. I wasn't running a fight club from my loft. The only skeleton in my closet was my father, and he was good and dead now.

"And you participate in triathlons."

I didn't expect that one. Maybe he was thinking I could run, swim, or bike back to Boston tonight.

"Not just triathlons," Lauren said. "Those crazy Ironman competitions like Will and Wes."

She was disappointed that her brothers were still deployed on top secret missions and weren't joining us for the holiday, but I was relieved I was only facing unfriendly fire from only one Halsted.

"I usually get a few miles in each day. Up for a run in the morning?" Bill asked. "Maybe some ocean swimming? You can't get much of that in Boston."

Feats of strength. Perfect. Why couldn't I just let him win a round golf?

"Definitely," I said.

"Good," the Commodore said, smiling. "Looking forward to it."

Yeah. I'd be lucky if I didn't have to wrestle a pod of humpback whales tomorrow.

"THAT WENT WELL," Lauren said as the door closed behind us.

She kicked off her sandals and headed for the bathroom. I seized the opportunity to bang my head against the casita's door.

"I mean, overall, it wasn't *bad*," she called.

I banged my head again.

"Yeah, sweetness, if I had seven margaritas, I'd be saying the same thing." I nursed a single beer through dinner. Didn't seem wise to meet my future in-laws while rocked off my ass on the best tequila Mexico could offer. "Which part went well? When your father announced that he had me investigated? Or when he suggested that your engagement ring was intended to make up for a small dick? Or maybe the fact he glared at me for three straight hours like he was trying to decide how to kill me?"

"But my mother loved you." Lauren leaned against the door frame and gestured with her toothbrush. "Give him some time. He's surprised. We've been in Cabo for like eight hours and he just met you. You'll grow on him."

She vanished behind the bathroom door, and I flopped onto a wide leather chair in the living room. Moonlight sparkled on the Pacific no more than twenty feet away, and I exhaled. The worst of it was over, the 'hi, how are you, I'm Matt and I'm marrying your daughter' was behind us. Now I just needed to survive the next ten days.

But I couldn't relax. I'd been on edge for the past month, but *this*—this tension gnawing at the base of my skull—was different.

"Hey," Lauren murmured as she approached. Her hands

dropped to my shoulders. "Everything is going to be fine. There's no bite to his bark. You know that, right?"

I nodded, and closed my eyes while her fingers teased apart the bunched, knotted muscles. Several quiet minutes passed, and her ring tickled my earlobe, catalyzing my tension into hunger.

This is what I need right now. She is what I need.

"Bedroom," I murmured.

Standing, I caught Lauren around the waist, tossed her over my shoulder, and marched out of the living room.

"Is this some kind of Walsh family holiday tradition?" she asked.

"No," I said. Her sundress was over her head on the ground before her ass hit the bed. "This is me taking what's mine."

I stripped down and crawled onto the bed, stalking Lauren until she reclined against the bank of pillows. There was no mistaking her heavy-lidded gaze or the way her breathing hitched when I dragged my cock along her leg. I ran my nose across her shoulder, up and down her neck, between her breasts, surrendering to the staggering pull I felt toward her.

"Tell me what you want," she whispered against my ear.

Hooking my fingers in her panties—God, those lacy creations were going to give me a heart attack one of these days—I drew them down her legs and over my shoulder. Her bra was next, but instead of yanking it off, I twisted her wrists in the straps.

"What are you doing?" she giggled.

"You're all mine, sweetness." With her hands positioned over her head and blessedly bound, I smiled. "But if you touch me right now, I'll explode. Don't even think about moving."

Lauren laughed beneath me, her body vibrating with loose, drunken giggles that spiked desire through my veins. "And what would be wrong with that?"

"Ordinarily? Nothing. But right now?" I licked each of her nipples, leaving them taut and shiny. "I'm in charge. You basically gave me a hand job under the table while your father was plotting my execution. And I had to sit next to you while you wore that little dress, and I wanted to lean over and lick your tits every forty-one seconds. So now I'm tormenting you."

"Oh really?" Nodding, Lauren curled her leg around my waist, locking me against her center. Instinct had me grinding on her, and I realized I was probably the one who required the restraints.

LAUREN

SOMETIMES, Matthew's eyes shifted between several shades of blue. They brightened when he was happy and laughing, almost a cornflower color. While he worked and solved problems, they tended toward grayish slate. And now, even with his head bent over my breasts, I knew they were nearly midnight blue, dark and serious as intensity consumed him.

Drinks and dinner with my parents was rough. Matthew was quite accustomed to being one of the most affable Walsh brothers, and he didn't know the first thing about being the least popular guy in the room. But he held his own and took the best my father could give without breaking a sweat.

Now I figured we'd get naked and forget all about it.

"We told your parents that we're engaged," he murmured against my belly button. I needed him a few inches lower, I needed those tiny kisses and licks and bites where I was aching for him.

"Mmhmm. And look, my father didn't castrate you. I'm really pleased about that."

Matthew glanced up at me with a rueful smile. "So when do I get to marry you?"

For a full day after I said yes, I wrestled with gravity. I couldn't determine whether I was floating ten feet off the ground or flattened by the weight of this decision. I assumed responsibility for arranging Angus's funeral, and that busy work provided the cover necessary to panic without anyone noticing.

But it wasn't panic, not exactly.

It was realizing that Matthew was part of me, and I was part of him, and not only did we want each other but we *needed* each other. Sure, we knew how to kick ass on our own, but doing it with him was the only option worth considering.

And maybe that was where the gravity pushed and pulled, because it was never a choice; it was *always* Matthew and me. While he arrived at the conclusion more quickly that I did, I was there, and I was owning the shit out of it now.

I grinned, my leg tightening around his waist. He was erect and ready, the hot weight of his cock sliding over me, just waiting for the right moment. "When do you want to marry me?"

He dipped to my chest and took a nipple in his mouth while his hips moved against me, urgent and impatient. I could translate his touches, his movements, and I knew he was going to fuck me hard and fast, and I knew he wasn't waiting much longer.

With his mouth on my breast, he said, "As soon as you'll let me. I know you probably want—"

"Is tomorrow too soon?"

I felt his lips curve into a smile, and he wrapped his arms around me, my breath vanishing as he squeezed my ribs. I didn't want to talk about this without my hands on him, and I laced my arms around his neck, urging all his weight onto me.

And then he bit the underside of my breast.

I couldn't explain why his teeth drove me wild or why the bolt of pain electrified my desire. The sensation had me arching off the bed, moaning, begging for more. For his fingers, his mouth, his cock—anything, everything. All of him for all of me.

"Oh, sweetness," Matthew growled. "You drive me so fucking crazy."

"But you love me."

He nodded, shifting until he was there, pushing inside me. "And you love me."

"More than I can even explain," I whispered. He anchored my legs around his waist and thrust forward, filling me. Goosebumps spread out across my skin, every tingle gathering, aligning in my center. I felt him everywhere, stretching me, owning me, adoring me.

A sob caught in my throat, and I wanted to remember

every ounce of this moment, every drop of warmth radiating from us. I wanted to keep it in a safe place alongside his bites and growls forever.

It was overwhelming and suffocating and perfect.

"We did it all backwards," Matthew groaned. Each word was punctuated with rough thrusts that had me seeing stars.

"That doesn't mean it was wrong," I said.

He pulled all the way out, watching his body separate from mine before snapping forward, then repeating the process. Matthew slipped two fingers into my mouth and growled, his eyes narrowing and head falling back as I sucked.

"I want to do this right. A real wedding," he said.

His fingers retreated from my mouth and he fastened them to my clit. "We'll do the wedding thing, and then we'll do the marriage thing."

His lips were on me, all over my throat, my mouth, and his kisses mixed with my obscene words and filthy requests and promises of a forever we'd create. There was nothing to hold back, not anymore.

"And I'm going to build you that house. And we'll have a dog and babies, and we're going to do it right."

He lifted my hips higher and—oh God, oh fuck, oh *yes yes yes yes*—his eyes held mine for a heavy moment before leaning down and kissing me, swallowing my moans as he drove deeper.

"I can't wait, sweetness. I need you with me."

His fingers dug into me, pulling at my hips and shoulders, demanding everything, and I didn't want to deny him anything, ever. Teeth scraped over my nipples, and tiny explosions erupted under my skin, each one triggering another. The waves of my orgasm crashed over me, spreading, multiplying until I was dissolving in Matthew's arms.

He stilled, his body rigid while he roared against my shoulder. It was my turn to hold him tight, and I squeezed my legs around his waist, keeping him deep inside me.

"Holy fuck, Lauren," he groaned. "You're going to kill me. And I'm going to enjoy it."

We stayed there, panting and clinging to each other, still joined.

"Memorial Day," I murmured. "On Cape Cod. But I don't want to wear a white dress. Maybe yellow. Or pink."

Matthew lifted his head from the crook of my shoulder, running his thumb over my kiss-swollen lips with a smile. "That's when I can marry you?" I nodded and sucked his thumb into my mouth. "Okay. Wear whichever color you want, sweetness. I'll be there."

"Merry Christmas, Mr. Walsh."

Matthew's lips curled into a devious smile. "Merry Christmas, Mrs. Walsh."

another epilogue

FOR LAUREN, ON VALENTINE'S DAY

I like numbers. That should come as no surprise to you. Today, there are a few numbers I want to tell you about.

953: Number of days we've been married. That's two years, seven months, and twenty seven days.

1: I remember that first day like it was yesterday. I remember us sneaking away from the resort to get lunch (and shots of tequila) in town before the wedding, I remember getting under your dress ten minutes before the ceremony, and when you walked down that aisle, I remember hoping that you wouldn't realize that I didn't deserve you until after the vows.

4: You tripped down a mountain in Switzerland on our honeymoon. I should have expected that. What I didn't expect were the dirty looks the innkeepers gave me when they noticed your bruised knees.

98: We drank tequila on that day, and congratulated ourselves on surviving our first three married months. I can't remember why we doubted ourselves.

364: You brought home a mini-replica of our wedding

cake on that day, and confessed to eating the anniversary slice that we saved in the freezer after a rough day at school. I really loved licking that frosting off you.

502: Three of your teachers went home with the stomach flu that day, and I taught first graders about triangles. It wasn't until then that I realized I didn't know nearly enough about geometry if I couldn't explain it to six-year-olds. It was the most difficult thing I've ever done.

731: I watched you walking along the beach that day. I counted the freckles on your calves (I've always loved your freckles. Have I told you that?) We went back to Chatham for our second anniversary, and you were intent on finding some seashells for Judy's new craft project, and I couldn't remember what my life was about before you and your freckles.

899: That day was our third Christmas Eve together. There are many reasons why that day was memorable but it was then that I noticed how much you'd changed my family. You convinced Tiel that we're all bark and no bite (well...maybe a little biting). Patrick and Andy are still Patrick and Andy because you wouldn't let them walk away from each other. Erin likes you, and she doesn't like anyone. You brought Will to Shannon, and that's probably bad news for me, but my sister has never been this happy. None of this would have happened without you.

0: The number of times we've managed to celebrate Valentine's Day without one of my siblings (or Nick) rearranging our plans. As you might have heard, you're bossy as fuck. You're adorable and perfect, and you're bossy as fuck. Now, don't misunderstand: I love your bossy ass. I also know you claimed you'd be helping Shannon pack her apartment this weekend, but I'm taking you to Vermont.

We're putting that obscene lingerie you have hiding in the closet to use and getting a legitimate Valentine's holiday on the scoreboard. Get ready.

There are so many more days to come, sweetness.

- Matthew

Thank you for reading *Underneath It All*! I hope you enjoyed Matt and Lauren. If you loved the heat and heart, steam and sass in *Underneath It All*, you'll love Andy and Patrick in *The Space Between*.

A brilliant, alpha architect. A smart, sultry apprentice. What could possibly go wrong?

Patrick

That hair.

That fucking hair.

It was everywhere, always, and I wanted to tangle my fingers in those dark curls and pull.

And that would be fine if she wasn't my apprentice.

Andy

One incredibly hot architect with the most expressive hazel eyes I ever encountered and entirely too much talent in and out of the bedroom wasn't part of my original plan.

With Patrick Walsh leaving love notes in the form of bite marks all over my body, it seems my plan was undergoing some renovations.

The Space Between is available now!

Join my newsletter for new release alerts, exclusive extended epilogues and bonus scenes, and more.

If newsletters aren't your thing, follow me on BookBub for preorder and new release alerts.

Visit my private reader group, Kate Canterbary's Tales, for exclusive giveaways, sneak previews of upcoming releases, and book talk.

also by kate canterbary

Vital Signs

Before Girl — Cal and Stella

The Worst Guy — Sebastian Stremmel and Sara Shapiro

The Walsh Series

Underneath It All – Matt and Lauren

The Space Between – Patrick and Andy

Necessary Restorations – Sam and Tiel

The Cornerstone – Shannon and Will

Restored — Sam and Tiel

The Spire — Erin and Nick

Preservation — Riley and Alexandra

Thresholds — The Walsh Family

Foundations — Matt and Lauren

The Santillian Triplets

The Magnolia Chronicles — Magnolia

Boss in the Bedsheets — Ash and Zelda

The Belle and the Beard — Linden and Jasper-Anne

Talbott's Cove

Fresh Catch — Owen and Cole

Hard Pressed — Jackson and Annette

Far Cry — Brooke and JJ

Rough Sketch — Gus and Neera

Benchmarks Series

Professional Development — Drew and Tara

Orientation — Jory and Max

Brothers In Arms

Missing In Action — Wes and Tom

Coastal Elite — Jordan and April

Get exclusive sneak previews of upcoming releases through Kate's newsletter and private reader group, The Canterbary Tales, on Facebook.

about kate

USA Today Bestseller Kate Canterbary writes smart, steamy contemporary romances loaded with heat, heart, and happy ever afters. Kate lives on the New England coast with her husband and daughter.

You can find Kate at www.katecanterbary.com

facebook.com/kcanterbary

twitter.com/kcanterbary

instagram.com/katecanterbary

amazon.com/Kate-Canterbary

bookbub.com/authors/kate-canterbary

goodreads.com/Kate_Canterbary

pinterest.com/katecanterbary

tiktok.com/@katecanterbary

Printed in the USA
CPSIA information can be obtained
at www.ICGtesting.com
CBHW010811180224
4373CB00032B/57